SAFE
AND
SOUND

SAFE
AND
SOUND

a novel

LAURA
McHUGH

RANDOM HOUSE

NEW YORK

Copyright © 2024 by Laura McHugh

Published in the United States by Random House, an imprint and division of Penguin Random House LLC, New York.

RANDOM HOUSE and the HOUSE colophon are registered trademarks of Penguin Random House LLC.

Library of Congress Cataloging-in-Publication Data
Names: McHugh, Laura, author.
Title: Safe and sound: a novel / Laura McHugh.
Description: First edition. | New York: Random House, [2024]
Identifiers: LCCN 2023017580 (print) | LCCN 2023017581 (ebook) |
ISBN 9780593448854 (hardcover) | ISBN 9780593448861 (ebook)
Subjects: LCSH: Sisters—Fiction. | Missing persons—Fiction. | Small cities—Fiction. |
City and town life—Fiction. | LCGFT: Detective and mystery fiction. |
Thrillers (Fiction) | Novels.
Classification: LCC PS3613.C5334 S24 2024 (print) | LCC PS3613.C5334 (ebook) |
DDC 813/.6—dc23/eng/20230414
LC record available at https://lccn.loc.gov/2023017580
LC ebook record available at https://lccn.loc.gov/2023017581

Printed in Canada on acid-free paper

randomhousebooks.com

2 4 6 8 9 7 5 3 1

First Edition

Book design by Jo Anne Metsch

For Mom,
who let me read whatever I wanted

AMELIA

&

KYLEE

ONE

Aunt Elsie sat on her mobility scooter in the laundromat parking lot amid piles of dirty snow, wearing white sandals and her good Easter dress despite the bitter wind that swept down Main Street. She pushed her glasses up as she eyed the gathering crowd, adjusted the wilted red carnation pinned at her breast. Her boyfriend, Jimmy, slumped against a tree behind her, looking like a misshapen fungus growing out of the trunk. He held a posterboard sign with STILL MISSING neatly lettered at the top in blood-red marker, a blown-up photocopy of Grace's senior picture pasted below. Jimmy was more than twenty years younger than Aunt Elsie and might have been mistaken for her son if most folks in Beaumont didn't already know every twig on every branch of everyone else's family tree.

Days ago, Kylee and I'd stretched across the hood of my car in tank tops, gazing up at the budding trees. My face still stung with sunburn. It had been a fool's spring, typical of Missouri in March, and now everything was dead again, the tender buds frozen, blossoms shriveled and brown. Every living thing that had sprung forth in hope had been taught a brutal lesson. As daylight faded, the wind picked up, rattling crumpled beer cans along the gutter. At the front of the crowd, Aunt Elsie began to speak, her voice brittle to the point of cracking.

"Six years ago tonight, my daughter was taken from me, snatched away in the dark. Grace was my whole world, and you have no idea how much I miss her every single day. Six years on, and we've still got nothing but questions, but I will never give up hope that we'll find her. One way or another, we'll bring her home."

Aunt Elsie held the vigil every year, and every year, she said we'd bring Grace home, but the ironic part was that what Grace had wanted most was to get away from here. She was always telling me and Kylee that we had to get out before we got stuck, that there was no life for us in Beaumont. There was no choice but to leave and not look back. Otherwise, we'd be married and pregnant and working at the meatpacking plant before we were old enough to buy beer. We didn't really get it back then—we were only ten, eleven years old when she disappeared—but I did now. Cutting Road circled around town, from the hospital to the meatpacking plant to the graveyard, and that was life in Beaumont from start to finish. You were born at Beaumont General, worked at Savor Meats, and then ended up in Beaumont Memorial Cemetery. It was like the kiddie-car ride at the county fair, where you've got your own steering wheel and you can turn it all you want, but there's only one way to go, the track laid out before you got there. Not much changed from one generation to the next, except the spring Grace vanished, the hospital had been shuttered, the building abandoned. Kids broke in to get high and have sex. If they got pregnant, they'd have to go to Springfield to give birth. The only babies born in Beaumont now were born at home.

Kylee stood next to me, scanning the crowd. A few of Grace's old classmates had come, folks from Elsie's church, kids from our high school who hadn't known Grace but knew the stories. She served as a cautionary tale, one inevitably brought up after dark at sleepovers and drunken bonfires. While fool's spring kept us from being too optimistic, Grace's disappearance warned the young girls of Beaumont not to get too big for their britches. *You think you're better than this? You want out? Be careful what you wish for.* They didn't have to say the last part out loud: *Look what hap-pened to Grace Crow.* The vigil had been shrinking each year, but there were more people than usual tonight.

"I told you the bones'd bring people out," Kylee said. "They think it's her."

It happened every time human remains were found somewhere in Missouri and it made the news. The rumor mill roared back to life, certain it must be Grace. It never was. This time, though, the bones were found uncomfortably close to home. Two weeks back, a skeleton had been dis-covered on an old farmstead near the county line where one of the Savor plant managers was building a new house. A long-abandoned farmhouse and barn and other outbuildings were razed to make way for construction, so it was possible the bones were from a family grave. Or they might belong to a missing person who hadn't been missed. The farm wasn't far from the interstate—it could be a runaway or transient or addict whose vanishing went unnoticed, ungrieved, the bones left without a name. Still, there was a flicker of possibility that it might be her, that we would finally know. A pilot light sparking and shuddering in my heart.

"Please join me in prayer," Elsie said, raising her bare arms, pale flesh billowing.

Some of the kids whispered and snickered as Elsie began to pray, but most everyone else dutifully closed their eyes, making it easier for me to look them over, take stock of them. I always wondered, at these gatherings, whether the person who took Grace stood among us. As a kid, I'd imag-ined a stranger with blood under his nails that would never wash away. Elsie thought it must've been one of Grace's customers at the Waffle House, a man passing through on the interstate who'd followed her home. Mama snorted at that. *What, you think people you know won't hurt you?* She wasn't impressed by alibis, and rightfully so. Even if there was bad blood between you, you'd have to be a real piece of shit for your own fam-ily not to lie and vouch for you around here.

There were no strangers among us tonight, though some familiar faces were missing. Mama hadn't shown up, even though she knew how much it would hurt Elsie. It was no surprise. She didn't care for memorials, vigils, whatever you wanted to call them. Prayers made her antsy. Even getting her to church for a funeral was like trying to force a feral cat into a cage. She'd practically spread-eagle her body against the doorframe to avoid going inside. I didn't see Mrs. Mummer either—Grace's favorite teacher, and mine and Kylee's, too. And for the second year in a row, Levi hadn't come. We couldn't expect him to mourn his high school sweetheart forever, even if we wanted him to. Still, it felt as though Grace deserved at least that much, for everyone who loved her to mark her absence, to remember what we had lost.

Aunt Elsie began to tell her favorite stories about Grace: how she would pretend to read an encyclopedia while sitting on her training potty; how she had saved me, her cousin Amelia, from drowning when I was four years old. Kylee pulled away from my side and drifted into the crowd, her black jacket and dark hair ceding to the shadows. Smoke leaked from the cracked window of one of the parked cars, someone inside sucking a cigarette, maybe waiting on their laundry, maybe here for the vigil but not willing to brave the cold. It was one of those ridiculously long cars from the seventies that was probably impressive when it was new, and now looked like something an aging backwoods pimp would drive. That was probably a fair description of half the vehicles in Beaumont, though.

A movement caught my eye, someone waving from the curb. Ketch, his head freshly shaved. I'd been staring right past him without realizing. He had to work, so I hadn't expected him to come, but he must've stopped on his way. He'd be leaving for boot camp soon, something he'd been waiting to do for as long as I'd known him. For kindergarten graduation, our teacher had asked each of us what we wanted to be when we grew up, and our responses had been printed in the program, which I had recently unearthed while cleaning out a drawer. The girls had wanted to be princesses and singers, except for me and Carly Greer. Carly said trucker, probably because her dad was a trucker, and I said dancer, because I thought that was what my mom did on the stage at Sweet Jane's. Mama had snort-laughed when she saw the program, and it took me years to realize what was funny. Most of the boys wanted to be football players or NASCAR drivers. Ketch said soldier. With graduation looming, none of our class-mates had a chance in hell of appearing on *American Idol* or winning a football scholarship. Even the most modest aspirations had escaped our reach. Carly Greer wouldn't be driving a semi anytime soon; she'd lost her license and was on house arrest at the Happy Trails mobile home park, her teeth rotting out of her mouth. I'd graduated a semester early so I could go full-time waitressing at Waffle House. Ketch was the only one who'd man-aged to follow through on his dream, the only one on his way out of town.

Kylee and I talked about leaving all the time, but it had begun to feel like something we only talked about instead of something we would actu-ally do. Like how Aunt Elsie kept saying she was going to stop feeding the stray cat that came around, because she didn't want it to get too comfort-able and decide to stay, and now it had birthed two litters of kittens and they all lived under the porch, multiplying, while Elsie sewed little catnip toys for them and bought bulk cat food in huge bags from the feedstore. That was how things happened. We weren't those people until we were. Years from now, Kylee and I'd probably be talking about leaving while we waited in line to buy scratcher tickets at the Kum & Go on our way home from the meatpacking plant to fix store-brand SpaghettiOs for our kids.

We weren't like Grace. She had real plans. A scholarship to a school out of state, the first in our family to get into college. My only plan was to wait around for Kylee to graduate, because I couldn't leave without her. That was another thing Grace had taught us: stick together. I was working to save up money so we could afford to start over someplace else, but I barely had the time or energy to dream about where that place might be or how a different life would look. It was hard to plot a path to some unknown destination, and all too easy to keep waking up in Beaumont every day, to stay on the ride and follow Cutting Road to its end.

Kylee reappeared, followed my line of sight. "G.I. Joe." She let out a low whistle and I elbowed her. "Such a shame," she said. "I'll never get why you didn't hit that."

"It's not like that with us, Ky, you know that."

She rolled her eyes. "You're both idiots."

"It's called being friends. You should try it sometime."

Ketch and I had been friends since we were assigned to sit next to each other on the bus in kindergarten, alphabetical order by first name: Abel Ketchum, Amelia Crow. Most of the other kids had on brand-new, first-day-of-school outfits. My dress, same as everything else in my closet, was an old hand-me-down from Grace. Ketch's shirt looked like it had been handed down from a long-dead cowboy, a threadbare Western style with snaps instead of buttons and a pointy collar. His jeans had dirt on the knees. A kid leaned over our seat, his nose pinched shut, and said, "Ew, what stinks?" Ketch looked down at his hands, which had slid forward to cover the stains on his jeans.

"You do," I said to the kid. "'Cause you're an asshole." Mama might not have taught me how to tie my shoes or tell time, but I'd received an advanced education in insults and curse words. The kid punched the seat and the bus driver yelled at him to sit down.

After lunch that day, I saw Ketch in the office. I'd been ratted out by the boy on the bus, and the principal had tried to explain to me what kind of language was and wasn't appropriate for school. Ketch was there, wearing a different outfit than the one he'd worn that morning, and we walked back to class together. The other kids said he peed his pants and that's why he had to change, but he told me the truth: that the school nurse was washing his clothes for him, because his house had a dirt floor and no running water, so his mom couldn't keep up with the laundry.

He was always honest with me. I trusted him as much as I trusted anyone aside from my sister. I was going to miss him.

Aunt Elsie wrapped up her sappy stories, most of which would have had Grace rolling her eyes or shrinking in embarrassment, and her tone shifted as she spoke of the night Grace was taken from us. "It rained that night," Elsie said, pausing to compose herself. I remembered. It was a cold, ceaseless rain that flooded Cutting Road and washed away the low-water bridge, along with any evidence of Grace's departure. We might have simply thought that she'd walked home that night, tried to cross the creek, and drowned, if not for the blood in the kitchen.

I remembered how the wind funneled under the eaves and filled the farmhouse with a damp chill. Grace was watching us that night while Mama worked late at Sweet Jane's. She fed us dinner, and after we ate, she took us upstairs to get ready for bed, helped us pick nightshirts from a drawer of free promotional tees Mama had brought home from work, each one advertising a different beer or liquor, Bud Light or Milwaukee's Best or Jose Cuervo tequila. She braided our hair, mine French and Kylee's Dutch, because my little sister and I always wanted the same thing, but different. Grace tickled our backs and fluffed the quilts just right, snapping them out and then letting them drift down over us. After she left the room, I could still feel her fingernails gently tracing wings across my shoulder blades. Later, when the police officer carried Kylee and me out of the house, he told us to close our eyes, but I didn't, and I could still see it. Grace's blood. Pooled on the kitchen linoleum, spattered on a cabinet. One haunting red handprint on the doorframe. She had vanished while we slept, and neither of us heard a thing.

"There's always a chance," Elsie said, "that the phone'll ring, that we'll get answers." I knew she was waiting for that call now, probably flinching every time her cell jangled with its old-fashioned rotary ringtone, because either way, if the bones were Grace's or they weren't, it wouldn't be the answer she wanted.

Elsie finished with a final prayer and we made our way to the front to say goodbye. Jimmy had set down the sign so he could play games on his phone, and he didn't bother to look up from *Fruit Ninja* or whatever dumb thing had him mesmerized. I leaned in to hug Elsie. Her bare arms were cold as a corpse, but she smelled of warm, familiar things, bacon grease popping in a cast-iron skillet, coffee brewing in her yellow kitchen.

"I'm sorry Mama couldn't make it," I said.

"Me too." She'd put on mascara for the occasion, and it was smeared out from her eyes in tearful streaks. "Shannon's Shannon. But, you girls."

She smiled wistfully at me and then Kylee, who backed out of reach. She wasn't a hugger. "You're always here for her. Grace loved you both so much. She'd do anything for you. I know I can count on you. It means a lot, knowing you're here, that you're not going anywhere."

I squeezed her hand. "Sorry we have to run. I've gotta get to work."

"Careful walking home." It wasn't something said as an aside. She meant it.

Most of the cars had already cleared out, including the one I'd seen earlier, the street nearly empty. We crossed Main, past the last streetlight and into the darkness. Elsie's words hung in my head. *You're not going anywhere.*

"We won't be here much longer," I said.

"Hell, no."

"We're leaving and we're not looking back."

"No, ma'am. Can't look back."

"What happens if you look back?" I said. It was a game we played: What was the worst that could happen if you stayed in Beaumont?

Kylee ran a finger across her throat. "You'll be bleeding out hogs for the rest of your life."

"You'll be slinging Natty Light at the titty bar," I said.

"You'll be screwing your boss in the Waffle House parking lot between shifts."

"Jesus, Ky, really?"

"Sorry, it's gotta be something bad," she said. "So you don't look back. You don't want to look back and see Alan's hairy ass. It'll turn you to stone."

"I will never hook up with Alan, I promise you that."

"Nobody *plans* to do that shit, Amelia. It happens. Worse things happen."

I didn't know if she was thinking about Aunt Elsie, but I was. Diabetic feet, her back and knees wrecked from work, boyfriend a worthless walking mushroom. Her beloved brother, our uncle Norman, never calling or coming to visit. And her daughter missing. Dead, most likely, but no body to bury. Couldn't get much worse than that. Elsie looked back all the time, though that wasn't why she was stuck. It would never occur to her to leave.

Kylee stopped in the middle of the dirt road and turned toward me, her face pensive in the darkness, her long hair a banner in the wind. Mama had told her if it got any longer, the Pentecostals were going to take her in.

"Some girl at the vigil was talking about the bones."

"Yeah, half the town's probably talking about it."

"She said she *saw* them."

"So what if she did?"

"I don't know," Kylee said. "Just pisses me off. People acting like they know things about Grace when they don't."

"Forget it. We've heard it all before. Most of the folks talking about her never even knew her."

I linked my arm with my sister's, the two of us braced against the wind. I didn't doubt that Grace was dead, because if she were alive, she'd have come back for us. She wouldn't have disappeared without saying goodbye, wouldn't have left us here in the place she warned us to leave. We cut through the woods, past the ruins of the old barn that had burned last fall, past the neighbors' rusty cattle gate, their driveway flanked by two whiskey barrels full of pansies. The flowers were shriveled, frostbitten. They wouldn't survive. Another year of fool's spring, of false promise and hopes dashed. It happened time and again, and we never learned.

TWO

Waffle House was lit up like a bug zapper, the big yellow sign drawing truckers to the outer road off the interstate, a greasy glow spilling out of the windows into the dark parking lot. It was the quietest part of the night, after the dinner crowd regulars had gone home and before the drunks started to arrive. Javi nodded hello from the grill when I walked in. Alan was doing some kind of weird standing push-ups against the counter. He was always calling himself a "gym rat" and talking about hitting the gym after work. The gym, as far as I could tell from pictures he'd shown me, was located in a dark corner of his basement and contained a weight bench, a full-length mirror, and a rusty chest freezer. He had invited me, on more than one occasion, to come check it out, which I always found an excuse not to do.

Alan stopped flexing and combed his fingers through his mustache, which had grown bigger and bushier as the hair on his head disappeared. The mustache was so massive now that you could barely see his mouth move when he talked. "Hey," he said. "Your sister want to put in an application? Another waitress quit and we're gonna need somebody in the afternoons."

"I'll check," I said, not meaning it. Kylee did not have it in her to be a waitress. She lacked the ability to tolerate bullshit of any kind. If a trucker snapped his fingers at her and called her "sugar tits," Kylee would probably get arrested for smashing a coffeepot into his skull. She preferred the outdoors and the company of horses and was perfectly happy to keep mucking stalls for our neighbors, which she'd been doing since she was thirteen.

I started on the never-ending side work: marrying ketchups, wiping down salt and pepper shakers, filling creamers and sugars and syrup jugs. Javi whistled to himself, as he often did when the jukebox wasn't playing, a monotonous tune I didn't recognize. Alan sidled up next to me while I balanced one ketchup bottle atop another, mouth to mouth, watching the red sludge flow from one to the other like the world's slowest hourglass—an accurate measure of Waffle House time. Alan's hand snaked up to my shoulder and rested there.

"I appreciate you coming in," he said. "I'm sure it's a difficult day for you, the anniversary and all."

"Thanks," I said. I stared at his freckled arm, willing it to shrivel up or catch fire or, at the very least, fall back to his side so his hand would no longer be in contact with my body. I hadn't had a choice about coming in for my shift. Alan had turned down my request to take the night off.

"Grace was a hard worker," he said. "Always willing to go the extra mile. She had a real future here. She was looking into the manager trainee program, did you know that?"

"No," I said. I didn't believe him.

Alan's glasses had slid down his nose, the frames slick with grease. He squinted and leaned closer. He was forever leaning closer. "I've been thinking, there might be a path to management for you, if you're ready to put in the work." His hand dropped down, grazing my backside. Javi cleared his throat and Alan straightened up, giving me a last once-over before disappearing into his office to do whatever he did in there with the door closed. My guess was internet porn.

Alan had gone home by the time the night crowd started to arrive. A half-dozen high school kids banged in the door after midnight. A few of them piled into a booth and the rest started slamming quarters into the jukebox and arguing as they punched the buttons. They were loud, and sloppy drunk, leaning on one another, tripping over their own feet. I recognized one of the girls from the vigil. She wore a purple coat with a fur-trimmed hood. I had seen her around town, but she wasn't from Beaumont. We rarely got new kids here unless their parents came to work at Savor Meats. She must've landed effortlessly in the popular crowd, with her highlighted hair and clothes you couldn't buy at Walmart and the simple fact that she came from someplace better than here. She was laughing so hard she was practically choking, her mouth wide, her perfect teeth no doubt a result of expensive orthodontia.

"Ready to order or you need a few minutes?"

The guys ignored me, but the girl sat up straighter and squinted at me, catching her breath. "Hey, you're her cousin," she said. "Grace Crow's cousin. Right?"

Mariah Carey belted out of the speakers and the guys groaned. "I told you, you hit the wrong one!"

"I'll give you a few minutes," I said.

"No, wait," the girl said. "I'm Olivia." She paused as though that should mean something. Her friends stared at their menus, glassy-eyed. One of the guys shouldered in front of her, pushing her back.

"Gimme the waffles and grits. Extra butter."

I leaned in, making eye contact with the girl. "You have something to say?"

She opened her mouth to speak, but hesitated just long enough for the guy to interrupt her again.

"You didn't ask what kinda meat I want," the guy said, stabbing the menu with his finger.

"Sausage," one of the others chimed in. The guys howled, miming blow jobs. *Dewayne wants sausage!* Dewayne lunged across Olivia to shove his buddy out of the booth, crushing her in the process. She pushed him off.

"You can all fuck off." I turned away and they started hollering.

"Bitch, wait! Where's my grits!" Raucous laughter quickly dissolved into a collective groan. Somebody was puking. I could smell it, hear it splatting on the floor.

Javi came out from the back. "We got a problem here?"

"No," I said. "They're gonna leave before I call the cops."

A red-headed girl in a letter jacket was the only one who looked worried at the mention of police. "Guys," she said. "My dad'll take my car away again." The puker got up and ran out the door, holding his mouth, followed by Letter Jacket, and the rest reluctantly shuffled out after them, mumbling slurs, leaving behind puddles of gritty snowmelt and vomit.

"Assholes."

Javi rolled his head from side to side to crack his neck. "I'll get the mop."

Mariah finished singing and "Waffle Home" came on, the song that always made me want to strangle whoever had played it. As I scrubbed out the booth, I found a soft purple scarf stuffed into the crack between the seat and the wall. It matched Olivia's coat, and it felt expensive—something she might want back. I tucked it into my bag in the break room. Whatever she had wanted to say to me, it was probably best that she hadn't gotten it out. It was unbelievable what spewed from people's mouths when it came to Grace—offensive comments, idiotic theories, questions they had no right to ask. *Were you scared? How much blood was in the kitchen? How did you not hear anything?*

It wasn't something I talked about much with anyone but Kylee. I would never forget how it felt, waking to screams, my sister clutching my arm in the darkness. I'd thought it must be Grace screaming, and I wanted to run to her, but then I recognized our mother's voice. She'd hollered that way before, during a fight with a man who left a dent in the paneling where she'd hurled him against the wall. If you cornered Mama, she was all fangs and claws. No one laid a hand on her without her dishing it back. The scream came again, raw and primal, and Kylee and I crawled into the closet and clung to each other, hidden beneath a pile of dirty laundry.

We didn't know until later that our mother had come home to find the door ajar, rain blowing in. She'd seen the blood before crossing the threshold and screamed, dialing 911 as she staggered through the kitchen and living room, expecting to find our bodies. When she raced upstairs to our empty bed, she feared it was too late. That whoever had taken us would kill us, if we weren't already dead. She stood outside in the rain, numb, not realizing we were alive until the officer who found us spoke into his walkie-talkie. *The Crow sisters are here,* he said. *Safe and sound.*

The same phrase was used in the newspaper article. The two young daughters of Shannon Crow, found safe and sound in an upstairs bedroom. *Thank God the children were spared!* people would say, as if Grace wasn't a child herself. As if Kylee and I were fine because we hadn't been touched.

We weren't fine. We had lain sleeping while someone attacked Grace in the kitchen below us and dragged her out of the house, leaving her blood in puddles and smears. My mental snapshot of the crime scene was as vivid as ever, refusing to fade with time. That bloody kitchen was a room in my head, always waiting for me to open the door and turn on the light.

At the end of my shift, I drove home along Cutting Road, fog rising up from the creek as I neared the house. Lamplight illuminated the broken bedroom window upstairs, the glass held together with a spiderweb of duct tape. One of Kylee's old boyfriends had been throwing rocks at the window to get her to sneak out and woke me up instead, not realizing we shared a room. Kylee and I had shared a bed, too, for the first nine years of her life, until someone from Aunt Elsie's church gave us a castoff. The frame was Pepto pink with fancy spindles, and we had fought over it until Mama threatened to chop it up for kindling. We didn't stop fighting until she stomped upstairs, axe in hand. I let Kylee have the bed because pink was her favorite color, but in the years since, she had been slowly coloring it black with a Sharpie.

I brought in the mail. There was a card from Mrs. Mummer addressed to me and Kylee, and a letter from the landlord. Mama was probably behind on the rent again. I dropped the letter on the kitchen counter and tore open the card. It had a picture of a mother duck surrounded by baby ducks on the front. Mrs. Mummer apologized that she wasn't well enough to attend the vigil and asked us to stop by and see her as soon as we could. She still wrote in print after a lifetime of teaching kids who hadn't yet learned cursive.

The stairs creaked as I walked up, and Kylee called out to make sure it was me. I asked her once what she would do if I didn't answer, and she'd pulled a deer-skinning knife out from under her pillow.

"Back already?" she said. She was propped up in bed with a book she was supposed to be reading for English class, but it sat unopened in her lap. "I thought you might hit the gym with Alan after work."

"Kylee."

She smiled sweetly, setting the book aside. "I mean, who could blame you. That *mustache*."

"You're lucky I'm too tired to throw something at you." I changed out of my uniform, debating whether I should toss it in the laundry before the whole room began to reek of cooking oil.

"All right," she said, clapping her hands. "Forget about Alan. On to more important things. Show me the money!" She did a drumroll.

I took the tip jar out from under the bed and dumped in a couple of handfuls of change, along with a dozen dollar bills. "We'll be moving outta here in no time."

"Dang," Kylee said. "You'd make more on the overpass with a cardboard sign. You'd have to unbutton your shirt a little. Or a lot."

"It was dead most of the night," I said, stretching out on the bed. "Some kids from the vigil came in, though. That girl you were talking about earlier, the one who said she saw the bones . . . did she have a purple coat?"

"Yeah, I think so."

"She was there. Asked if I was Grace's cousin."

"And?"

"I don't know. Whatever she was gonna say, she didn't get a chance to say it. Okay if I turn out the light?"

"Sure." She twisted her long hair around her fingers. I switched off the lamp and closed my eyes. My limbs felt heavy, as they always did after a late shift, like I was temporarily paralyzed. I was too tired to brush my teeth, let alone take a shower, though I knew if I didn't, the Waffle House odor would leach into the sheets, and my pillow would smell like hash browns in the morning.

"Mimi," Kylee said. She was the only one who still called me that. It had been one of her first words; our mother claimed she'd said my nickname before she said "Mama." "I have to tell you something."

"Yeah?" I rolled onto my side to face her in the darkness. I could barely make out her open mouth, the hollows of her eyes.

"I think I'm gonna drop out."

My pulse thumped in my stomach, my throat. "No, you're not."

"I can do the GED later. Still get the diploma. It's no big deal."

"Why would you do that, Kylee? You only have one year left." ·

"What does it matter?" she said.

"It just . . . does."

"You left school early to work," she said. "That's all I'm doing."

"It's not the same. I did that so we'll have enough money to leave when you're done with school. And I graduated. If you quit now, you'll never finish."

Kylee's bed creaked as she got up. "So what, Amelia? What do I need a high school diploma for? I'm not going to college. I'm not going anywhere. You know it's true. This is it. We can say whatever we want, pretend we're making plans, but we're stuck here, same as every other asshole in this place. Might as well get on with it. I'm gonna get a real job so I can at least move out of this house."

"No," I said. "Don't be stupid."

"I'm stupid?" She pulled on a pair of jeans, grabbed her phone from the nightstand. "What's your plan, exactly? You think you're gonna move to some other town down the interstate and work at some other Waffle House with a boss no different than Alan? You think your life'll magically be better just because you're not here?"

"You can't quit. I won't let you."

"I don't need your permission. I don't know why I even fucking told you." The room shuddered when she slammed the door.

I curled up against the wall, pulling the quilt to my chin. If Kylee quit school, that was another square blacked out on her Beaumont bingo card: High School Dropout. We didn't have room for mistakes, because we'd been born with a row nearly full. Dirt Poor. No Dad. Mom Who Works at a Strip Club. Beaumont Roots Five Generations Deep. Now Kylee only needed one more—Shotgun Wedding, Meth Addiction, A Job at Savor Meats—and bingo, it was guaranteed we'd never leave. I'd thought I had more time to figure something out, that I was doing all I could. We couldn't go anywhere without cash, so I'd been working and saving as much as possible and had a decent amount in the bank. I'd repeated Grace's warnings over and over, to my sister and myself, but it hadn't been enough. I'd failed. Kylee was right—I didn't have a plan. As much as I might have wished to be, I wasn't like Grace. She figured out what she wanted to do and did it, despite everyone telling her it was impossible. *And look where that got her.* The bitter voice of Beaumont whispering in my ear, no matter how many times I told it to shut up.

I listened for a creak on the stairs, but Kylee didn't come back. There was little insulation in the house, nothing but rotting wood and failing shingles between me and the night air, and frost flowered on the slanted wall above my bed as the condensation from my breath began to freeze. The crystalline pattern gleamed in the moonlight. *Look for small wonders. See the Beautiful Now.* Grace had taught us that. That there were tiny miracles amid the mundane; that beauty could be found in even the darkest places if we knew how to look. Her voice was still in my head, all the little things she'd taught us carrying more weight as time passed, rather than fading away.

She'd been a second mother to us from the time we were babies until the night she was taken, watching over us until the very end, a debt we couldn't repay. And maybe that was another reason it felt impossible to leave. Didn't we owe her something? Grace couldn't escape, so we would stay, going to the vigil every year, feeling guilty that we couldn't help her—that despite all she'd taught us, we couldn't even help ourselves. Maybe if she was finally found, if the bones were hers, it would set us free somehow. Not that Grace was haunting us. I didn't believe in spirits, in some ghostly in-between. We haunted ourselves with her memory, and there was no easy cure for such things.

THREE

Kylee wasn't home when I woke up, and she didn't answer my texts all day, so I walked down to our neighbors' farm, where she mucked stalls after school. She was out in the paddock with a chestnut quarter horse, feeding it carrots and talking to it as though it might talk back. The horse nickered, and Kylee smiled and stroked its flank. I called her name and waved.

My sister had always been happiest and most at ease around horses. She was a rodeo baby, born during the annual Midland States Rodeo, which took over Beaumont one week a year. There was a grand parade down Main Street with miles of horses, more than a thousand of them, the riders carrying colorful flags, all decked out in cowboy hats and boots and shiny belt buckles, the outlines of tobacco cans in the back pockets of their Wranglers. We would sit on the curb in front of the laundromat and watch them flow by in an endless stream, a river of horses. When she was little, Kylee thought the parade was for her, that the horses came for her birthday. She had a pink cowboy hat with a plastic tiara on the brim that Uncle Norman had given her, and pointy-toed boots that she insisted on wearing long after she had outgrown them, jamming her blistered feet in and never complaining. Mama was fond of the rodeo, too. When so many cowboys came to town, some were bound to find their way to Sweet Jane's with money in their pockets.

Kylee led the horse back into the barn and then emerged a few minutes later, stomping mud off her boots. "Hey," she said.

"Hey. I know you're mad at me. Can I talk to you for a minute?"

"I guess."

We started down the road, the sun warm on our faces in the cool air. "I was thinking," I said. "About what you said last night. You're right—I don't have things figured out any better than you do. I'm gonna work on that. And I know I can't stop you from dropping out if that's what you want. I just hate to think of you stuck at Savor or some other shitty place, wearing an ugly uniform, doing something you hate every day. That's what I'm doing, and it's not so great. You've got your whole life to work a soul-sucking job. You're almost done with junior year. Can you at least finish the semester? Maybe think about it over the summer before you do anything?" I figured that might give me enough time to come up with a better plan, to convince her—and myself—that we could make it someplace else.

"You're telling me you don't love working with Alan?" Kylee said. The smallest smile touched her lips. As quick-tempered as she might be, she could forgive me just as fast.

"Just say you'll think about it."

"Fine," she said. "I'll think about it." She hooked her arm around my neck. "Hey, where'd you get this?" She rubbed her cheek against the purple scarf. "It's soft as a fucking angel wing."

"It's Olivia's. The girl we were talking about?"

"You stole her scarf?" She sounded both surprised and impressed.

"I didn't *steal* it, I found it at work. If I run into her, I'll give it back."

"Maybe you'll run into her tonight," Kylee said. "There's a party at that house out past Windy Hill. You should come."

"Are you only asking me because you need a ride?"

She pinched my arm. "You need to get out. Have some fun. All you do is work and go running with Ketch."

I'd avoided parties since I finished school. I hated bumping into people I hadn't seen in a while, because they always asked if I was still working at the Waffle House. It shouldn't have bothered me. There was no shame in honest work, certainly not in Beaumont, where there wasn't much to choose from. Nobody batted an eye when I said yes, but that was the problem; they didn't expect anything different from me, anything more than a job serving grits. Part of me felt like I should expect more from myself. Grace would have. I knew what she would say: *Get out. Don't look back. It's not too late.*

The party was way out in the sticks, and I hoped I had enough gas to get us there and back. Kylee yanked the rearview mirror in her direction and dabbed a dark ruby stain on her lips.

"Not like I'm driving or anything," I said.

"Relax. You want some?" She swiped the stain onto my lips without waiting to see if I'd say yes, then tugged my jacket open to see what I was wearing. "Oh, Lord," she said, jabbing a finger into the Beaumont High Cross Country logo on my T-shirt. "That's what I smelled. Didn't even change after your run. You really fix yourself up for a party."

I had meant to change, but forgot. Not that it mattered. "I'm not trying to impress anyone."

"What do you do when you *are* trying?" she said. "Put on deodorant? At least take down your hair." She tugged at my ponytail and pulled the elastic out before I could swat her.

We passed the old Windy Hill Church, the ruins encased in vines. There was a cemetery there, too, its occupants largely forgotten, the gravestones covered with lichen that had devoured their names. Kids snuck Ouija boards out there and pretended to talk to the dead, snapped selfies in the dark to see if the pictures revealed ghosts. Kylee and I had been there a couple of times. She'd punched a girl who tried to conjure Grace.

Kylee rolled my hair tie onto her wrist. "Remember how Grace used to braid our hair at night and we'd take it out in the morning so it'd be all crimpy?"

"Yeah." We had undone the braids every morning except for the morning after she disappeared. That time—the last time—we didn't want to take them out until Grace came back. We left them in as long as we could, until Mama finally forced us to wash our hair.

"Do you think she knew somebody was coming for her?"

"Maybe," I said. "If she was scared, she didn't let on."

"She wouldn't have. Grace never acted scared."

"No."

"She didn't even scream," Kylee said. "We would've heard her."

People wondered how we could have slept through the attack, and the only thing that made sense was that Grace had protected us. Kept quiet so we wouldn't wake up and hear her terror, or sneak down the stairs while the killer was there. She had done what she could to keep us safe, even as she fought for her life.

"That girl," Kylee said. "Scarf girl. What was her name?"

"Olivia?"

"O-livia." Kylee said it in a snooty voice. "If I see her, I'm gonna tell her she's got no right talking about our cousin. I'll wrap that scarf around her neck and choke her if I have to."

"Kylee Jane! You're not choking anybody."

"I probably won't have to," Kylee said. "She gets close enough, your BO'll knock her right out." This time, I managed to smack her arm.

"Hey," she said, squinting. "What the hell is that?"

Someone had marked the narrow dirt road we were looking for with a sagging helium balloon, the way you might tie one to a mailbox at the end of your driveway for a baby shower or a kid's birthday party. Except this balloon was tied to a mangled roadkill carcass—a headless deer.

"Fucking psychos in this town," Kylee said.

We parked in a muddy field with the other cars and started trekking up the hill. The abandoned house was part of somebody's grandparents' farm, the woods grown up around it so that it was no longer accessible by vehi-cle. That made it harder to haul in kegs, but easier to avoid getting busted. I'd only seen the house at night and imagined daylight wouldn't do it any favors. The windows were stuffed with moldy cardboard, the wood soft with rot. With any significant rain or snowmelt, a small creek would run under the floorboards. Tree roots were probably the only thing keeping the whole place from sliding down the hill.

Through the trees, we spied a barrel fire burning out front, the silhou-ettes of people chugging beer from plastic cups. When we reached the clearing, I thought I saw Levi at the edge of the woods, but the figure sank back into the shadows before I could be sure. The door was propped open with a large rock, music spilling out of the house. Someone called Kylee's name, and she waved, rolled her eyes, and dragged me inside. The house was lit only by lanterns and phones and gaps large enough to let in moon-light. Beneath top notes of smoke and spilled beer, the place had a deeply earthy smell, dampness and dirt and decay, like the forest itself. Something caught in my hair, and I swiped at it, startled.

"Hold still," Kylee said. "It's just old wallpaper." She peeled off a dan-gling strip and handed it to me, the pattern of faded yellow flowers spotted with mildew. Someone had found it pretty once, had chosen it for the walls of their home. They'd be long dead by now, the wife who picked it out, the husband who had put it up. Kylee turned back toward the kitchen, where a couple of guys were shotgunning beers, and I grabbed her wrist.

"Did you see Levi outside?" I asked.

"No. But if he's here, I bet Tyson's here, too. I never see him out by himself."

I'd noticed Levi at a few parties with his brother over the years, but he never appeared to be having a good time. I assumed he'd gone out with other girls since Grace, though there hadn't been anyone serious unless he was very good at keeping secrets, which was hard to do in this town.

"Come on," Kylee said. "I know there's people you don't want to see, but we have to get at least as far as the keg."

"Can you bring me a drink?" I said. "I'm gonna wait for Ketch."

"You mean, you're gonna hide here in this dark corner so nobody sees you?"

"Yeah. Pretty much."

"Fine. But you have to drink whatever I bring you."

"Sure. Whatever." I leaned back against the wall, pretending to look at my phone whenever I saw someone I recognized. I could hear Kylee laughing in the kitchen. She was taking her sweet time, and I began to wonder if she was ever coming back for me. She finally returned with a cup in each hand.

"Here you go."

I sipped the drink. "This isn't beer."

"You said you'd drink it no matter what."

"I still want to know what it is."

"Liquor," she said crisply. "It was served out of a garbage can, if that tells you anything. Drink up." She tapped her cup against mine and chugged. I swallowed as much as I could in one go. It tasted like someone had mixed Hawaiian Punch with Jägermeister. Kylee wiped her mouth and patted my shoulder with her sticky hand. "All right," she said. "Don't have too much fun." She wove through the crowd and out of sight.

I downed the rest of my drink, and the room began to close in on me as more bodies packed inside, heat and sweat building beneath the jacket I stupidly didn't want to take off now that Kylee had made me self-conscious about how I looked and smelled. I left my cup on the floor and slipped outside, grateful for the chill. A handful of people gathered around the fire, passing a pipe and laughing at something on somebody's phone. I wandered around the side of the house where I thought I'd seen Levi earlier and nearly ran into a guy taking a leak. I turned and headed back, sticking to the edge of the woods, beyond the light of the fire.

"Amelia?" A figure stepped out of the trees.

"Hey. Levi?" He looked different than I remembered from the last time I'd talked to him. His dark hair was longer, past his chin, pushed back from his face. I was always startled to see that he'd aged. Somehow, I expected him to stay frozen in time, to look the same as he had when he was with Grace. He'd be around twenty-four now. Too old, maybe, for a high school party, and from the way he was hiding in the shadows, it didn't seem as though he wanted to be here. Tyson must have dragged him along, same as Kylee brought me.

"It's been a while," I said.

"Yeah." He shoved his hands into his jacket pockets. "How's your family?"

"Fine." Silence stretched between us while I tried to decide whether or not to mention Grace. "We missed you the other night," I said finally. "At the vigil."

Levi rubbed the back of his neck, his gaze dropping to the ground. "Yeah. Sorry about that. I, uh . . . I wanted to be there, but . . ."

"Hey, no—I'm sorry. I shouldn't have brought it up. You don't owe us an explanation or anything. It's just, fewer people show up every time . . . people who actually knew her. I hate to think of her being forgotten."

"No chance I'll forget," he muttered. There was an edge to his voice, anger or pain or something else, I couldn't tell. He managed a strained smile, his eyes reflecting firelight. "Good to see you, Amelia," he said, backing away. "You take care."

I knew that boyfriends and husbands were usually the first to fall under suspicion when a woman went missing, but I'd never been able to imagine Levi hurting Grace. The first time we met him, Grace took us to the Baylors' farm. Kylee was always asking for a horse back then, and Levi brought a pretty paint horse into the paddock for us to ride. I remembered the way Grace looked at him as he led the horse in his mud-caked boots and dusty jeans, his sleeves rolled up, the sun shining on him. She wasn't watching me and Kylee on the horse; she was watching Levi, and I knew then that she loved him. I had loved him, too, in the way that a girl with no good men in her life might love the first man to be sweet to her, to help her onto a horse.

As I crossed the yard, a herd of younger kids flooded past, bumping into me without slowing down, in a hurry to get to the alcohol. One guy stumbled over my feet, and the girl behind him grabbed my arm for balance. She stopped while the others moved on.

"Hey," she said. Her breath was fruity and sharp. She'd already been drinking, something with a bite. She reached out and clumsily touched my lips. "What're you drinking?" she said. "Stained your mouth." Firelight illuminated one side of Olivia's face, her skin sparkling like a *Twilight* vampire from an excess of shimmery highlighter. Her fingers trailed down to the scarf. "I have the exact same one!"

"It's yours," I said. "You lost it. At the Waffle House." I unwound the scarf and draped it around her neck. Olivia took a slurp from an insulated mug, the kind that's supposed to keep your drink cold all day long. No plastic cup for her.

"Wait." Her eyes widened, attempted to focus. "I know you."

"Yeah. Grace's cousin."

Olivia wobbled and then steadied herself. The girl had worn wedge heels to a party in the woods.

"I need to tell you something," she said.

Someone called her name and she swiveled her head like an owl, trying to locate her friends. I grabbed the scarf and drew her close, nowhere near choking her as Kylee had suggested, but bringing us nose to nose, so she wouldn't get distracted.

"Go on and say it."

"I saw her," she breathed. "Grace."

"What did you see?"

"Her body," Olivia said. "They were moving dirt with the bulldozer where they're building our barn. My dad said I could get a horse when we moved here."

"I don't care about your horse," I said. "How do you know it was her?"

Olivia stifled a burp. "Well, the head—the *skull*—was sticking out of the tarp. And I thought there was a wig, at first. It was like her hair was in a ponytail and the whole thing had come off in a big clump. It was all dirty and nasty, but you could still tell what it was. It was long and dark . . ." She stroked my hair where it hung over my shoulder. "Just like yours."

"Liv. Come on." One of her friends had come to retrieve her.

"I'm really sorry," Olivia said, squeezing my hand. "I thought you should know." I let go and she staggered away, the end of her scarf dragging in the dirt.

She hadn't sounded as though she was making it up or joking around, though brown hair didn't mean much, if that was even what she saw. Anything dug out of the ground would be coated in filth and likely hard to identify at a glance. Still. She had seen the remains. A ponytail, long and dark, same as mine. The same as Grace's.

I headed for the house, and Ketch was there, waiting by the door, dressed in the familiar uniform he'd been wearing since middle school: faded jeans, combat boots, camouflage jacket. I couldn't help smiling when I noticed he had on a Beaumont Cross Country shirt, too. Kylee would for sure have something to say about that.

Ketch's hand rested at his hip, right where his pistol would be, beneath the jacket. He'd saved up for it working as a janitor, cleaning the school and the police station at night, and he'd originally bought it for his mother, for protection, in case his dad came back. She wouldn't touch it, though, so he'd started carrying it himself, and now he took it practically everywhere—even on our runs, sometimes, though so far he hadn't found cause to use it on the trail. He'd declined to shoot a rattlesnake coiled in our path one day, insisting we leave it alone, that we could safely make our way around.

"Hey," I said. "Have you seen my sister?"

"I just got here," he said. "Do you want to check inside?"

"Not really. But I guess I will."

Kylee wasn't in the front room or the kitchen, so we pushed our way to the back of the house, into a bedroom with a swollen, rotting dresser against one wall. Water had tracked down from ceiling to floor, dark stains blooming on the wallpaper. Levi's brother, Tyson, stood in the center of the room, telling an animated story to a pair of enthralled high school girls. He took up more space than Levi in every way. Taller, broader, louder, more gregarious, constantly shifting back and forth, gesturing with his hands. He always looked like he'd left home in a hurry: face unshaved, boots untied, shirt unbuttoned, his wavy, wheat-colored hair hastily finger combed. Luckily for him, he made messy look good. Tyson didn't notice me as I moved past him to reach Kylee, who was in the corner with a guy I recognized as one of Olivia's friends from the Waffle House. The puker.

"Do you have any cash on you?" Kylee asked, grabbing my sleeve.

"What for?"

The guy smirked.

"You know Robby?" Kylee said.

"Sort of. I cleaned up his puke the other night."

Robby's face pinked up. "Look, you want the Adderall or not?"

"Hey, hey, hey." Tyson pushed into our circle and clapped a meaty hand down on Robby's shoulder. He acknowledged me and Ketch, but his gaze fell on Kylee and stuck there. "How's it goin'?"

No one said anything at first. Kylee and I had known Tyson since we were little, when Grace would take us to the Baylors' farm, and over the years, he might smile and wave whenever we saw him out, but that was the extent of it. He'd never really talked to us the way Levi did.

"I gotta go." Robby shrugged out of Tyson's grip.

Tyson cracked a grin. "Sorry to scare off your friend," he said. "I saw you girls over here and wanted to say hello."

Kylee ignored him, staring after Robby, probably hoping she'd catch him before he sold his stash to someone else.

"I been hearing all the talk since they found that body," Tyson said. "I know it's gotta be hard for y'all. Everybody thinks it's their business, but none of them knew her the way we did."

Kylee gave him a once-over and deadpanned, "We? Who're you, again?"

Tyson dropped his chin to his chest. "That's fair," he said. "I haven't been around, haven't checked in, and I should have. I'm sorry about that. Not trying to be an asshole here. But me and Grace, we were close—real close. She practically lived at our place when she wasn't taking care of you girls. I've been thinking about all the times she brought you out to the farm."

Kylee chewed her lip, unimpressed.

"Kylee, you knew your way around horses, even back then. Remember that time you helped me groom Midnight?" He cackled. "Told me I wasn't cleaning his hooves right."

"You weren't," Kylee said.

Tyson grinned. "Still full of sassafras. I love it."

Was he flirting? Was she into it? Whatever was happening, I didn't love the way they were eyeing each other, like they'd forgotten Ketch and I were standing there. Kylee hadn't even made a snarky comment about our matching shirts.

"So, I know you do some work for your neighbors," Tyson said. "If you're looking for a summer job, we could use some help at the farm. If you're interested."

"I might be."

"Tell you what. How about you think on it and gimme a call. Can I see your phone?"

Kylee hesitated a moment and then handed it over. He tapped around on the screen and then his own phone dinged. "Now you've got my number," he said.

Kylee checked his message, a hint of a smile playing on her lips. I nudged her.

"We better get going. I've gotta work a split tomorrow."

"We just got here," Kylee said.

"Hey—I can give you a ride later," Tyson said to Kylee. "If you want to stay."

"Yeah," she said. "Thanks." Zero hesitation. Not even a glance in my direction.

"I'll get her home safe," Tyson said, raising his beer. "Don't worry. My killjoy brother's driving."

I couldn't tell whether Kylee was only using Tyson for a ride or if she had something else in mind. Not that it mattered. She never took my advice when it came to guys. I wanted to tell her what Olivia had said, but that could wait. The house was too crowded. Ketch forged a path for us, and we made our way outside and back down the hill through the woods. I didn't see Levi, but I imagined him there, alone amid the trees in the darkness, waiting for his brother. Ketch walked in front, holding branches aside so they wouldn't slap me in the face.

"Have you heard anything at the station yet?" I said. "About the remains?"

"They're working on an ID, is all I know."

"Could you maybe ask David?"

I hated to put Ketch in that position. He and his cousin weren't close, and David could be a real prick about favors—he'd recommended Ketch for the janitorial job and still felt that Ketch owed him. But they were family, and that meant something here, and David was the only cop I knew who might spill something before it went public.

"I can try," he said. "No promises."

"They probably have pictures, right? From the scene, or from the morgue or whatever? I want to see them."

"You sure about that?"

"Yeah," I said. "I heard something. I don't know if it's true. I need to see for myself." I wasn't sure what such a picture would reveal to me. You could easily identify the women in our family in old yearbooks and newspaper clippings and photo albums—we all had the same dark hair and green eyes and tilted smiles. I wouldn't recognize my cousin in these photos. But maybe it was something I could feel; maybe I would know it was Grace, even laid bare in her naked bones.

FOUR

ylee was asleep when I got up, and I had no idea when she'd gotten home, so I didn't bother waking her to tell her where I was going. I knew I couldn't convince her to go along. She'd warned me that Mrs. Mummer was way sicker than she let on—that if she couldn't make it to the vigil, she must already be tits-deep in the grave. Kylee didn't want to see her that way.

Mrs. Mummer lived in a redbrick bungalow on Sycamore Street, and usually the front yard was filled with birds swarming her numerous feeders, but today the yard was quiet, the feeders empty. A sturdy woman in a blue smock answered the door, some sort of nurse or home health aide, and I knew as soon as I saw Mrs. Mummer in a hospital bed in the middle of her living room that Kylee had been right. She looked like the last tiny doll in a set of nesting dolls, the final iteration of her human form after all the other versions had been peeled away. Over her nightgown she wore one of her bright hand-knit cardigans. It hung loose on her skeletal frame. She held out her frail arms to embrace me. "How are you, Amelia!" Her breath rasped in her chest, but she still managed the exclamation point. "Thank you for coming, dear."

"It's so good to see you," I said, though it was hard to look at her. I didn't want this version of her to exist in my head. I started to ask how she was doing, but didn't get past the "How . . . ?" because it was a stupid question and we both knew the answer.

"I'm all right," she said. "Let's just get that all out of the way. I'm not scared. I'll be with my daughter soon. And I pray that, in death, earthly mysteries are revealed." Mrs. Mummer's knobby fingers spidered beneath her collar to extract the necklace she wore in memory of her daughter, Charlotte, who'd died in childhood. In addition to the angel pendant with Charlotte's name engraved on the back, there was a silver butterfly I hadn't seen before. She held it up for me. "This is for Grace," she said.

She might as well have kicked me in the gut. It hurt to breathe. "You know you were her favorite teacher," I said. "I mean, mine and Kylee's, too. But Grace, she was always telling us things you'd said or done, all the way back before we even met you. She taught us to look for small wonders when we were little. It stuck with her, all of it. She never forgot."

Mrs. Mummer folded and unfolded her hands. They fluttered in her lap. "She asked to come home with me, once, and I have always wished that I could have said yes."

"I bet kids asked you that all the time."

She shook her head. "No. This was different."

"What do you mean? She wanted to go home with you for real? To stay?"

"I believe so. In the moment, anyway. She was serious. Something had brought her to that point, for her to ask me that."

There had been times when I daydreamed about going to live with some other family, one that had name-brand cereal, a place where my sister and I wouldn't wake up to strange men in the house. Sometimes, when we were growing up, I had wished we lived with Aunt Elsie. Her house felt warmer, safer, more cheerful. Maybe that was only because Grace was there.

"I could tell something was wrong," Mrs. Mummer continued. "But she wouldn't say what. She was crying. I had no idea what was going on, nothing I could report. I tried reaching out to her mother, but she was working all the time. Couldn't make it to the parent-teacher conferences. I didn't get anywhere, and Grace—I felt that I failed her. So I did everything I could to make school a happy place for her. I kept up with her all those years and tried to be there for her. I didn't know what more I could do. It seemed that things got better at home, later on. She regained her confidence. I believe it was sometime after you and your sister came along."

It was hard to imagine Grace lacking confidence. She had always seemed strong to me. Driven.

"I was so proud of her, of everything she accomplished," Mrs. Mummer said. "It still pains me, though—how she reached out to me and I couldn't help her."

She watched me expectantly, her mouth pinched as she wrung her restless hands. It hit me, why she'd asked me to come. She hadn't wanted to visit, or apologize for not being able to attend the vigil. This was her version of a deathbed confession, and she'd summoned me here to absolve or punish her for some imagined sin. I was hardly a moral authority, but I was here, and she was waiting.

"Grace loved you," I said, trying to sound both comforting and wise. "I'm sure she didn't hold that against you. She never mentioned it, not once."

"No," Mrs. Mummer said. "She wouldn't, I suppose. It's been on my mind lately, that and something else. I wanted to talk to you about it, since I might not get another chance. I don't want to leave anything unsaid."

"Sure," I said. "What is it?"

She pulled a tissue from the sleeve of her sweater and dabbed her nose. "I'm not sure if you're aware, but I was on the Bender Scholarship committee Grace's senior year. I took Mr. Copeland's place because his son, Dallas, was eligible, and it was a conflict of interest. Did you know Mr. Copeland?"

"I never had him as a teacher," I said. "I think he'd retired by then."

"Well, you know the scholarship usually goes to the valedictorian, though that's not in the rules. And Mr. Copeland was pushing for his son to get it."

All I knew about the scholarship was that it was funded by one of the few wealthy families in Beaumont, the one that owned part of Savor Meats. I hadn't paid much attention because I wasn't planning on going to college right away and was never within spitting distance of being valedictorian.

"Grace and Dallas were neck and neck for head of the class. There was a bit of a rivalry, you could say. She didn't mind it, I don't think, because it pushed her. She was competitive. She liked to win. Remember the reading caterpillars that tracked all the books you read? Grace's must have been three times as long as anyone else's. There wasn't enough room on the wall."

"I'm not surprised," I said. My own construction paper caterpillar, when I was in Mrs. Mummer's class, had more than the minimum number of segments only because Grace read with me every night. They were short, simple books, but I never would have read them on my own.

"Copeland was the only biology teacher, and Grace and Dallas were both in that class, and I know at one point she thought he wasn't grading her fairly. That he was favoring his son, so he'd come out on top. Copeland had an ego as big as a barn. I don't think he wanted his boy shown up by a girl from a family of factory workers. Grace didn't give up, though, no matter what he did to throw her off. She kept her grade up. Then . . . come gradua-tion, she was gone, and Dallas got it all anyway. It never sat right with me."

"I didn't know anything about that," I said. "Grace never talked about it."

She balled the used tissue in her fist, each bone in her hand visible through her thin skin. "Those remains," she said. "The ones on the news. They were found on the old Copeland farm. Land got sold to a developer, but it was in their family for generations. They still owned it back then."

"Are you saying . . . you think her teacher might've killed her just so his kid would win a scholarship?"

"I don't know," she said. "I've got no proof of that. But when I heard . . . I felt I should tell you. I wish I'd spoken up at the time. Said something to the man. He was out of line, the way he ran his class, that much was obvi-ous, but . . . I didn't want to cause a fuss." She paused to sip from a plastic cup with a straw. "When you're dying, Amelia, you remember your regrets.

They crop up, like stones in the river when the water gets low. Try to have as few as possible."

"I'll do my best," I said.

That brought a faint smile. "I know you will." She had always told us in class not to worry about a score, just to do our best and be proud of that.

She ran her fingers along her necklace and then gingerly pulled it over her head and handed it to me. "I want you to have it."

The chain was still warm from her skin. The charms dangled from my palm, catching the light. "Are you sure?"

"I'm sure. It's a reminder. The importance of family. I don't have anyone to leave it to. When you die alone, everything dies with you."

"Mrs. Mummer . . ." I didn't want to cry. I wanted to run out the door and keep running.

"It's all right, Amelia," she said, her voice soothing and warm. It took me right back to grade school, Mrs. Mummer praising my use of color in an art project gone horribly wrong, giving me an extra star and a hug. Now here she was facing death all alone, still comforting me. "Our earthly life is temporary, same as a butterfly," she said. "There's beauty and bitterness. Feel it all. That's how you know you're alive."

I called Ketch as soon as I left, because I didn't want to go home, didn't want to be alone. He was already at the trailhead when I arrived to meet him, pulling his laces tight, tying double knots. We ran in silence for the first few minutes, the woods closing around us, mud caking our shoes and spattering our legs.

"I'm sorry," Ketch said. "That's gotta be hard, seeing her like that."

"Yeah, she was still in teacher mode, though. Telling me everything'd be okay. She didn't seem that upset about dying. She wanted to talk about Grace, mostly. She thinks her biology teacher might've killed her—I guess the bones were found on his property. Did David say anything about that?"

"No. But . . . I did get a picture," he said. We stopped in the middle of the trail.

"Why didn't you say something when I called?"

"You were already upset," he said. "About Mrs. Mummer. And I didn't know how to say it."

"Say what?"

He took out his phone to show me. At first, I wasn't sure what I was looking at. There was no skull, nothing that resembled human remains. Only a tarp, partially shredded, a couple of pieces of plastic, and what might, with some imagination, be a clump of hair. There was no gut feeling. I didn't feel anything at all.

"Is that it? Where are the bones?"

"I didn't see them. David showed me this and I took a picture of it with my phone when he wasn't looking."

"This is . . . her hair?"

"David said it's a wig. That real human hair would decompose after a year or two." He tapped the screen, enlarged the photo. "And those are breast implants."

The flicker of hope went dark. I barely felt it, the tiniest light burning out. "It's not her."

"No. But they think they know who she is. There're serial numbers on implants, apparently. David mentioned the name 'Brielle.' They're trying to track down next of kin. You can't tell anyone until they go public. Not even your sister."

"This girl—she was murdered."

"Yeah. I mean, somebody hid her body, so I guess so. You okay?"

It wasn't Grace in that grave. She wasn't the only girl around here who'd disappeared and never made it home. Now there were two. Were there more? Grace was still missing, but her voice boomed in my head louder than ever. *Get out. Don't look back. You can't stay here.* "Come on," I said. "Let's keep going."

We crossed a gully carved through the trail by spring rains. There was only a thin stream of meltwater in it now. Ketch grabbed my hand and we jumped it together.

"Who am I gonna run with when you're gone?" I said.

"I don't know, but I'd feel better if you weren't out here alone."

"There's never anybody out here but us."

"I know. That's what worries me."

"I'll be fine," I said.

"You could come with me."

"Come with you? What, you mean join the army?"

He kept his pace, eyes on the trail. "I mean, after basic training. If you want to go where I'm going. It'd be easier, maybe, to know someone there."

"You know I'm waiting for Kylee. So we can go together."

He sidestepped an outcropping of rock. "Just saying. It's an option."

The trail narrowed to a single track and I cut in front to take the lead, pushing myself uphill, dodging the tree roots that snaked out of the hillside, waiting to snare an ankle. Ketch was right at my heels, and I knew without looking that he made the climb seem effortless, that his pulse and breath remained steady, that he would catch me if I tripped or slid backward.

"What do you think it'll be like?" I said. "Living someplace else? Somewhere other than here?"

"I'm not sure," he said. "Probably something like when Dorothy lands in Oz. Lots of singing. Bright colors."

"Great. Maybe we'll get hearts and brains and courage and whatever else we've been lacking in Beaumont."

"That's only if you're from Kansas," he said. "We're from Missouri. We'll be lucky to get a can of Bud Light and a bootstrap."

I watched my footing in the dead leaves, eyes on the ground, wondering what might be hidden beneath the soil. Somewhere below us, in the valley, in the woods, in the fields, in the river, Grace waited to be found—and maybe she wasn't the only one. We reached the top of the hill but didn't pause to admire the view. We ran like our lives depended on it, churning mud, focused on our breath, the rhythm of our bodies, the distance we had yet to cover.

FIVE

When I got home, Kylee was in the kitchen running Granny
Crow's old stand mixer. I'd never seen her bake anything in
her life, but from the mess of bowls and utensils on the
counter and the flour spilled on the floor, it appeared she was making
something from scratch.

"What are you doing?"

"It's Tyson's birthday. I'm baking him a cake."

"Are you serious? He's way too old for you. Please don't tell me you
hooked up with Levi's brother last night."

"I'm just being nice! I can be nice, Mimi."

"Right," I said. "You've never made *me* a cake. I'm shocked we even
have the ingredients."

"Me too. This stuff doesn't expire, right?"

"Guess you'll find out."

Kylee poured the batter into a pan and went to the sink to wash her
hands, tracking flour across the linoleum. It made me think of a crime
scene, dusting for footprints.

"I went to see Mrs. Mummer," I said.

"Tell me I was right. She's half dead and you wish you hadn't gone."

"You were right. But I'm glad I went. She gave me her necklace." I held it out for her to see. "The butterfly's for Grace."

"Damn. You start bawling?"

"Almost." I poured a bowl of cereal and reached for the milk that sat out on the counter, but Kylee snatched it away.

"I need that for the frosting." She popped the cake into the oven and set the timer.

"She told me some things about Grace. Didn't want to die with anything weighing on her conscience."

"What could she possibly have on her conscience? She forget to put a star on her paper one time?"

"She had suspicions about one of Grace's teachers." I explained about the scholarship, and the remains being found on Copeland's land.

"So you're telling me sweet old Mrs. Mummer thinks this guy might've killed Grace?" Kylee dumped half a bag of powdered sugar into a bowl, and a plume of sugar dust billowed out.

"She's not sure, she just wanted us to know. In case it meant anything."

"Wait, was Copeland's kid named Dallas?"

"Yeah, I think so."

"I know that name." She dribbled some milk into the sugar, and then tipped the jug and cursed when she poured too much. "Here." She handed the bowl to me. "Add more sugar and keep stirring till it looks right."

I took the spoon, but I didn't bother stirring. I doubted we had enough sugar left to firm up the soupy frosting, and I couldn't care less how Tyson's cake turned out. Kylee grabbed her phone, and after a minute of clicking and scrolling, pointed at the screen.

"This is him. Says he's from Beaumont."

I read his Facebook profile out loud. "Dallas Copeland. Future doctor. CrossFit fanatic. Coffee connoisseur."

"Jackass," Kylee added. She scrolled through his page. He was sporty and clean-cut, and showed his teeth when he smiled. He loved to brag about how little sleep he got and how much coffee he drank, and he obsessively posted maps of his runs, along with occasional gym pics, which elicited a chorus of heart-eyes and fire emojis. According to his bio, he was attending med school at the University of Missouri in Columbia.

"Let's message him," she said.

"What? Why?"

"Maybe he knows something! Look, Mrs. Mummer's as close to a saint as you can get in Beaumont. I was a nightmare in her class, and she still made cupcakes for me to hand out on my birthday because she knew Mama wouldn't do it. She gave you her dead daughter's dress when you didn't have anything to wear for the holiday pageant and wasn't even mad when you got paint all over it. For her to basically accuse somebody of murder, she's gotta mean it. She's on her deathbed saying this is important. What if she's right? What if this is it? You want her to die not knowing? Catfishing this guy is literally the least we can do."

"Yeah, but there's something else," I said. "I wasn't supposed to tell you."

"When has that ever stopped you?"

"You can't tell anybody. Ketch'll get in trouble."

She pulled an invisible zipper across her lips.

"It's not Grace they found out there. It's some other girl. So who knows if it even has anything to do with Copeland."

"Maybe he killed them both," she said, pinching my arm. "He could have a whole graveyard out there that they haven't found. What if they're not even looking? Come on, Mimi. Let's live a little. Do something for once instead of just talking about it."

I recognized the gleam in her eyes. Our whole lives, I'd tried to talk Kylee out of things and she'd tried to talk me into them. Sometimes her ideas were flat-out crazy, but this time I knew she was right. Not that it mattered what I thought. When she was determined to do something, it was nearly impossible to stop her. In that way, she was more like Grace than she realized.

"Okay," I said. "I'm in. Let's do it." Kylee clicked the Message button and started typing.

Hi Dallas, I'm a student at Beaumont High and I'm interviewing former graduates for the school paper—I'd love to interview you! It'll only take a few minutes and would really mean a lot. Thanks! Kylee Jane.

"What if he figures out you're Grace's cousin? You think he'll talk to you?"

"He's gonna be so excited to brag about himself that he won't be thinking about anything else. My last name's not on the account, anyway, and I never post on here."

"What are you gonna say if he does talk to you? You can't just ask him if his dad killed Grace."

"You ease into it," she said. "Treat him the same as you would any other man. Flatter him so he gets comfortable. Figure out what matters to him, what he's got to lose, and then use it against him. Turn up the heat and see if he sweats. Easier than boiling frogs."

"Sounds like you know what you're doing."

"Hey, I learned from the master," she said. "Can't say Mama didn't teach us anything."

SIX

When I got to Waffle House for my evening shift, it felt like I'd never left. It didn't help that my job had infiltrated my dreams. I'd wait tables all night in my sleep and then wake up and start over again. I didn't drink coffee, but I'd poured so much of it that the smell brought a looming sense of dread. The one good thing about waitressing was that a busy shift left little room in my head for anything else. I didn't have time to think about Mrs. Mummer or buried bodies while I ticked through a running list of endless tasks, my mind on autopilot. By the time my break rolled around, I needed to get out of the building, away from the grease and glaring lights and the never-changing jukebox songs I'd heard a thousand times.

It wasn't exactly quiet behind the restaurant, though the drone of interstate traffic was almost soothing. The night air was humid and stank of garbage that had been fermenting in the dumpsters, but at least there was a breeze. I counted that as my small wonder for the day. I closed my eyes and leaned against the wall in the darkness, trying to convince myself that I wouldn't be serving waffles for the rest of my life, that I wouldn't always be surrounded by the stench of garbage and grease.

The scritch of a lighter startled my eyes open. The flame illuminated Javi's face as he lit a cigarette.

"Hey," he said. "Didn't mean to interrupt. This is the only spot Alan lets us smoke."

"It's okay," I said. "I was just trying to pretend I wasn't here."

"Same."

"At least there haven't been any assholes tonight."

"Not yet." He took a drag, blew the smoke away from me. "So . . . what was the deal the other night? I thought you might start throwing punches. You know those kids?"

"Not really. They were . . . talking about Grace. You know. That stuff in the news."

Javi flicked his cigarette, nodded.

"Hey . . . you worked with her, right?"

"Yeah. I did."

"Can I ask you something? Did she ever talk about one of her teachers? Mr. Copeland?"

"Nah, we didn't talk about school much," he said. "I dropped out."

"Oh. Were you working her last shift?"

He cleared his throat, twisted his wedding ring around his finger. Smoke hung in the air around him.

"I'm sorry. You've probably been asked that a million times. I just wondered if maybe you noticed anything. Maybe her teacher came in, offered her a ride."

Javi looked off toward the interstate, a stream of red taillights disappearing over the hill. "I gave her a ride to your place after work that night. Figured you knew that."

"Oh. I probably heard it at some point, but I've heard a lot of things . . . hard to keep track of which parts are true and which ones were made up."

"Lot of shit got made up," he mumbled.

"Like what?"

He didn't respond right away. His cigarette burned closer to his fingers, until he finally dropped it and stamped it out.

"You don't know?" he said.

"Don't know what?"

He bent to retrieve his cigarette butt. "That first day, they thought it was me. Cops said maybe I came on to her in the car, got mad when she turned me down. That I could've gone back later that night after she put you and your sister to bed. I was sleeping next to my pregnant wife, but they said maybe I snuck out without her knowing and got back before she woke up. Wife told me I should've known better. Asking for trouble giving some pretty white girl a ride. They wanted to search my car, but that made it worse because I'd cleaned it out. It was raining that night, and there was mud on the floor mats. I keep my car nice. That set them off. They were looking for blood. My wife was so scared she went into labor early."

"Javi, I'm so sorry," I said. "That's awful. I'm guessing they talked to everybody who worked with her that night?"

"They talked to Alan, sure. But they didn't check *his* car for blood." Javi didn't raise his voice, didn't have to. The well-earned bitterness came through in his tone.

"Did Alan give her rides sometimes, too?"

Javi grunted. "She said she'd rather die than catch a ride with him."

"So . . . they didn't get along."

"You know how he is. He'd get real close, brush up against her from behind, act like he didn't mean to. Shit like that. He'd offer to drive her home and get bitchy when she said no. And he was always trying to get her interested in the management program. He lied when he told you she was into it. He'd push her to talk about it in his office. Caught him jerking off in there one time after she left."

"Seriously? Did you tell the police all of that?"

"You think they were asking me about Alan? I was trying not to get thrown in jail. They talked to the waitresses. They'd all seen the same things. If the cops wanted to dig into Alan any more than they did, they would've."

"Do you think . . . they would've found something, if they did?"

Javi took out another cigarette, checked the time, put it back. A door slammed, and both of us flinched. Footsteps approached from the other side of the wall, from the direction of the storage freezer, and Alan appeared, dangling a giant key ring. He propped his hands on his hips and puffed his chest. He was probably flexing his arms, too, though I couldn't tell in the dark.

"Checking inventory," Alan said, unprompted. He zeroed in on Javi. "Your break about up?"

Javi bristled but didn't say anything. They exchanged a long look and Javi went back inside, leaving me alone with Alan.

"Didn't think you were a smoker, Amelia."

"No, I just needed some air." Alan came closer. He was always and forever coming closer.

"You shouldn't fraternize with him," he said.

"What?"

"I'm looking out for you, Amelia. You'll have to trust me on this."

"I don't know what you mean. We were both on break. This is the break spot." He was close enough now that I could smell his sweat, his mustache wax.

"Break's over. Coffee won't pour itself."

Javi was waiting for me inside the back door, index finger pressed to his lips. "Do you think he heard us talking about him?" I whispered.

"Look, forget what I said about Alan. It's not worth it. Just do your job, let it go."

"He told me not to talk to you."

"He's the boss." Javi strode off, putting distance between us as quick as he could.

SEVEN

ylee was at the kitchen table the next morning, fishing pickle slices out of the jar with her fingers. "There's nothing to eat," she said. "Mama still hasn't been to the store."

I checked the fridge anyway. A dried-up bottle of Sweet Baby Ray's barbecue sauce. Half a stick of butter. A lone hot dog in a cloudy plastic bag that appeared to be growing mold.

"You hear back from Dallas Copeland yet?"

"No," she said, licking pickle juice off her thumb. "I'm stalking him on Facebook and he hasn't checked his messages yet today. But I'm betting he will after his morning run. He'd be really easy to take out—his schedule, his location, it's all on there. He's on the Grindstone Trail right now. Can't take ten steps without posting a little map of his progress so people can clap for him."

"Well, let me know what he says. I asked Javi last night if Grace ever talked about Mr. Copeland, and it got kinda weird. Did you know he gave her a ride that night?"

"Her teacher?"

"No, Javi. The police questioned him. He'd scrubbed his floor mats and they thought that was suspicious, but he said he was just cleaning off the mud, that he was home with his wife."

"That's totally suspicious! You really believe he's that anal about his floor mats?"

"He was worried they'd target him, and he was right. He acted like Alan might have had something to do with it, actually. He was upset they didn't really look into him."

"Maybe he's trying to push suspicion off himself onto Alan, and it works because Alan's a creeper."

"It's possible, I guess, but Javi doesn't seem like the violent type. He's always nice at work."

"Of course he's nice at work. He's not gonna act all murdery around you when he knows you're Grace's cousin. Did Ketch say if they got ahold of that Brielle girl's family yet so they can tell everybody they ID'd the remains?"

"You talking about Brielle Becker?" Mama had materialized at the foot of the stairs.

"Who's that?"

"Girl I used to dance with." Mama bugged her eyes. Her makeup was smeared, and it was hard to tell whether she hadn't gone to bed yet or went to sleep without washing her face. "Well?"

"Kylee was talking about somebody from school."

Mama cocked her head like a rooster that was about to make use of its spurs. "I *heard* you talking about *remains*, and I *heard* you say 'Brielle,' and I don't know anybody else with that name around here. Now, I keep a roof over your head, so you best not lie to me, or you'll be the ones fixing to walk with the Lord."

"That girl," Kylee said. "The one you know. She get her boobs done?"

"Yeah, so what?"

"You can't say anything to anybody," I said. "Not Aunt Elsie, not some random guy at work. Swear it."

Mama looked around the kitchen, put her hand on a nearly empty bottle of Captain Morgan. "I swear on all that's holy."

"Ketch's cousin said the body they found isn't Grace. They think it's a girl named Brielle, but I don't know the last name. All I know's she had breast implants and a wig."

"Shit." Mama slumped against the counter. "She wore a wig at work, sometimes. You know, switch things up, blond to brunette. That sucks. I mean, it's not like dancers never meet bad ends, but she was just a kid."

"When did she go missing?"

"I didn't know she did. Haven't thought about her in years. She always talked about going back home, some shithole even smaller than here, figured that's where she went. She had a granny back there, I believe, never told her where she was, what she was doing. Didn't want anybody to find out she was stripping. Dancers come and go, you know? Can't always keep track. We only hung out after work one time, but I'll never forget it. Probably wouldn't remember her otherwise." She opened the fridge, grunted, slammed it shut.

"What happened?"

Mama smirked. "Well, you know your boss, Mr. Mustache? He came into Jane's one night and got hammered."

Kylee made a retching sound. Plenty of men in town had seen our mother onstage at one time or another, even if they were only dragged there, embarrassed, for a bachelor party. It was something you got used to and put out of your mind, but I hated the thought of Alan watching Mama take her clothes off.

"Brielle was giving him some attention and he was stuffing cash in her ass crack. Your uncle Norman was in town and we went drinking out by the stockyards with a bunch of people after work, and Alan shows up, expecting Brielle to treat him all nice for free when she's off the clock. Wouldn't take a hint. Norman finally grabbed him by the balls and told him to leave her the fuck alone. Your uncle's a grade A asshole, but he can be a real hoot when he gets going. Alan slithered outta there on his hands and knees. Some of the funniest shit I've seen."

Kylee kicked me under the table. I knew exactly what she was thinking. "Was that the last time you saw Brielle?" I asked.

"Nah. We were still laughing about it the next day. Joking about Alan's nutsack, wondering if he had a mustache on his dick. Didn't see him back at Jane's for a good long while after that. Not sure he ever did come back." She grabbed the Captain Morgan bottle by the neck and headed for the stairs.

"Mama," Kylee called after her. "You going to the store today?"

"Why would I?" she said, thumping up the steps. "You're letting a perfectly good hot dog go to waste."

"A raccoon wouldn't eat that!" Kylee hollered, but Mama had already shut her door.

"So maybe Javi's not wrong about Alan," I said. "He was probably pissed at Brielle after getting humiliated like that. Maybe Grace pissed him off, too. Javi said Alan was always offering her rides, trying to get her to do his management program, and she said no every time. Maybe that's all it took. I'm gonna tell Ketch, and he can tell David."

"I mean, yeah, tell the cops," Kylee said, "but if they didn't go after Alan when Grace disappeared, why would they now? Some story about him getting his nuts grabbed probably won't cut it. Uncle Norman's not around to back it up, so they'd have to take Mama's word, and you know how likely that is. She's lied to the police a few too many times."

She was right. And maybe it was only a coincidence that Alan was connected to two girls who'd gone missing. In a small town like Beaumont, everybody was bound to be connected somehow, paths constantly crossing, the branches and roots of our family trees tangling in common ground. We had no proof that Alan had anything to do with what had happened to Brielle or Grace. But if he had killed them both, he might be the type to keep evidence of his crimes.

"Remember that *Dateline* we watched about the serial killer from Wichita?"

"BTK?" Her eyes narrowed. "He and Alan have a lot in common, actually. Both uptight nags with gross mustaches."

"You know how he kept all those souvenirs from his victims? Pictures, underwear, jewelry, driver's licenses?"

She pinched my arm. "You think Alan has a little something stashed away in his lair?"

"We're gonna find out."

EIGHT

Javi avoided me at work, not even saying hello when I arrived. He finally made eye contact at the end of my shift, frowning and shaking his head when I followed Alan out the door. I wasn't sure if he was worried or just thought I was stupid, but if anything happened to me, there would be a witness who knew where I'd gone. A grin had crept across Alan's face when I told him I wanted to hear more about the management program. That was all it took for him to invite me over, to offer to give me "a leg up." The way he said it turned my stomach.

I'd always found Alan creepy, but he was ridiculous enough that I'd never quite been afraid of him. That probably gave him an advantage—anyone he targeted would underestimate him. I'd have to keep my guard up. I parked on the street and fluffed my hair, applied some of Kylee's strawberry lip gloss. Alan's yellow ranch house appeared perfectly ordinary except for the enormous, overgrown evergreen shrubs that blocked the front windows and most of the door. A reservoir of dread pooled in my stomach. If he was capable of killing someone, should I really be alone in his house with him? "You can do this." I said it out loud to myself like an idiot. A little fear was good. It'd keep me sharp. Grace never let fear get in her way, and neither could I. She had saved my life once, if not twice. She had jumped into a pool that had always scared her, fought a murderer without letting herself scream. All I had to do was smile and fake enthusiasm about restaurant management.

Alan was waiting at the door to let me in. He extended his arm with a flourish. "This is my place," he said, the words landing awkwardly.

The living room was a study in browns. Beige walls, tan curtains, dirt-colored carpet, the furniture blending in like desert camouflage. A pair of khakis lay in a heap on the floor in front of the couch, as though he'd let them drop and stepped out of them. I didn't want to think about him sitting there watching TV in his underwear or, even worse, *not* in his underwear. The room was as drab and depressing as the countryside in winter, when the trees shed their leaves and the fields were shorn bare and every desolate thing lost its color. The old-fashioned pictures of flower bouquets and bowls of fruit on the walls looked out of place. They reminded me of the ones Mama had inherited from Great-Aunt Iris's house and eventually tossed in the Salvation Army dumpster.

"Wow," I said. I couldn't think of any compliments that would sound sincere, so I nodded at the television. "That's a big TV."

He beamed, his head bobbing. "It's four-K."

"Oh. I bet that was expensive."

"You bet your ass it was."

"So, where's the weight room I'm always hearing about?"

"You want to see it? I can give you the grand tour." He flexed his arm for effect and pointed toward the stairs.

"Yeah," I said, doing my best to appear excited without going overboard. "Sure."

He led me down into the basement and switched on the light, illuminating a windowless room that was even more depressing than the one upstairs. The low ceiling had been painted the same mushroom brown as the walls. "My man cave," he said. "I keep my CD collection down here." He paused so I could feign interest in his choice of music. Lots of ancient hip-hop and rap, unsurprising given the tunes he was always humming at work, elevator-music versions of old Nelly and Flo Rida songs that were probably popular when he was in high school. One time I'd caught him singing "Low" out loud in his office: *Apple Bottom jeans, jeans, boots with the fur, with the fur!* I'd tried to record it for Kylee but couldn't get my phone out fast enough.

"Home office," he said, flapping his hand at a closed door and continuing down a dark hall. "And here's the main attraction." He flicked on a fluorescent light in the unfinished space. "I upgraded to a Bowflex."

"Cool," I said. Alan's home gym looked every bit as creepy as I'd imagined. A hot water heater, a washer and dryer, and a rusted chest freezer lined one wall. Laundry was piled atop the freezer, including dirty socks and a set of wadded-up bedsheets. "What's over there?" I asked, pointing to the back side of the basement where the light couldn't quite reach.

Alan's mustache lifted as his mouth stretched into a grin. "Postworkout soak."

"No way."

"Yes way."

I followed him to a bulky hot tub in the far corner, distracted for a moment by the pegboard on the wall. He pulled a chain and a lightbulb flared. The dark shapes hanging on the pegboard became handsaws, pruning shears, an assortment of hammers. My feet rooted to the floor and refused to move. Alan had set up his hot tub next to his workbench and a wall full of weapons. If he wasn't a killer, he lacked any awareness of how disturbing this looked. Had he brought women down here before? It was hard to imagine that they wouldn't run away screaming. I wanted to run myself, but I couldn't, because I had just found what I was looking for. While Alan removed the cover from the hot tub and bragged about its features, I leaned against the walkout door and reached behind my back to unlock it.

"This is a really great setup, Alan," I said, hoping my voice sounded normal.

"Thank you. I had a feeling you'd appreciate it. I know you care about keeping in shape. I see you out running all the time."

"Oh." I didn't recall ever seeing Alan on the trails, though I didn't always pay attention. I ran to relax, to forget about other things. He'd be the last person on my mind. It made me uneasy to think that he'd been lurking and I'd failed to notice.

"You should be careful out there," he said. He wagged his finger dangerously close to my face, and I wanted to slap it away. If he tapped me on the nose, I wouldn't be able to stop myself. "Running's not safe for a young woman alone," he continued. "Remember that girl in Iowa that got raped and killed on her evening jog, found her in a cornfield?"

"Um. Yeah, I remember." As if he had to remind me of the terrible things that could happen, like I didn't already think about it all the time. As if Grace, and now Brielle—what was left of her—weren't always on my mind.

"We can head upstairs," Alan said, "and I'll grab us some drinks."

I followed him, texting Kylee to let her know that I'd left the basement door unlocked, and that he had proudly shown me everything except for his office, the only room with the door closed.

It was a relief to get out of the basement. Alan poured us iced teas, and when we sat down on the couch, he noticed the discarded khakis on the floor and tried to surreptitiously scoot them under the coffee table with his foot. The coffee table had a glass top, though, so I could still see them. The tips of Alan's ears turned pink. The last thing I wanted was for him to feel embarrassed, humiliated. I smiled, avoided looking at the floor.

"Hey, do you mind if we turn on some background music?" I asked, hoping to provide cover in case Kylee made too much noise rifling through his things in the basement. "It relaxes me after a long shift."

"I totally get it," he said. "I'm the same way. I've got the perfect playlist on my phone." R&B music started playing, and Alan hummed along. "This is Boyz II Men," he said. "Classic." *I'll make love to you*, the singers crooned. *Like you want me to.* "All right." He clapped his hands. "Let's get down to business."

I tried to pay attention as he droned on about the responsibility of management, the weight on your shoulders, all your employees looking to you for guidance. That part was hilarious, because none of us relied on Alan for anything except a paycheck, and waitstaff barely made two bucks an hour, so the check wasn't much. We did our work and tried to avoid him. He went on to talk about the perks of the job. The opportunities. I was shocked that he was actually talking about work. I had expected him to dive right into a sleazy proposition, a blow job in exchange for a recommendation letter, something along those lines. The more he talked, the less interested I became in any type of management, and my enthusiasm had already been at basement level to start with. Boyz II Men continued to play. It wasn't so much a playlist as the same four songs on repeat.

Alan wrapped up his lecture by listing the qualities of a good candidate, and it made me wonder why Javi hadn't applied. He'd been at Waffle House for years, and I'd never known him to call in sick or slack on the job. He could run the whole kitchen on his own without complaint. Maybe he wasn't interested. Or, more likely, Alan hadn't given him the chance. Instead, he offered the opportunity to a mediocre waitress who hadn't earned it and didn't want it. I doubted, though, that Alan had any real intention of helping me or anyone else get a promotion. He'd invited me over to see what he could get out of it. I was counting on that.

"Hey, could I use your restroom, Alan?"

"You bet," he said. "It's the door by the basement stairs."

I paused by the stairwell to see if I could hear anything, but Kylee was being quiet. Alan's bathroom had beige walls and carpeting and a bouquet of fake daisies on the counter. The toilet lid had one of those covers made of shag carpeting (also beige, because of course). I tried not to think about how many other people had sat on it.

Almost done? I texted Kylee.

Not even close, she replied. *Doing God's work here.*

I waited a couple of minutes before flushing the toilet. The little rose-shaped soaps in the dish by the sink were coated with dust. I let the water run long after I'd finished washing my hands, and still there was no text from Kylee. I opened the cabinet under the sink out of curiosity and shuddered when I opened a set of hot rollers and saw silver hairs tangled in them. Obviously not Alan's. I hoped he wouldn't get suspicious about me being gone for so long, but he struck me as one of those guys who didn't know, and didn't *want* to know, what women did in the bathroom. Maybe he thought I was freshening up for him.

I half expected Alan to be lurking outside the door when I finally opened it, but thankfully he was still in the living room, waiting. When I reached for my tea glass, I noticed the khakis had disappeared from beneath the coffee table. "Could I maybe get another drink, Alan?"

"Sure," he said. "No problem."

"I'll come with you," I said. "You can show me the rest of the house."

Alan's kitchen was tidy and granny-ish, with yellow gingham curtains and a macramé owl on the wall above the little breakfast table. The salt and pepper shakers were ceramic toadstools with polka-dot tops. I was starting to think the previous homeowners had died and left all their belongings behind, like when Elsie inherited Granny and Grampa Crow's place. Maybe Alan's granny had passed away and left him the house. Or maybe he killed her and dismembered her in the hot tub.

"I do have beer," Alan said, opening the refrigerator. "I know I'm your boss, but we're off the clock now, so . . ."

"I'm not much of a drinker," I said. "One beer makes me tipsy."

Alan popped the top on a Bud Light and handed it to me faster than I'd ever seen him do anything. He watched eagerly as I took a sip.

"Come on," he said. "Down this hall are the bedrooms."

There was nothing in Alan's two guest rooms except for stacks of empty boxes, though there were several framed family portraits on the walls, the kind people used to take at Sears or J.C. Penney, everyone dressed in turtlenecks and pointy-collared jackets and plaid pants, all the colors faded into shades of brown and orange. None of the people particularly resembled Alan. I hoped the house truly had belonged to a relative, because if these were pictures of strangers, it was disturbing that he hadn't taken them down. Alan seemed to be waiting for a reaction before moving on, but I didn't know what to say about an empty room, so I smiled and chugged my beer. I peeked at my phone. Kylee still hadn't texted. Alan and I were nearing the end of the hall and the end of his tour, and I knew the last thing he was going to show me. He opened the final door.

"And, this is my room," he said, stepping inside.

I stood at the threshold, taking it in. I'd braced myself for something weird, shiny satin bedding, or a black light, or maybe some Boyz II Men posters, considering "End of the Road" was playing for the seventh time, but in reality, Alan's bedroom resembled a sad, anonymous motel room. A pilled brown comforter. Flat, worn-out pillows. Heavy drapes. An ancient clock radio. It lacked even the borrowed personality of the other rooms, having nothing on the walls. You couldn't tell, from looking, what kind of person slept here, or if anyone slept here at all. I imagined Alan spending his nights in the basement instead, alone in his grotto with his Bowflex and hot tub and '90s R&B albums.

Alan leaned against the dresser and set his drink down on a doily, leering at me. "You feeling it?" he said.

"What?"

"The beer. You drank it pretty quick. You can sit down if you want, if you're feeling woozy."

"Thanks, Alan," I said. I was not the least bit woozy, and I was not about to have a seat on Alan's bed. I slumped against the doorframe a bit for effect, but kept my feet planted right where they were. I wouldn't take a single step into that room as long as he was inside it, unless Kylee slammed a door downstairs and I had to throw myself at Alan to distract him. He looked pleased with himself, with how things were going, and I had the urge to slap the sick smile off his face.

"Hey, did Grace ever come over here?" I asked. Alan's dumb grin faded away. I squeezed the beer can, opening and closing my fist, feeling the metal give and spring back. "You know, to talk about the management program?"

"No," he said. "She was going to, but she . . . never got the chance." He moved toward me, closing the distance between us. "I'm glad you're here, though, Amelia."

"I'd . . . love another beer," I said. "But you're right, I might need to sit down. Would you mind getting one for me? And maybe a glass of water, too?" I needed him to get out if I was going to search the room. The dresser wouldn't take long, but there was also a closet.

"I've got another case of Bud in the basement," he said. "I can bring it up."

"Oh—no, that's okay. Maybe I shouldn't." My phone vibrated. Kylee, finally. "Hey, I'm sorry—it's my sister," I said. "I've gotta go pick her up. She needs a ride."

He touched my elbow. "You shouldn't drive if you've been drinking, Amelia."

I stepped back and gently tugged my arm away. "It's sweet of you to worry, Alan, but I'm fine. I don't have far to go."

"Let's talk again," he said. "Maybe this weekend? Or early next week? We can pick up where we left off."

"That sounds great," I said, backing into the hall. "Thanks."

Kylee called before I even reached my car. "What is up with the fucking murder tub?" she said. "You could have warned me. He could be chopping up bodies in there. Making human stew."

"I know," I said. "I thought the same thing."

"Well, there was nothing in his office about Grace or Brielle or anybody else. No newspaper clippings. No diaries. No pictures or jewelry or underwear. Nothing personal at all, really. Just business stuff. Spreadsheets. Scratch paper with a bunch of numbers on it. Stupid motivational posters about success or whatever. A couple old *Hustler* magazines with the pages stuck together. The exact kinda shit you'd expect from him."

"Yeah."

"But there was one surprise," she said. "I checked the freezer. It looked big enough for a body, right? So, I opened it up. There were a ton of those Hungry-Man frozen dinners in there, all the same kind—Salisbury steak with gravy. But that was just on top. There was something else underneath, some kind of false bottom. So I pried it up. That's what took me a while. And I've gotta say, our boy Alan has a secret."

My first thought was that Kylee had found the old lady who'd owned the house before Alan. The one whose hair was still stuck in the hot rollers. "Don't be dramatic," I said. "Just tell me."

"I'm trying! The freezer was stuffed with plastic-wrapped packages. Some of it was meat. But it didn't look like . . . a head or arms or . . . you know, anything human. Though I couldn't really check all of it, so I can't say for sure."

"Kylee."

"I mean, that's the kind of thing we're looking for, right?"

"Was that it? He likes meat?"

"No," she said. "The other packages, the ones that weren't meat—they were full of cash. Stacks of it."

"Cash? How much?"

"I didn't have time to count it, Mimi!"

"I know, I mean—was it, he doesn't trust the bank, so he keeps his savings in there, or more like he robbed an armored truck?"

"It wasn't millions of dollars. It was all wrapped up, so it's hard to say, exactly. But it was more cash than you'd expect that backwoods Waffle House fuck to have in his freezer."

I stopped at the end of the block for Kylee to get in the car. "Where would Alan get that much money?"

"Nowhere good," she said, "if he's hiding it."

I'd thought Alan might have killed girls who'd rejected him, but maybe it wasn't that simple. Maybe there was something else going on. "Do you think it's connected, somehow? Grace was smart. Maybe she figured out he was doing something shady and he didn't want it to get out."

"I don't know," Kylee said. "You know what's fucked up, though? It made sense that it could've been a stranger, some guy off the interstate, totally random. Because who around here would want to kill Grace, right? Who didn't love her? But as soon as you start looking at people she knew, it's not hard to find more than one who might've wanted her dead."

It wasn't just Grace. It could be the same for any of us. On an ordinary day in our dead-end town, we might cross paths with someone we'd known all our lives, someone who secretly harbored a desire to slit our throats, drag us off into the dark.

Get out, Grace had told us. *Before it's too late.*

GRACE

NINE

Someone had been in the house. She could feel it when she walked in the door after the school bus dropped her off. And now confirmation that it was more than a feeling: The toilet seat was up, and her mother hadn't said anything about guests.

She went to check the spare bedroom, just in case. It was a room with dreary brown wallpaper where a succession of elderly relatives had come to live out their last days. Great-Grandma and Great-Grandpa Crow had passed away within weeks of each other in the double bed, followed by Great-Aunt Iris, who had come to recover from a broken hip and died before it could heal. Her mother frowned when Grace called it the dying room, despite Grace pointing out that they also had a living room. While it smelled irrevocably of mothballs and Lysol and ointments—scents she associated with old people and death—not every guest came there to die. Elsie was prone to taking people in. Once, a man Elsie was seeing had moved his three kids into that room, only to leave them behind a week later when he found a new girlfriend. Elsie had continued to care for them until their mother could be tracked down, frying up packs of cheap hot dogs for dinner and making sure they all did their homework and took their baths. Most recently, the room had housed the family of a Congolese coworker from the meatpacking plant whose trailer had burned down. Elsie didn't care what the neighbors had to say about that. Nowadays, she worked the line alongside folks from countries she'd never even heard of. If someone needed your help, you helped them. There were a few times when Elsie should have been more discerning about houseguests, but that wasn't her nature. She'd probably let a vampire in, Grace figured, if it was down on its luck.

Grace stood outside the door at the end of the hall, wondering who might be inside. She pressed her ear to the wood and listened, holding her breath. Nothing. She pushed the door open to see the neatly made bed, the cross on the wall, the tissue box with its crocheted cover on the night-stand. No one was there.

She crept through the narrow kitchen, where her A+ spelling papers hung on the fridge, and out to the backyard, but there were no cars parked in the gravel drive or behind the shed. The plastic lawn chairs were empty. Trees crowded along the fence, evergreens with drooping boughs and massive oaks that blotted out the sun in summer, ensuring that the water in the aboveground pool was always a bit too chilly. The pool was still half full, one wall bulged out like it was about to collapse. It needed to be drained before winter, but they hadn't gotten around to it. Grace hesitantly stepped onto the rickety ladder to peer over the edge. Dead leaves and acorns and bugs floated in the muck, along with a faded pink pool noodle. Someone had flicked in a couple of cigarette butts.

She walked around to the front of the house, the porch still draped with the fake spiderwebs and rubber spiders they'd put up for Halloween. In the distance, she could make out the hazy smokestacks of Savor Meats, where her mother wielded the sharpest of knives, carving tendons from chunks of flesh as they zipped by on a conveyer belt all day long. It was a step up from her previous job of cutting out tongues. Elsie wouldn't be home until later, after dark.

Grace wasn't scared to be in the house by herself. Elsie was always tell-ing people how responsible she was, how mature for a grade-schooler. She could make dinner on her own, but it almost seemed to hurt Elsie's feelings; her mother insisted on cooking, even when she was bone-tired from work. She'd fry up a skillet of bologna and potatoes, swallow a couple of ibuprofen with a diet soda, and fall asleep in the recliner with the TV on, the cold of the meatpacking plant radiating off her like an iceberg had settled in the living room. She lamented her aching joints, though she was careful to never speak ill of her job, as though Savor Meats was a vengeful god that might strike her down for being ungrateful. The meatpacking plant gave her insurance and reliable hours and the best pay she could get in Beaumont without a high school diploma, providing for her family while it broke her body down part by part.

Grace cleaned up the dishes and spent the evening finishing her last library book. Her teacher, Mrs. Mummer, let her check out extra books, but she still always ran out before library day. At bedtime, her mother came to tuck her in and hear her prayers, same as always, yet something still felt off. In the darkness, she thought again of the dying room, of the spirits that might have gotten trapped there. She'd read a book about hauntings, how hard it was to undo them. Grace peered out the window to the backyard. The stagnant water in the pool shone black in the moonlight. The door to her room wasn't locked, nor were the doors to the house. Elsie didn't think you needed locks in Beaumont. Whatever it was had already found a way inside, whether it was a ghost or something worse. There was nothing to do but wait and see if it would show itself.

Grace pulled the covers up over her face and tried to sleep, but there was a humming in her ears, electricity in the air, like bad weather coming.

TEN

Grace woke with a stomachache, a dull pain gnawing her gut. Her bedroom door stood open, a strange scent in the air. Whatever had been in the house had come back. She crept down the stairs and into the darkened living room, where the drapes had been clumsily bunched up in a late-night effort to avoid being woken by the morning sun. She smelled him before she saw him, a distinct, complex odor that could be dissected into several identifiable scents and a few rancid unknowns. Notes of engine grease and motor oil. Marlboro Reds. Fried bologna. Old Spice. It wasn't a ghost or vampire who'd opened her door while she slept. It was Uncle Norman. He lay sprawled across the couch, his bare feet sticking out over the armrest, her mother's pink bathrobe draped over him in lieu of a blanket. She would have preferred a vampire.

She moved closer and studied his face, mouth agape, lips crusted, eyelids fluttering. He groaned and rolled over, the robe sliding off him and down to the floor, and she skittered out of the room. Her mother hadn't said anything about Norman coming to stay, but he likely hadn't given any warning. He showed up when he wanted and stayed as long as he liked.

She wasn't sure how long it had been since she'd seen him last. A year, maybe?

Elsie was always overjoyed to see her big brother, no matter how long it had been. He was a hoot when he wanted to be, the most charming person in the room until something set him off, but even then, Elsie catered to him. She kept a bag of corn chips in the back of the cabinet so she could be ready to make Norman a Frito pie whenever he unexpectedly appeared. That was what family meant to her. You welcomed them home, no matter how long it had been. You cooked their favorite meal, even if they'd never do the same in return.

Usually, Elsie would be up making breakfast by now, but the kitchen was empty. Norman's work boots had been kicked off in front of the stove, his dirty tube socks rolled into balls on the table, his jeans draped over a chair. As if he'd come in the back door and undressed on his way to the couch. Pabst Blue Ribbon cans lay crumpled on the counter alongside an empty liquor bottle and two glasses.

Grace got ready for school quietly so as not to wake them, and all day she prayed Norman would be gone again when she returned. She got her hopes up when she came home and saw the empty couch, but then she realized that was a bad sign: he'd moved his things into the bedroom. He was dressed, at least, when he joined them at the dinner table that evening. He wore a stained trucker hat from Beaumont Motors that was molded to his head and a T-shirt that read "Workin' harder than an ugly stripper." He attacked the Frito pie, gulping it down like a buzzard, telling Elsie that nobody nowhere could cook as good as her. Elsie giggled and blushed, the way she always did when there was a man in the house. Norman drank beer after beer, filling them in on what he'd been up to since he'd last been home. Driving a truck. Roughnecking in an oil field. Pouring concrete. Most recently, before getting fired for stealing an umbrella out of a car, which he denied—*What do I want with a fucking umbrella?*—a stint changing oil at Jiffy Lube. Elsie always said, "Language!" when Aunt Shannon cursed in front of Grace, but she didn't seem to notice when Norman did it. F this and f that, and she just tittered and refilled his plate. She didn't even ask Grace how school was that day, how she'd done on her spelling test. Norman's best magic trick was making everyone else invisible when he appeared.

"Now, this one!" Norman said, swinging around to bug his eyes at Grace. "Look at that. She done grew up on me while I was gone."

Elsie blinked, suddenly remembering Grace was there. "She's doing so good in school. Teacher wrote on her report card that she wished she had a whole class full of Graces."

"That right?" He raised an eyebrow at Grace and turned to nudge Elsie. "You sure she's one of us?" They busted out laughing and Norman winked at Grace before going back to ignoring her.

Aunt Shannon showed up when the plates were being cleared, her long hair pulled into a high ponytail, her skintight jeans and low-cut tank covered by a loose flannel shirt that hung nearly to her knees. "Hey, brother," she said, barely glancing at Norman, who was draining another beer. "You save me some scraps?"

"There's some left on the stove," Elsie said, running hot water in the sink. Shannon scraped around in the pot and ate chili off the serving spoon. Norman came up behind her, grabbed her like he was giving her the Heimlich, and pecked her cheek.

"Jesus!" The spoon clattered to the floor and she shook Norman off her.

He cackled and got three more beers out of the fridge, cracking Shannon's open in a peace offering.

"Good to see ya, sis."

"Elsie made me come," she muttered, but Grace was the only one who heard. Elsie was on her knees, retrieving the dropped spoon and sponging up the mess.

"You still workin' the pole at Sweet Jane's?"

Shannon flipped him off and Norman chuckled.

"Aw, come on, now," he said. "Let's turn on some music and play some cards." He switched on the kitchen radio and fiddled with the dial until he found the classic rock station.

"What kinda cards you playing with three people?" Shannon said.

"Gracie can play!" Elsie said. "I taught her spades."

Shannon eyed her skeptically. "She can be your partner, then."

The four of them sat around the table, making their bids and slapping down cards, the grown-ups getting louder and sloppier as they worked their way through the case of Pabst. Grace kept score on her Hello Kitty notepad and quietly nursed a Mello Yello. At first, she'd been excited about being included in the game, but an hour in, she wasn't even enjoying winning. No one was paying attention to her, despite her being on a team. Norman was chain-smoking Marlboro Reds, the tiny kitchen thick with smoke, and Elsie didn't so much as crack a window. She was too busy laughing at everything her brother said. Shannon didn't find Norman near as funny, her face rarely relaxing from its perpetual glower. When she stripped off her flannel, Norman grabbed her bare arm, twisting it to see her tattoos.

"What the ever-lovin' fuck is this? Some kinda voodoo crap?"

She jerked away from him, knocking over an open beer and soaking the pile of cards in the middle of the table. Elsie snatched them up and grabbed a dishtowel to dry them off. "Least I don't have my ex's name on my private parts," Shannon said.

Norman sucked his teeth, his eyes glinting, and Elsie stood at alert, ready to referee if his humor turned and things got ugly. Beer pitter-patted down onto the floor. A seemingly endless guitar riff played on the radio, and nobody moved, like they were all waiting for the chorus to start.

"It's my bedtime," Grace blurted. "Goodnight, Aunt Shannon. Goodnight, Uncle Norman."

"I'll be there to tuck you in soon," Elsie said.

The bathroom door opened while Grace was brushing her teeth, but it wasn't her mother. "I gotta piss," Shannon said, unzipping her jeans. Grace finished brushing and moved out of the way for Shannon to wash her hands. Her aunt caught her staring. "What?"

"Norman's dumb," Grace said. "I like your tattoo."

"Thanks, kid," she said. "It's a Viking symbol, see?" She ran her fingernail down her forearm. Her skin was orange from self-tanner. "It's for protection."

"Does it work?"

Shannon pursed her lips in the mirror, fussed with her fake lashes where the glue was coming loose. "Can't hurt, right?"

"How long do you think he'll stay?"

Shannon wobbled and sat back down on the toilet. Her breath was sour, her voice a gritty whisper. "Norman, he's like a locust. You know about locusts, right?"

Grace nodded. In the Bible, God sent them to destroy everything.

"Okay, so you know how they crawl out of their holes every few years and they're loud and annoying as fuck and they leave their nasty shells everywhere to remind you how shitty they are even after they're gone?"

"I think those are cicadas."

"Whatever. You know what I mean. He's like one of them bugs. Comes up out of the ground every so often, makes a mess, disappears. Now, when he goes underground, he might be gone for years. Sometimes it's so long you almost forget, and then he shows back up, same old asshole you remember. No telling how long he'll stay," she said. "But it's always longer than you want."

ELEVEN

Grace dug a stick into the side of the pool where it bulged out. She would have rather been indoors, reading, but Uncle Norman was there. Already, the house had begun to smell like him, the dying room emitting a musk that reminded her of the goat pen at the county fair. She would have preferred the medicinal odor of Bengay and Vicks Vapo-Rub that used to linger in the room, the overpowering mothball scent of Great-Aunt Iris's ancient sweaters.

The back door opened and Norman tromped across the yard, carrying a bucket. "I'll shore that up, come spring," he said. "You and me'll go swimming." He clamped his arm around her shoulders. She didn't want to think of him still being here in the spring, or the summer, when she would be out of school.

"Let's do your mom a favor, get this pool drained out." Norman was trying to appear useful around the house, changing the oil in the car and burning the trash, but usually only when Elsie was there to see it. Grace's mother was working overtime because Norman was here to keep an eye on Grace and also because Norman needed money to pay someone back. For what, she didn't know. Aunt Shannon had rolled her eyes and muttered to Grace that Norman always needed money, and there was no way in hell she would give him a goddamned dime.

Norman opened the drain plug and some foul water sluiced out, but not all of it. "We've gotta get in there, clean up the gunk," he said. He climbed in first and helped her off the ladder into ankle-deep water. She shuddered. The pool made her uneasy. It smelled like sewage. They gathered clumps of slimy dead leaves and dumped them over the edge, one armload after another. Grace squatted down to retrieve a cigarette butt. Marlboro Red.

"Hey," Norman said. "Get that pile over there."

Grace scooped it up before she saw it. A drowned squirrel among the leaves. It was only recognizable because of its tail. She wanted to drop it, but her arms wouldn't move. She looked up at Norman. He was watching her, and she knew he must have seen it, told her to pick it up on purpose.

"Jesus," he smirked. "Get a sense of humor."

He grabbed the squirrel, and as he slung it over the edge, something foul and wet splatted across her face. Norman cackled like an old witch, nearly doubled over, and she scrubbed her eyes with her sleeve, trying not to cry. The stench was soaking into her clothes, her skin.

"All right," he said. "We better get cleaned up before your mama gets home. Bath time."

Back in the house, she headed straight to the bathroom. Norman followed her in and closed the door behind them, dropping the hook into the eye latch to lock the door. She watched as he shucked off his filthy flannel shirt and jeans and got the water started, and then knelt down to help her get undressed, his fingers slipping beneath her waistband to unbutton her jeans.

"I can do it myself," she said.

"Oh, that's right." He grinned and held his hands up in a don't-shoot position. "Sorry. I keep forgetting what a big girl you are now. You were just a little thing last time I was here. I gave you baths all the time back then, remember?"

She did not. She didn't remember him having anything to do with her at all back then. Mostly what she remembered about Norman's visits was him being the center of attention, her mother fussing over him.

"Go on, then," he said, making a show of shielding his eyes to give her privacy. She undressed and put her clothes in the hamper like she was supposed to. When she turned back around, Norman was eyeing her. He dipped his hand into the water to check the temperature. "You like bubbles?" he asked.

She nodded. His smile was too big. He squirted shampoo into the stream of water and it churned into foam.

"Mm, strawberry, smells nice," he said. "Ready?" Before she could protest, he'd lifted her up and placed her in the tub. "Make room for me," he said, sliding his boxers down so they fell to the floor. "Only tub in the house, so we gotta share."

She stared at his body, at the thin white scar on his stomach. There was a woman's name tattooed in heavy script on his lower belly—"Annalise"— and a dark nest of hair beneath it. He eased himself into the hot water, his legs stretched to either side of her. The clawfoot tub was slippery, and when she tried to scoot back, away from him, she only ended up sliding closer. He grinned, grabbed her foot, and pretended he was slipping, too, sliding under, bumping against her, sloshing water over the side. He popped back up and shook his wet hair, laughing. The bubbles had already deflated to a swirling gray scum on the surface, and she watched the patterns as the water settled.

"You know, me and your aunt Shannon used to take baths together when we was kids. There's this game we'd play where we'd wash each other. I'd wash her hair, she'd wash mine. I know you can do it yourself, but it's more fun this way."

She kept her eyes on the water. She wanted to go to her room and close the door and be alone with her library books. Mrs. Mummer let them pick out anything they wanted. Grace had chosen a science fiction story with robots on the cover, a guide to marsupials, and a book from the I Survived series, about the Children's Blizzard, where hundreds of people had perished. She wondered how much longer until her mother would be home.

"Here," Norman said, handing her the shampoo. "You can do my hair first." She reluctantly stood up and when she started to slip, he put his hands on her hips to hold her steady. "I won't let you fall. Squirt it on there and rub it in real good."

She upended the bottle and squeezed a generous blob onto his head.

He grinned. "I'm gonna smell pretty as a princess, ain't I? Go on, use both hands, gotta get the grease out." When she was done, he let go of her to duck underwater and rinse.

"Now turn around here, I'll do yours." He pulled her between his legs and washed her hair, dripping soap in her eyes.

"Bodies next," he said. "And dang, am I dirty."

At his direction, she took the washcloth and scrubbed his face, rubbed the bar of Ivory soap across his chest. He made a big show of it tickling.

"Don't forget down below," he said.

She swiped the washcloth down one hairy leg. "All done."

"Hey," Norman said, smiling carefully at her. "It's okay. It won't bite." She didn't move. He took her hand in his and placed it between his legs, giving a gentle squeeze. "See? Okay, your turn," he said.

"I'm ready to get out."

"You gotta get clean." He wasn't smiling anymore. "You want me to tell your mama you wouldn't behave?"

Her mother was across town, working late to give Norman money that he owed to someone else. There was nothing she wouldn't do for her brother. Grace knew that she would not come bursting through the locked bathroom door. She would not even be thinking about Grace right now. On the line, it was very important to focus on the task at hand. Your life depended on it. You had to pay close attention to the sharpness of your blade. The sharpest knives were actually the safest. Dull equaled dangerous. She had taught Grace that, when she started leaving her home alone, so she wouldn't cut herself slicing an apple after school. She probably thought her daughter was safer now, with someone there to watch her.

Norman wrung out the washcloth. Grace closed her eyes and imagined waking up in the morning to find him gone, returned to the ground like Shannon said, like the cicadas, nothing but an empty shell left behind—so small and insignificant, she could crush it with her fingers.

TWELVE

Mrs. Mummer was Grace's favorite teacher. She spoke in exclamation points and played music during quiet time—*Peter and the Wolf*, or a CD of rainforest sounds or ocean surf—and if you leaned in close, she smelled of gingerbread. Her bulletin board featured smiling owls with big happy eyes, and the reading logs were caterpillars taped to the wall. When you finished a book, you could add a new construction paper circle to your caterpillar with the title of the book written on it. Grace's was already the longest, so long she was running out of room to add more.

Mrs. Mummer looked like a grandma, though she didn't have any grandkids, because her daughter, Charlotte, had died suddenly from a heart condition that she'd probably been born with but didn't know she had. Mrs. Mummer wore loose dresses and bright cardigan sweaters that she knit herself and thick glasses with tortoiseshell frames. The only jewelry she wore was a necklace with an angel pendant, her daughter's name inscribed in tiny letters on the angel's gown.

On this bleak Monday morning, Mrs. Mummer brought out the glass aquarium that had previously held Harold, the class turtle, who had died after eating an eraser. Now the aquarium held fat striped caterpillars chewing milkweed leaves. *There's new life in the classroom!* Mrs. Mummer said. *Real caterpillars! Welcome our monarch friends!*

Grace listened, rapt, as Mrs. Mummer explained the metamorphosis that would take place. How the worms would build cocoons and emerge as delicate butterflies. She kept her eye on the aquarium each day, waiting, but when the caterpillars finally made their cocoons, it happened overnight and she missed it. *Don't be sad that we didn't see it happen!* Mrs. Mummer said to the class. *Be excited that we can witness one of life's beautiful mysteries!*

Grace was determined not to miss the moment when the butterflies emerged. She pressed her face to the glass one day after school, thinking she saw movement in one of the cocoons. She didn't want to go home. Norman was there. She asked Mrs. Mummer if she could stay and watch, just for a little while, even though she would miss the bus and have to walk, and Mrs. Mummer said, *Of course! You can stay while I finish grading papers!* She turned on the CD of ocean sounds and handed Grace a peppermint from the bowl on her desk.

Minutes later, Grace knew she hadn't imagined it. The cocoon was moving. Its occupant was struggling to break free.

"Look," Grace said.

Mrs. Mummer looked up from the papers, blinking, a sheet of glittery star stickers in one hand. Mrs. Mummer was always generous with the stickers.

"Something's happening."

Mrs. Mummer hurried over and squatted down next to her. "Oh!" she said.

"What do we do?" Grace asked.

"We bear witness!" Mrs. Mummer said. "If you pay attention, the universe will show you small wonders! Tiny miracles! We keep our eyes open and see the Beautiful Now!"

Together, they watched as the wet butterfly emerged and tended its silken wings. Everything slipped from Grace's mind except for the Beautiful Now, until Mrs. Mummer glanced at the clock and began the process of unlocking all her joints so she could hoist herself up off the floor.

"Time for you to be getting home!"

A lump formed in Grace's throat at the mention of home. Her mother was working late, and she would be home alone with Uncle Norman.

"Can I stay here with you?"

"Oh, I have to go home, too! I don't live at the school!"

Grace's ears burned. Of course her teacher didn't live at the school. She knew that. Desperation forced the words out of her constricting throat. "Can I come home with you, then?"

Mrs. Mummer pressed Grace's hand between her two warm palms. Behind her smeary glasses, her eyes were watery. "I wish that you could," she said. There were no exclamation points in her voice. Her words sounded sad and hollow without them. "But you have a home, and a mother who would miss you terribly if you weren't there."

Grace didn't mean to cry, but her vision blurred, and she couldn't hold it in. Mrs. Mummer hugged her, her soft cardigan blotting the tears.

"Is there a reason you don't want to go home?" Mrs. Mummer asked.

Grace thought of Norman's hands. The calluses across the arch of his palm, the split nail, the cracked skin on his knuckles. No words came out. They swelled in her throat but couldn't find their way to her tongue.

"How about this," Mrs. Mummer said. "Let's sit together for one more minute." They sat in the little chairs, Mrs. Mummer dwarfing hers and spilling over the sides. She held Grace's hand. "Look at the butterfly," she said. "Let everything else go. Live in the moment, and take slow, deep breaths." They sat together breathing, watching the butterfly, listening to the sounds of sea gulls and ocean surf from Mrs. Mummer's CD until Grace stopped crying.

"Now, every day," Mrs. Mummer said, "try to find a moment like this. Pay attention, and the world will reveal its small wonders. There will be days where you might not be able to find a single one. It's not that the beauty isn't there, it's just . . . sometimes you can't see it. But, Grace? You have to keep looking."

Grace took a deep breath and tried to hold the fleeting wonders in her heart. Butterfly wings. The warmth of her teacher's hand. The crashing waves of a distant sea far, far from home.

THIRTEEN

Elsie was over the moon to have Norman back home. She had expected to live out her life surrounded by family, and she was still heartbroken over the untimely loss of her own mama and daddy before Grace was born. Granny and Grampa Crow had drowned crossing the low-water bridge in a hundred-year flood not long after Shannon, their youngest, had moved out of the house. Elsie had been shocked by their deaths, having clung to the childish idea that her father was invincible, though from the stories Grace had heard, she was not at all surprised to learn how her grandparents had died. According to Aunt Shannon, their daddy always thought he knew best, ignoring any evidence to the contrary. He lacked the fear and humility that gave people common sense, incorrectly assuming he could hold his own with the very elements of the earth. He was the one who'd stand outside and watch a tornado bear down instead of heading to the root cellar. He'd burn the fields on a windy day, walk on a frozen pond without checking the thickness of the ice. He had survived many things that might have killed him. Snakebites. A fall from the roof. Fireworks exploding in his face. But when he drove into the swollen river with Granny, assuming they could make it across, the swift water swept their truck away and swallowed them up, spitting them out lifeless on a distant bank.

Elsie had wanted big family dinners, a whole page of Crows smiling in the church directory, but all she had left was Norman and Shannon and Grace. She was gravely disappointed that her siblings hadn't yet managed to get married or have kids. Norman had come close once, Elsie told Grace. Now that he was back, Elsie believed that her brother might finally settle down and give her the extended family she deserved. Grace hoped she was wrong. Every day, as she rode the bus home from school, she prayed he would be gone—that he'd go back underground, like the cicadas, like Aunt Shannon said—but it hadn't happened yet.

The bus wheezed to a stop at her driveway, and there was Uncle Norman's truck, parked by the shed same as it had been every day that week. He'd found a job pouring concrete for a contractor he'd worked with in the past, and he claimed there was plenty of work to go around, yet somehow he was always at the house when she got back from school. It was three forty-five. She calculated the minutes until her mother would be home. She could stretch out her chores and hope that he would leave her alone. She would wash the breakfast dishes, run the vacuum, carry firewood, set out scraps for the stray cats. She would tell him she had to study for a spelling test, though that wasn't true. She had already memorized the words.

He was sitting in the middle of the couch, shirtless, when she walked in, a king on his faux-leather throne. He patted the cushion next to him. "C'mere. Lemme show you something." He was smiling, but that didn't mean he was going to be nice. If anything, the smile was reason to be wary.

She moved as slowly as she could toward the couch, pretending she was walking through quicksand, that it would suck her down into the floor before she reached him, but it didn't. She sat as far away as possible, but gravity and the slick upholstery made her slide toward him. His hairy arm touched her skin and she flinched.

"Look here," he said, holding out a picture. "She's pretty, ain't she? Not as pretty as you, though."

A naked girl, maybe ten or eleven years old, stood in a half-plowed field. It looked like spring, the sky a bright, bitter blue, the ground damp and newly greening. A breeze blew the girl's golden hair over her shoulder and it streamed out behind her. She held a white ferret to her chest. Grace wondered if the girl was cold, if her bare feet had gone numb in the raw, stony earth.

"Who is she?"

Norman smirked. "Nobody you know."

Grace studied the girl's face, trying to read her expression, but her eyes revealed nothing. Aside from the lack of clothing, the picture was ordinary. Perhaps the girl had simply been playing in the fields with her ferret, and her mother made her stop for a picture. Elsie had taken dozens of photos of Grace holding kittens over the years. When she looked back at them, Grace couldn't remember the kittens' names or anything special about the occasion. Maybe it was the same with this girl. Maybe she was older now and didn't even remember the photo being taken. Uncle Norman tapped the photograph, his fingertip blotting out the girl's face.

"We're gonna take some pictures today," he said.

Grace stiffened. "I have homework."

"Come on," he said, chuckling. "It'll be fun." When she didn't get up, he grabbed her by the arm.

In the dying room, with its brown wallpaper and the crocheted tissue box on the nightstand, Grace thought of a show she'd seen on PBS about death rituals and burial practices. She had learned about mummification, embalming, cremation. She imagined her organs being removed, preserved in clay jars, her hollow body packed with sawdust and salt. She envisioned her blood draining away on a cold metal table, chilled embalming fluid pushing through her veins. She imagined a rush of flames, a blinding heat that would consume her flesh and turn her bones to ash. As Norman posed her for his pictures, she played each scenario over and over in her head, each one painless, because her body had gone numb. You couldn't feel anything when you were dead.

She focused on her imaginary death to escape the sensation of being eviscerated while still alive. That was how she felt when Norman looked at her, when he snapped a picture, when he repositioned her limbs. There was no anticipation of the relief she imagined in death, because there was no end in sight.

She did not know what would happen to the pictures, where they would go, who would see them. If men like Uncle Norman would stare at her body, if girls like herself would look into her eyes and try to guess what lay within them. Would they see what she was seeing, her own death playing out? Perhaps her expression, her pose, her imagined life would seem ordinary. She would be skin on paper. A character in a book. Grace, as she knew herself, would not exist to them. They would take from her picture what they wanted. Like the girl with the ferret, they would not even know her name.

FOURTEEN

Grace froze on her way down the stairs. There were noises coming from the kitchen. Norman had left right after breakfast, or so she thought. Maybe he'd already returned. She was going to sneak through the living room and out the door to wait for the school bus, but then she heard someone mutter, "Christ on a cracker," and knew exactly who it was.

Aunt Shannon was digging through the kitchen cabinets, poking her finger into the peanut butter jar, shaking a box of saltines to see if there were enough left to bother with.

"Hey," she said. "Elsie said I could stop by for breakfast, but there's nothing left." She surveyed the empty skillets, paper towels translucent with grease.

"Uncle Norman ate all the bacon," Grace said. "And the eggs."

Shannon pursed her lips. "Course he did. Aren't you supposed to be at school or something?"

"The bus comes at seven thirty."

"Feels later than that," Shannon said. "I've been up all night. Since when do you have granola?" She opened the bag and sniffed it. "How old you think it is?" She popped a piece in her mouth and immediately spit it into the sink. "Don't eat this," she said to Grace, shoving the open bag to the back of the cabinet. "Three family-size bags of Fritos? Jesus, is she making Norman's favorite supper every damn night? Does he not know how to feed himself?"

"Aunt Shannon, who's Annalise?"

Shannon tore open a package of beef jerky. "Where'd you hear that name?"

Grace said nothing. She'd never heard anyone say the name aloud. She had only seen it written on Norman's skin, on a part of his body she wished she hadn't seen.

"You hear Elsie talking about her?" Shannon said. "I'm surprised she'd even say her name with Norman around. He gets pissed if anybody brings it up."

"Why? What did she do?"

"She was Norman's girlfriend, way back when. Real serious deal. Tried to marry her, but her mama wouldn't sign the papers."

"Why not?"

"I dunno, maybe she didn't like him, or maybe it was because her daughter was fourteen fucking years old and she didn't want her kid getting married in middle school to some asshole in his twenties."

Grace thought of the blond girl in the picture Uncle Norman had shown her, and her stomach hollowed out. Could that have been Annalise? That girl had looked younger than fourteen. Maybe the photo had been taken years earlier, though.

"Did she have a pet ferret? A white one?"

Shannon's face wrinkled up. "What? Look, I don't know what kind of animals she had or what color they were or anything about her except she was young and dumb enough to get mixed up with Norman somehow."

"What happened after they couldn't get married?"

"All I know is Norman wouldn't leave her alone, and her mom got fed up. They had to move to get away from him."

Grace couldn't help picturing Annalise as the girl with the ferret, whether it was her or not. She didn't believe that girl would ever want to marry Norman. He had probably tried to force her into it. Annalise managed to escape, but Norman hadn't let go of her. He still possessed her, in a way. Wherever he went, he took her name along with him, down in the dark, secret place she was certain Annalise would not want to be.

"Where did she move to?" Grace asked.

"You think she told us? What good would it do to move if he knew where she was going?" Shannon put down the jerky and turned to look at her. "Why're you so interested in Annalise, anyway?"

Shannon waited for an answer this time, her green eyes probing. Grace's breathing grew shallow. If Shannon looked hard enough, what would she see? Could someone tell what had happened to her just by looking? Grace had a recurring nightmare that everyone knew her secrets, and that fear had spread to her waking hours. She worried that when people looked at her, they would know. That they would not see *her*—the girl she had always been, the girl she was on the inside—but the girl in Norman's pictures. She worried that even if Norman left, even if she could get away from him, she would carry the mark of what he'd done to her, indelible as any tattoo.

FIFTEEN

One frigid morning when Elsie's back was acting up, she asked Norman to drop Grace at Sunday school. The old Dodge pickup kept stalling out and he was cussing: *Motherfucker-bitch-cunt-whore.* Like the truck was a woman who'd done him wrong.

"Listen," he said, jabbing a finger in Grace's face. "I gotta pop the hood. When I tell you to give it gas, give it gas." He threw the door open and icy air billowed into the cab. She had no hat, and her ears ached from the cold. She scooted into the driver's seat, her feet stretching down to reach the pedals. The hood creaked up, and through the gap, she could see Norman, a disembodied slice of him, leaning over the engine.

"Now," he said. "Give 'er some gas." She tapped the gas pedal. "Floor it!" he hollered. She stomped down until he yelled, "Godammit! Let off!"

She spied his fingers, etched black with grease, and she could smell him in the cab despite the winter wind. Marlboros and sweat and stale beer. Her stomach twisted into a tight knot. She imagined herself trying to loosen it, reaching into her gut and pulling it apart, like untangling a necklace.

"All right," he called. "Punch it." Her hand rested on the gearshift.

Some of the letters were nearly worn off, but she could still make out the D. She knew how to do it, how to change gears. Aunt Shannon had let her drive in the field behind the house. She imagined the truck lurching forward, bashing Norman in the chest and rolling over him as he fell to the ground. No one would believe it was anything other than an accident, that a child, especially a girl like Grace, would do such a thing on purpose. She could hardly believe it herself.

"Come on!" Norman bellowed. "Now! Now!" Grace gripped the knob, her teeth chattering. She could do it. She wasn't afraid. But if she ran over Norman and he survived, he might well kill her. That thought seemed to come from somewhere outside herself, but it took root, and she knew it was true. It was enough to loosen her grip on the gearshift, to deflate the swell of courage in her chest.

"Goddammit!" Norman pounded the truck with his fist and she revved the engine until the sound drowned out his voice.

She tried to look for something beautiful, like Mrs. Mummer had said. The windshield was streaked with dirt. Beyond it, the sky colorless and empty of birds. The bare trees bent to the wind for fear of breaking. If there was beauty, she couldn't see it.

SIXTEEN

Aunt Shannon either didn't know she was pregnant or didn't tell anyone out of fear that she'd be forced to switch from dancer to cocktail waitress at Sweet Jane's and take a hit on tips. They finally took her offstage around month six when they started getting complaints, and she went into labor at work two months later while serving a round of Alabama slammers.

Elsie picked her and the baby up from the hospital the next day and insisted on bringing them to the house so Shannon could eat some soup and take a nap. Shannon was still wearing her work shirt from the day before, a Budweiser tee that had stretched out to accommodate her pregnant belly, but she'd traded her booty shorts for a pair of Elsie's pajama pants. She looked ready to fall asleep at the kitchen table, except Elsie wouldn't stop chattering.

"My friend Dodie was working last night when you got to the hospital. She said a man dropped you off and left, and you made a scene, hollering at him that he was a coward, afraid to tell his wife."

Shannon smirked and adjusted the pillow she was sitting on. "Your friend Dodie sounds like a nosy bitch with no sense of humor."

Elsie frowned at her. "Language!"

Shannon rolled her eyes. "He's a regular, likes to joke around. Nice enough guy. I was just getting him back for something he said on the ride."

"What did he say?" Grace asked.

"I'd guess nothing worth repeating," Elsie replied.

Grace peeked at the baby, still bundled in the carrier. She was tiny, jaundiced. "Aunt Shannon, aren't you gonna tell us what you named her?"

"No name yet."

"You can't leave the hospital without naming your baby," Elsie said.

"Sure you can," Shannon said. "'Cause I'm here, and I didn't do it."

Elsie ladled potato soup into a bowl and set it down in front of Shannon. "What about the paper they give you to fill out?"

Shannon shrugged. "Paper said Baby Girl Crow."

"So her name is . . . Baby Girl."

"No, it's not. That's just what they have on there till you do the name."

"Shannon, you'll have to get that legally changed. It'll cost you a hundred bucks. You should've been thinking of a name all along."

"Jesus," Shannon said, pushing her soup aside and getting up from her chair. "I thought you brought me here to *rest*." She disappeared down the hall into Elsie's bedroom, leaving the baby behind in her carrier. The door slammed shut.

"She's wore out," Elsie said. "Needs some sleep, is all."

"Too bad Uncle Norman's here, or they could stay in the spare room."

"Shannon has her own place."

Grace knelt down on the floor to get a better look at the baby. "She needs a name."

"Yes, she does." Elsie sighed. "A family name would be nice. I always liked Iris."

"We should call her Amelia," Grace said. She was reading a book about Amelia Earhart and hadn't yet reached the chapter where the famous pilot was lost at sea. Amelia was brave and daring. She had left her midwestern home and gone on to see the world.

"I guess you can call her whatever you want till Shannon makes up her mind."

"Amelia," Grace whispered, touching the baby's forehead as though performing a baptism.

"Come on," Elsie said. "I'll show you how to make a bottle and change a diaper. Your aunt's gonna need our help."

When Shannon dragged into the kitchen the next morning, the baby was asleep in Grace's arms. Elsie had left biscuits and gravy—Shannon's favorite—on the stove for breakfast.

"I fed Amelia," Grace said.

Shannon nodded, eyes bleary. She fixed herself a plate and sat down to eat. Elsie's coffee cup was on the table, half full, and Shannon grabbed it and gulped down the cold dregs. She seemed more clearheaded by the time she'd finished eating and licked her fork clean. She looked at Grace and the baby as though just now realizing the baby was hers and that her little niece was holding it.

"Thanks for helping out," she said. "I got it from here." She grabbed the carrier, noticing the homemade nametag Grace had attached to the handle with packing tape. "Amelia?"

"Yes," Grace said.

Shannon shrugged. "Better than Baby Girl, I guess."

A week later, Shannon was back at work, still on cocktail duty, her breasts aching and swollen with milk. Elsie gave her cabbage leaves to tuck into her bra, and she and Grace took care of the baby on the nights when Shannon was working. Grace offered to keep the crib in her room. She didn't mind that Amelia was fussy and liked to be held all the time, that the slightest disturbance woke her up and made her cry. The baby was her personal security system, and Norman set off the alarm. If he tried to get Grace to put Amelia down, her colicky screams would drive him away. If he opened Grace's door in the night, Elsie would hear the baby's cries on the monitor and rush in to see what was the matter. Norman wasn't a fan of babies, and it seemed that Amelia could tell. Sometimes his voice was enough to set her off, or his smell if he got too close. Grace began to carry Amelia around in a sling strapped to her chest, and Norman spent less and less time at the house.

Eleven months later, Kylee was born, and she wasn't fussy like her sister. Elsie said babies didn't know what they were looking at, that they couldn't see very well, but Grace didn't believe her. Kylee stared intently, like an animal, her dark eyes watching, wary. She was quiet until someone touched her, and then she'd let out a banshee scream. Shannon rolled both babies into the living room in a one-seat stroller and left them with Elsie and Grace while she went to the hospital to get her tubes tied so there wouldn't be another one. She didn't come back to get them for a week, and Grace hoped she might not come back for them at all. She rocked them and sang to them and read to them from her library books every minute she wasn't in school.

Elsie was bursting with pride at the way Grace cared for her baby cousins. She took it as an indication that Grace would be an excellent mother and give her lots of grandbabies one day. She bragged to everyone that her daughter truly understood the importance of family, of being there for one another. *Family is everything,* she would say. She said it so much that one of her friends from church embroidered it on a pillow for her, and Elsie placed it in the middle of the couch. Norman had faded into the background like an old stain. Elsie ignored his complaints about the screaming and crying, the diapers and bottles all over the house. He didn't come home from work one night, and when Elsie gathered his laundry later that week, she found that his duffel bag was missing, along with some of his things. Grace hugged her cousins tight. She didn't know how long it would last, but for now, her tiny saviors had driven Norman underground.

"He'll be back," Elsie said.

Those three words settled into Grace's bones, a dull, arthritic ache. She was grateful for each day without Norman and constantly wary of his return. She'd lie in bed and sniff the air for the scent of motor oil or Marlboro Reds. She held her breath as she crept down the stairs, not letting her lungs expand until she was certain the couch was empty, the curtains open to the sun, the door of the dying room ajar so it could air out. The longer he was gone, the deeper she could push her fear, though it refused to go away. It lurked beneath the surface, a dark shape with jagged edges. Wreckage waiting to be dredged up.

AMELIA
&
KYLEE

SEVENTEEN

Kylee had been right about Dallas Copeland. She usually was, when it came to men. She knew what they wanted, which, admittedly, wasn't typically hard to guess, but she also knew how to get what she wanted out of them, a skill she'd inherited from Mama. Dallas had responded to Kylee's message, eager to do a video chat so he could show himself off. If his guard was up at all, it would likely give way once he saw Kylee. She'd glossed her lips and put on a clingy, cleavage-baring shirt that would've gotten her sent home from school, her dark hair falling in smooth waves past her breasts. There was some resemblance to Grace—the hair, the green eyes, the tilted smile we all shared—but not so much that Dallas would immediately guess they were related. I sat to the side, out of view. Kylee poked my leg, and her face lit up.

"Hi, there! It's so great to see you! Thank you *so much* for doing this," she gushed.

"No problem," he said. I couldn't see his face, but from his voice alone I could imagine him taking her in, trying not to be obvious about looking at her chest. "It's my absolute pleasure."

Kylee bit her lip and smiled. "Should we jump right in, Dallas? I saw on your Facebook that you're gonna be a doctor. That's *amazing*. I mean, *nobody* from here does that. *So* cool." Kylee tilted her head to the side, gazing at him with fake wonderment. She was too good at this.

"Well, I knew all my life I was going to be a doctor," he said. "I set my mind to it, worked hard, never gave up, and now here I am, top of my class in med school."

"That easy, huh?" Kylee teased.

He chuckled. "Well, it's definitely hard at times, a lot of all-nighters. And plenty of coffee."

I groaned and Kylee kicked my foot.

"Right," she said. "I bet. So, back in high school, you were valedictorian. You got the Bender Scholarship that year."

"I did, yeah. It was an honor."

"Was it even a competition? I mean, did you know you'd get it?"

"I knew I had a good chance."

"Sure. So, I went to the school library and looked you up in the yearbook, and no surprise, I saw you were voted Mr. Most Likely to Succeed! But what was up with that picture of you and Miss Most Likely? Looks like you can't stand each other. Were you bitter rivals or something?"

"No, I think everybody in our class got along pretty well. I haven't seen my yearbook since graduation, so I don't really remember the picture. They probably made us do some dumb poses. So . . . what did you want to ask me about? College advice? Words of wisdom for the graduating seniors?"

"Did you know her very well?"

"Who?"

"Grace Crow."

"I mean . . . we had a class together. And all those senior activities. You know how it is. Are you . . . are you doing a memorial piece about Grace or something?"

"Memorial?"

"You know, she, uh . . ."

"Yeah. Disappeared. Did you have any thoughts about what happened?"

"No. Only that it was horrible. Nobody could believe it. She had such a bright future ahead of her."

"She did. She was at the top of the class, right, same as you? I actually heard from somebody that your dad was her teacher. And that he was trying to make sure you beat her for valedictorian. Do you know anything about that?"

"Wait, what is this?" His tone had shifted. "Wow, I'm an idiot. Is this for a crime podcast or something? I didn't agree to—"

"Relax. I'm not recording you. I'm not writing anything about you for the paper or anywhere else. I'm Kylee Crow. Grace's cousin."

He didn't say anything right away. I imagined his face blanching as the resemblance began to hit him. "Shit. I'm . . . so sorry. For your loss. But I don't really have anything else to say."

"Look, I'm sorry I lied to you, Dallas, but this is important. You know they found a body, right? On your family's land."

He didn't answer.

"I know you know. Your dad must've told you."

"That's got nothing to do with me. My grandparents sold the farm a long time ago."

"We're not accusing you of anything." I scooted over so he could see me. "My sister and I are trying to figure some things out and we need your help. We can keep it between us."

His mouth opened but no words came out.

"Um . . . hi. I'm Amelia."

Dallas massaged his temples. "Anybody else there I should know about?"

"No," I said. "Just us. We were hoping you could talk to us about Grace's disappearance. We really appreciate anything you can tell us."

"There's not much to tell. I found out the day after, same as everybody else. I was home studying that night. My dad was in the basement grading papers."

"So you were each other's alibis," Kylee said. "That's convenient."

"We weren't suspects."

"It worked out pretty well for you that Grace was gone, though, didn't it? Your dad wanted you to get that scholarship, and you must've wanted it, too. Maybe nobody thought anything of it back then, but I wonder what people would think now if they heard it on a podcast, like you said, or on *Dateline* or something. What do you think would happen if people started talking about it? If you *did* look like a suspect? Would that hurt your medical career?"

"Yeah," he said. "That could ruin somebody, and I hope you're not threatening to do that, because I had no reason to hurt Grace. Neither one of us needed the Bender, and it didn't matter who got valedictorian—we already had scholarships from our top-choice schools. My dad was the only one who cared about it, and he'd already done his best to rig it so I'd win—he didn't need to kill her to do that. Grace and I didn't care about any of the high school bullshit by the end. Beaumont was already in the rearview mirror for us. We were ready to leave it all behind."

"How do you know what Grace cared about?"

He rubbed his eyes. "Okay," he said. "Okay. I know Grace cared about the two of you, because she talked about her little cousins all the time. She was worried about leaving you behind."

Kylee folded her arms across her chest.

"She was conflicted about it," Dallas continued. "Because she was so ready to leave. She thought her life was finally about to start."

"You were friends," I said. "You were close."

He looked down at his hands, rubbed his knuckles. "We were spending a lot of time together at the end, yeah. We got to be pretty good friends. We talked about things she couldn't talk about with anyone else."

"Like what? Was there anything she was worried about? Anybody bothering her? Did she say anything about her boss, maybe?" I asked. "Alan?"

"I don't remember her talking about her boss. She wasn't thrilled about having Jimmy at the house, I remember that. He was hanging around a lot, making her uncomfortable, staring at her. And there was something with her boyfriend. With Levi. That's the thing I keep coming back to. It was over between them, basically, but he couldn't accept it. Grace still cared about him, she just didn't want to settle down and get married like he did. She was waiting until she left to really break it off, but . . . something happened. She didn't want him to find out. Later, you know, I wondered, what if he did? What if he knew? How hard would he take it? Enough to hurt her?"

"What was it?"

"Are you really going to keep this between us? Because I'm only telling you if there's a chance it might help you somehow. It wasn't something Grace wanted getting out."

"We promise," I said. "You can trust us."

He didn't look so sure about that. He cleared his throat. "Okay," he said. "There was another guy."

"What do you mean? She was cheating on Levi?"

"It wasn't anything serious, I don't think. Just something that happened. She didn't want to hurt Levi, so she wasn't going to tell him. But I guess it's possible she did, or he found out some other way, and it set him off."

"Well, who was the guy?" I asked. "Maybe he was the one who got jealous, not Levi."

"She didn't say. But I don't think it was like that. I wish there was more I could do to help you. I still think about her, wonder what she'd be doing now."

"What about you?" I said. "What'll you do when you graduate? Are you coming back to Beaumont?"

"No. I'm going into neurology. I'm hoping to score a residency at a school out east. Johns Hopkins. NYU."

"Wow," I said. "That sounds like a big deal."

"Yeah," Kylee said. "I guess you won after all."

The glimmer of pride on Dallas's face quickly dulled. "I hope you figure it out," he said. "I wish I could do more to help."

"So, what do you think?" Kylee asked after signing off. "Do you believe him?"

"Hard to say. I mean, I believe he and Grace were friends. But he's smart, and he doesn't want any fingers pointed at him, so he's not gonna say anything that makes him look bad. He'd rather have us looking at Jimmy or Levi or some other random guy than him."

"I've never heard of Grace being with anybody but Levi. If there really was another guy, we need to find out who it was."

"Do you think Levi knows?"

Kylee clicked her nails on the tabletop. "Only one way to find out."

"You gonna ask him?"

She poked me in the ribs. "You are."

"No, I'm not. I can't talk to him about that."

"Come on, Mimi. He's always been extra sweet to you because you had that embarrassing little crush on him for so long."

"Kylee!"

She rolled her eyes. "Don't act like you didn't. Come with me to the river tonight. Tyson and Levi are out fishing and they're gonna have a bonfire."

"Won't it be weird if I come along? And how am I supposed to bring it up, anyway—'Hey, did Grace cheat on you?'"

"We'll get him drunk, loosen him up. People run their mouths when they're drunk. It won't be weird to bring up Grace, especially with the anniversary. Isn't that what you talk about every time you see him, anyway? Just push him a little, see how far you get. Feel him out, see how he reacts. Tyson and I'll be there, so you won't be alone with him if it goes bad."

"What's going on with you and Tyson anyway, Ky?"

"I'm having fun," she said. "It feels good." She pinched my cheeks. "Don't even give me that look. I'm just *living*, Mimi. You should try it."

EIGHTEEN

It was past dark when Kylee and I arrived at the river. The brothers sat on opposite sides of a small bonfire, a cooler planted midway between them.

"Oh, look," Kylee said. "It's the Baylor boys, sweet and sour."

"I'm the sweet one, right?" Tyson said.

Kylee popped the lid off the cooler and fished out beers for each of us. "We'll see."

She plopped down next to Tyson and I sat near Levi but not so close as to make it awkward. He cracked open his beer can and took a long slug without looking at me. Kylee and Tyson fell into an easy banter, teasing each other, laughing. The frequency with which Tyson's hand found its way to Kylee's knee, shoulder, wrist, and back left no doubt that he didn't merely see her as a friend, and certainly not as Grace's little cousin. Her long dark hair fluttered in the wind, and in the firelight her profile bore a striking resemblance to Grace's, though I might have been the only one who noticed.

I downed my first beer as quick as I could and grabbed another, because I needed a buzz to do what I was supposed to do. Tyson got louder the more he drank, flailing his arms as he bragged about the size of the walleye he'd caught earlier. Levi mostly stayed silent, only managing a halfhearted comeback when Tyson jokingly tossed an insult his way. I'd lost track of everyone's beer count by the time Kylee tugged on Tyson's shirt.

"Let's go get wet," she said.

"Yeehaw!" Tyson hooted. He got to his feet and then hesitated. "Levi? You all right there, brother?"

"Yeah," Levi said. "All good, brother. You?"

"All good." Tyson gave him a long parting look, and then he and Kylee took off down the shore, Levi staring after them long after they disappeared from sight, their laughter trailing back to us through the dark.

The breeze picked up, whistling through the trees and crackling the embers of the dying fire. A shiver twitched through me. "Probably one of the last nights we'll have this kind of chill," I said. It was the sort of thing a random old man might say to you in line at the Kum & Go to initiate an unwanted conversation, and I felt like an idiot saying it to Levi.

"Hey, you cold?" He glanced over as though noticing me for the first time. "You are. I'll stoke the fire." He shrugged out of his flannel shirt and got up to drape it across my shoulders, the scent of his body along with it.

"Thanks, Levi," I said, slipping my arms into the sleeves. I hadn't been able to tell until he got up to tend the fire, but he was unsteady, swaying. Drunk. Way drunker than me. I wondered if Kylee had told Tyson to pump him full of booze, though I doubted he would have done it if he knew the real reason—that we wanted him to let down his guard, tell us things he kept to himself.

Levi fetched two more beers and a nearly empty fifth of whiskey out of the cooler and flopped down next to me, maybe closer than he'd intended, our shoulders touching. "You don't have to drink if you don't want to," he said. "I just like to pretend I'm not drinking alone."

"No, hey, I've got you," I said, taking the whiskey and clicking it against his beer can. "Cheers." I unscrewed the lid and took a quick swig.

He raised an eyebrow, an endearing smile appearing unexpectedly. I hadn't seen him smile that way, unforced, in a long time.

"Now, I know you only did that for me, Amelia," he said. "I can tell by your face you're not a fan of bait shop whiskey."

"Is anybody? It's terrible."

"Not so bad when you're already drunk," he said. He took the bottle from me, our fingers touching, a zap of electricity running straight to my heart. He tipped up the whiskey and swallowed, unflinching. "Your sister says you're making plans to leave town."

"Yeah. We're saving up. There's not much of a plan yet, really. I don't know where we're going."

"Just start driving?"

"I don't know. Maybe."

"Wish I could do that sometimes." The wistfulness in his voice cut through me, slicing clean as a razor.

"You don't have to stay here. You could go."

"I'm never leaving," he said, laughing drily. "I didn't want to, before, and now I can't. I was born here. I'll die here. You know the old joke. It'll take me a lifetime to get from one side of town to the other. Cradle to grave." From the hospital to the cemetery. There was nowhere else to go. "My world is so small," he said. "I can see the whole thing from the end of Cutting Road. I used to think I wanted that. But now . . . this fucking place." Levi crumpled a beer can and tossed it toward the fire. "It's all gone to shit. Not much of a life. Nothing like the one I thought I'd have. That's the bitter fruit," he said. "My granny always says that. Whether we meant to or not, we planted those seeds, and this is what we got."

I reached out to him, wanting to comfort him, not quite sure how. My fingertips grazed the horseshoe tattoo on his forearm, which hadn't brought him the right kind of luck.

"I'm sorry, Levi. It's not fair how things turned out." I took his hand and squeezed it, and he let me. The sensation of his skin against mine was overwhelming. I ached for him, for what he'd been through, because we shared the pain of losing Grace. But beneath that was a different kind of ache. The guilty, thudding pulse of attraction. It wasn't right to want Levi, and I knew he could never want me back, but Kylee was right—I'd loved him, in a way, since I was a little girl.

"What we had," he said, "it couldn't last." I knew he was talking about Grace, though neither of us had said her name. "She didn't want to stay," he continued. "I couldn't see it, couldn't get *why*. Why she couldn't do it for me, for us. I know she loved me, same as I loved her. But I get it now. Why that wasn't enough." He had clasped his other hand on top of mine, holding on as though he needed something to keep him tethered. "I wish I could've seen it then. That it could never, ever be enough. And I shouldn't have tried to change her mind. I know what it means now, to be stuck here. To not have a choice."

His eyes met mine, and there was a desperation in his gaze, a savage need I wished I could fill. His lips parted and I wanted to kiss them. I wanted to take him into my arms, to feel the heat and weight of his body against mine. To comfort him, to be close to him, whether or not it was right. "What do you think happened?" I whispered.

"I know what happened," he said, releasing my hand. "Nobody could let her live her life. Nobody could let her do what she wanted to do. I wanted the saddle, the bridle, the stable, and she just wanted a chance to run free. I wish I could've thought of it like that, instead of being hurt by it. Because I understand the nature of a horse. But this . . . it's the last thing I wanted, for there to be nothing left of her. It's not what anybody wanted, but we're all to blame."

"You think you're to blame, Levi?"

He shook his head. "I'd never hurt her," he said, his voice catching. "I wasn't there that night and I wish to God I was. But there's all kinds of blame. And I live with it every goddamned day." He pushed himself up and nearly stumbled into the fire. "If you're gonna leave, Amelia, you should just do it. Before it's too late." Then he staggered off toward the woods, until the firelight lost him to the darkness.

NINETEEN

Kylee came home around ten the next morning, her hair twisted up in a messy bun. Mama was still asleep and I was on the couch eating cereal out of the box because no one had gone to the store for milk.

"Morning," Kylee said, grabbing the box from me.

"Glad to see you're alive," I said. "What happened to you and Tyson last night? You didn't answer my texts and I finally got tired of waiting."

"Yeah," she said. "Sorry."

"Sorry don't butter no parsnips," I said, mimicking Aunt Elsie. That's what she used to say when we'd apologize for breaking things at her house or getting permanent marker on the couch. Kylee smirked. Upstairs, Mama's door creaked open and then water started running in the bathroom.

"So? What were you doing?"

She flopped down next to me and pulled my feet onto her lap. "Do you really want me to tell you?"

"Is that a hickey on your neck? Seriously, Ky?"

"What?" She pushed down on my toes to crack them, one by one. "What's the problem? He's sweet when you get to know him. And it's not like we don't have anything in common. He's been around horses all his life. We went riding the other day, out at his parents' farm, and I had this flash of déjà vu, you know? Like I'd already been there. Like that was exactly where I belonged."

I'd never heard Kylee talk about a guy that way. She wasn't one to get dreamy-eyed. "I don't know," I said. "It's . . . Tyson. It just seems weird."

"Not as weird as your thing with Levi."

"I don't have a thing with Levi."

"So what happened when you were alone with him last night?"

"Not much." I could still feel him next to me, his hands clasping mine as we sat by the fire. I knew it didn't mean anything. He'd been drunk, and hurting. If I'd kissed him, he would've pushed me away, and I would've regretted it. Still, I'd kept his flannel, tucked it under my pillow so I could smell him as I slept. Kylee would tease me relentlessly if she found out. "We talked about Grace."

"And?"

"He blames himself for what happened. He was pretty upset."

"Did you ask him about the other guy?"

"No. I didn't get a chance. He took off into the woods and never came back. I don't know if I could have asked him anyway, though. If he didn't already know, it'd break his heart all over again. He seemed really regretful, but it was more like . . . he wished he could have kept it from happening. Oh, and right before he left, he said if we were gonna get out of here, we should do it before it's too late."

The toilet flushed upstairs and Mama came padding down. "Yeah," she said. "Best get out. You don't want to get stuck here like me, right? I can hear everything you say in this shitty house." Her breasts hung loose beneath an old Budweiser T-shirt, her long hair snarled in the back from sex or restless nightmares.

"Hey, Mama," Kylee said.

"Grace couldn't get outta here, and she had a brain bigger than the two of yours put together. You're not gonna make it ten feet past the welcome sign."

"You have a rough night?" Kylee said. "You look like shit."

Mama brandished her middle finger as she made her way to the kitchen, her legs wobbly. "Oh, I get it," she said. She bent to look in the fridge and we got a flash of her bare ass. "No. Fucking. Milk," she muttered. She pulled out the mostly empty jar of pickles, the murky green juice sloshing around as she waved it at us. "You think I'm a bad mother, a slut, a *failure*, right?" She struggled to unscrew the lid of the pickle jar and when it finally spun open, juice splattered the floor. "You think you're so smart, you'll drive on outta here and have some perfect life just because you say so—think you can yank up hundred-year-old roots and it'll be easy and it won't hurt and you're magically free of it all. But that's not how it works. No. It's not." She slammed the jar into the sink and then cursed at it, like she was angry it didn't break.

Mama's shoulders sagged, and I thought her tantrum was winding down, that she'd slink back up to her room, but instead she whipped around to face us, her cheeks flushed, fingers pointing at each of us, aimed at our hearts. "You'll be me one day!" she howled. "You don't think it'll happen, but it will. That's just how it goes. I didn't want to be my mother. I didn't want to be a mother at all, everybody expecting something from me, always making me feel like a fucking disappointment. You're just like me. You'll see. You will fuck. It. All. Up."

Kylee threw the cereal box at her and it smacked the wall, spilling brightly colored circles all over the floor. Mama stomped through them with her bare feet, crunching them into sugary dust, and then stormed up the stairs.

"What crawled up her ass?" Kylee said. "Her geezer boyfriend run outta blue pills?"

"Haven't seen that guy around in a while. Or any other guy either, actually. I've barely seen *her*."

"There was a car idling outside the other night. Big ugly thing. Looked like some old broke-ass, catfish sugar daddy."

I hadn't been paying attention. I had too many other things on my mind to worry about Mama and who she was screwing. I got up to fetch the broom. "She's lost her mind," I said. "No way we're gonna end up like her."

"I don't think she's crazy," Kylee said. "She's probably right."

"No," I said. "She's not." I offered Kylee a choice between the dustpan and broom, and she took the broom.

"I don't know if I can leave, Mimi. I don't think I can do it."

"What? You can't be serious. Is this about Tyson? Is he trying to get you to stay? Bribing you with horses?"

"No. Well, maybe. But that's not it." She swept halfheartedly at the cereal. "Sometimes I think . . . it was always gonna play out this way. It's destiny, or whatever you want to call it. You were named after Amelia Earhart, famous explorer, and I was named after a drunk stripper friend of Mama's who drowned on a float trip when her Mardi Gras beads caught on a dead tree underwater."

"That's not true!" I said, taking the broom and corralling all the crumbs she'd scattered. "I heard Aunt Elsie say you were named after a guy Mama was trying to pin paternity on. Kyle, add the 'e.'"

"Wow, thanks, that's so much better."

"You know I'm kidding! I think she just liked the name. It doesn't have to mean anything."

"Still. I'm not like you, or Grace. I never got into the small wonders, the Beautiful Now. I don't see things that way. None of that shit ever worked for me. I've always been more like Mama. That's just the way it is, whether I want it to be or not."

"You're not her," I said. "You're you." I finished sweeping and grabbed a dishrag to wipe up the spilled pickle juice. "And you're brave, same as Grace. You can't tell me you're scared to leave here."

"I don't know," Kylee said. "I try to picture myself somewhere else, living my life, and I don't even know what that looks like. I can't see it. I mean, can you imagine me stuck at a desk, working in an office? Or living in the suburbs, in a big house, taking my kids to soccer practice like some family on a TV show? It's not that I don't want those things, exactly. I don't even know how to want them. How do I know if I want something I've never seen in real life? I can see myself here. I can't say if that's what I want. But what if Mama's right and I can't ever be any other way."

Water splashed into the tub upstairs. Hopefully Mama was getting herself together. I grabbed Kylee's hand and crushed it in mine. "You don't have to decide your whole future right now, Ky. We just need the chance to see what's out there instead of taking whatever's dished up here. We've been going through the free lunch line all our lives getting the sloppy joe because that's what they give you, and it doesn't matter whether or not you like it, and there was no point thinking about what we'd rather have instead, because we never had a choice."

"I fucking hate sloppy joes," Kylee said.

"I know. Me too. And maybe we won't like what's out there any better. But we'll never know if we don't see it for ourselves. We can't stay here. We've gotta go."

"And don't look back," Kylee said.

"Yeah." I poked her in the ribs. She squirmed away and smacked my hands and I smacked hers back like we'd done since we were kids. Our play fighting had always driven Mama crazy, and sometimes we did it on purpose just to get a rise out of her, make her pay attention to us. "What happens if you look back?"

"You'll be a worn-out stripper covered in pickle juice, yelling at your loser kids with your ass hanging out."

"And nobody wants that." Here we were talking about leaving again, but it felt too precarious now. I was on a teeter-totter with her, doing my best to get her up off the ground, aware it wouldn't take much to tip her back down. I knew what would happen if she got too serious with Tyson. If he got her pregnant. If she went to work at Savor. If Robby sold her tainted pills. "Hey," I said, "I don't think we should wait for you to finish school."

"You were just lecturing me about not dropping out."

"I'm not talking about dropping out. As soon as you're done with finals, let's go. We'll have the summer to get settled. We can stay at campgrounds, sleep in the tent till we find a place. You can do your senior year wherever we end up."

"Are you serious right now?"

"Yeah."

"What about Grace?"

"We'll find out everything we can before then, and we'll pass it on to David and hope he does something about it."

"We're her family. Nobody's gonna care as much as we do. Nobody's gonna dig as deep. We can't count on anybody else for that. If we give up, that's it."

"We're not giving up," I said. "I want to find out who did this as bad as you do. But if we can't . . . this is what she told us to do, what she wanted for us."

"When have we ever been good at doing what we're told?"

"This is different."

Kylee slumped over the kitchen counter. "I'm starving, Mimi. Tell me I'll open the refrigerator and there'll be something good in there."

"Sorry," I said. "But I'm off tonight, and I know where we can get a decent meal and do some more digging."

TWENTY

A unt Elsie's living room looked the same as it had for most of our lives, except for a huge new TV balanced on a table that didn't look sturdy enough to hold it, tall speakers positioned on either side. She had probably bought them for Jimmy. Two well-worn recliners faced the television, and the clutter on the coffee table was arranged in neat piles: game controllers, remotes, paperback romance novels, a pair of yellow his-and-hers fly swatters.

Elsie was thrilled when Kylee and I called to invite ourselves over for dinner, unbelievably excited by the prospect of cooking her famous fried chicken for us, and it made me realize that we hadn't made any effort to spend time with her in a while. We'd assumed she didn't want us over with Jimmy around and Grace gone, but maybe it went both ways and she'd assumed we didn't want to come. Jimmy was napping when we got there and slept all the way through dinner, which Elsie apologized for. It didn't bother me one bit not to see him.

After we devoured Elsie's chicken and mashed potatoes and creamed corn and mopped up our plates with buttered biscuits, she opened the fridge to retrieve our dessert. A few of Kylee's and my school pictures were tacked to the door with alphabet magnets, along with Grace's from senior year, all of us with the same crooked smiles that had been handed down from our great-grandmother.

Elsie served us generous portions of homemade chocolate pudding in Granny Crow's custard cups, each with a fluffy blob of Cool Whip on top. Kylee scooped all her Cool Whip into her mouth at once and then reached her spoon over to try to steal some of mine.

"This was Grace's favorite," Elsie said. "She liked to eat it while the pudding was still warm." Her cell rang, loud as a fire alarm. She checked the screen and put it back down, disappointed. "Spam," she said.

Kylee kicked my foot. Aunt Elsie was waiting for a call that wouldn't come. It felt wrong not to tell her about the remains, that it wasn't Grace, though the news wouldn't give her closure, anyway. She'd still have all the same questions.

"I noticed Levi wasn't at the vigil," Kylee said.

Elsie spooned up a bite of pudding but didn't put it in her mouth. "He doesn't owe us that. I miss him coming around, though."

"Do you think they would've gotten married eventually?" Kylee asked. "They seemed perfect for each other."

"That's what I was praying for," Elsie said, pushing her dessert away, uneaten. "What more could a girl want? He had a good family, horses, land. And he loved her like the dickens. If she hadn't pushed him away, he might have been there with her that night. He would've come to drive her home in the storm. None of this would've happened. Heck, if she hadn't been so stuck on the notion of going off to school, she and Levi might've already got married by then, and this house'd be full of grandbabies now." She gestured at the empty chairs. "We'd all be here together. That's how it was supposed to be."

"Wait, did they break up?"

"No. Just going through a rough patch. Everything was college, college, college. She couldn't see what was important, what she had right in front of her. She would've come to her senses, though, soon enough, I know it."

Kylee dropped a bit of pudding on Granny Crow's flowered tablecloth as she took her last bite, and when rubbing it with her napkin only made it worse, she positioned her empty dish over the stain.

"Was Levi mad at her? Mad enough to . . . you know."

"Lord, no." She shook her head. "Not Levi. He was hurt. And who could blame him. But he wasn't giving up. He wasn't mad at her. That boy didn't have an angry bone in his body. And his family was so good to us afterward. His granny cleaned up your house before you went back, you know, so you wouldn't have to see all that . . . mess." She cleared her throat. "His mama brought casseroles, more than we could eat."

"Elsie . . . would it be okay if we looked around Grace's room?" I asked. "We've really been missing her."

"I know how it is," she said. "I used to go in there every day, lie on her bed, trying to feel close to her, flipping through her diaries. It was mostly old stuff about Levi, how in love she was. It's hard to read now. I don't go in there much anymore. Jimmy dusts for me, keeps it looking nice."

Kylee and I scooted back our chairs.

"Just . . . put everything back how it was," Elsie said. "I like to keep it exactly how she left it. So if she comes home, she'll know I didn't give up. That I had faith."

"We won't mess anything up," I said. "Promise."

Grace's door was closed. I couldn't bring myself to open it, so Kylee did, and we both paused in the doorway. At first glance, everything was the same as I remembered it. Double bed across from the window, bookshelves neatly organized, an assortment of neon highlighters in the Kum & Go mug on her desk, a poster celebrating Banned Books Week that implored us to *Read Dangerously!*

"Huh." Kylee broke the invisible barrier and took a step inside. "It doesn't smell like her anymore." She was right. It used to smell of Grace's favorite peach hand lotion. Now it had the vague musk of stale air and disuse.

The trophies on the shelf above the headboard were furry with dust, and the chenille bedspread, which Grace had always pulled tight, was rumpled as if someone had lain down on it. Apparently, Jimmy had been coming in here to nap when Elsie thought he was cleaning. Kylee beelined for her own favorite hiding spots, lifting the bedspread to slide her hands between the mattress and box spring, pulling out drawers and feeling underneath and behind them, taking shoeboxes down from the shelf in the closet. I went for the desk, sifting through the drawers, flipping notebook pages, fanning books open and shaking them to see if anything would fall out.

"Oh, God," Kylee said.

"What?"

"A whole shoebox full of dried-up corsages. Was Grace really that sentimental?"

"I guess she must've been. They're probably all from Levi."

"I hope you're finding something more interesting," Kylee said. "Because dead flowers is about all I've got."

I held up a small card I'd found stuffed in with a stack of old birthday cards and pictures. "Just this." I handed it to Kylee. On the front was a picture of cleaning products. Kylee flipped it over. There was a phone number scrawled on the back.

"What's this? A cleaning service? Was the other guy a janitor?"

"I don't know what it is. That's why it stuck out. Maybe it's nothing."

Kylee knelt in front of the bookshelf and pulled out Grace's journals. "I'd die if Mama read my diary."

"You don't have a diary."

"Well, no, but you know what I'm saying. I can't believe Grace left all of hers out on display where anybody could see them. Who does that?"

"People with nothing to hide? Or maybe people who're too smart to write their darkest secrets on paper."

Kylee slid a yearbook off the bottom shelf and held it up. The cover was glossy blue, BEAUMONT BUZZ centered on the front in white bubble letters, an angry cartoon bumble bee with balled-up fists posing beneath it. "Let's see who signed her yearbook. Maybe some of *them* weren't that smart."

Kylee and I sat on the rug together at the foot of Grace's bed and scoured the signature pages. There were lots of generic comments, things people wrote in yearbooks when they had nothing else to say. *Have a great summer! Stay sweet! Don't ever change!* I had expected something longer from Levi, but he'd simply signed it *Love always.* There was nothing out of the ordinary among the messages, nothing that hinted at a secret crush, a hidden grudge. Hardly any of it seemed personal at all.

Kylee ran a fingernail along the crease near the spine, where instead of using a Sharpie, someone had signed with a blue ballpoint pen. I read it aloud. "Good luck in all your future endeavors! Dallas Copeland."

"Future endeavors," Kylee said. "Yeah, that sounds like him." She flipped through to find the senior personalities. Best Looking. Biggest Flirt. Most Likely to Succeed was at the bottom of the page, and wedged into the crack, overlapping the group picture, was what appeared to be a proof from the same photo shoot. Kylee tugged it loose and held it up. This photo had a completely different vibe from the one printed in the book. While both poses were obviously staged, there was a raw intimacy to this one. Dallas was holding Grace, and it was clear from the looks on their faces, their parted lips, the way their bodies melted together that they were both feeling something more than friendship.

"Good Lord, they look like they're about to tear each other's clothes off!" Kylee said.

"Look, they're not in the group shot for some reason. I wonder why."

"I can guess," Kylee said, "after seeing this." She turned the picture over. On the back was a heart drawn in blue pen.

"It's him," I said. "Dallas is the other guy."

"He's not as smart as he thinks he is," Kylee said. "He let his dick get in the way."

"Or his heart," I said.

Kylee rolled her eyes. "I don't know why you're like this."

I snatched the picture from her and stuffed it into my pocket along with the card I'd found in Grace's desk. "Come on," I said. "Let's put everything back how it was." I pulled Grace's bedspread tight, smoothed out the wrinkles.

The house was quiet on our way down the stairs, the kitchen empty. "Aunt Elsie?" I peered down the hall. The bathroom door was open, and no one was in there. "Did she go to bed and not tell us?"

Kylee pushed past me. "Our old room," she said, opening the door and flicking on the light. "Good lord, check this out." The bedroom where we'd spent countless nights when Mama was working now belonged to Jimmy. A massive desk housed computer towers, dual screens, and a nest of cables and wires. There were superhero movie posters everywhere, shelves crowded with bobbleheads and toy figurines. The portrait of Jesus that had hung on the wall since the beginning of time had been replaced with a black-and-white boudoir-style photo of Elsie and Jimmy. Elsie was dressed in lingerie, and Jimmy wore what looked like a Speedo. The room stank of stale fast food and sweaty feet.

"This place has turned into a real house of horrors," Kylee said. She settled into Jimmy's gaming chair and spun around.

"What are you doing?" Jimmy filled the doorway, his eyes beading back and forth between the two of us, his hair matted from his nap. He wore a Spider-Man T-shirt—the kind with the muscles drawn on so you could pretend you had bulging pecs and a six-pack—and a pair of boxer shorts, his pale legs exposed. I couldn't recall ever seeing him without his jeans on.

Kylee leaned back in his chair, fiddling with the adjustable armrests. "Just hanging out."

"Don't do that," he said, pointing at the now-uneven armrests. "This is my office. It's private."

"Whoa," Kylee said. "This used to be our room. We didn't know it was your *office*."

"We were looking for Elsie," I said. "Where'd she go?"

Jimmy frowned, his cheeks flashing red. "Were you going through my desk?"

Kylee held up her hands. "Chill. Where'd you say Elsie went?"

"Back was hurting," he said, giving no further explanation. Maybe she'd taken a muscle relaxer and gone to bed without saying goodbye. Jimmy's weasel eyes were locked on Kylee, his face turning burgundy, then maroon as she stroked one of the drawer handles with her finger.

"We've gotta go," I said, extracting Kylee from the chair before Jimmy could have an aneurysm.

He moved toward us as we moved toward him, like we were doing a hostage exchange, and then he pushed past us to get to his desk. I caught a strong whiff of his body odor—rotting onions with a touch of Axe body spray.

"Good seeing you, Jimmy," Kylee said, pulling the door shut behind us. Out in the hall, she grabbed my arm. "What the fuck was that? Let's get out of here."

"Wait." I snuck down the hall to knock on Elsie's door. There was a dull hum coming from the room, a noise machine or a fan turned on high. I waited, knocked again, but she didn't answer.

As we drove off, we passed a car idling at the gravel turnout where Elsie's neighbor set up a card table to sell tomatoes every summer. The driver's window was rolled down a few inches, but I couldn't tell whether someone was inside, smoking a cigarette. It looked like the same car I'd seen at the vigil.

TWENTY-ONE

"Do you think we should check on Elsie today?" I said.

Kylee had her camera on selfie mode, making faces while we waited to connect with Dallas. "What, make sure Jimmy didn't kill her last night?"

"I know he's kinda spastic sometimes," I said. "But that was weird, even for him, right? Usually he's doped up, playing video games, barely looks at us."

"He doesn't want us anywhere near his desk, that's for sure."

"He's got a picture of him and Elsie in their underwear out on display. What could he possibly be hiding?"

"We'll ask Dallas," Kylee said. "After I'm done with him."

I shoved a pillow out of the way and sat next to her on the bed. "We need to hurry up with this before I have to get to work."

"Okay." Kylee clicked the button. "This ought to be fun." Dallas's face popped up on the screen.

"Hi, Dallas," Kylee said. I waved at him and he politely waved back. "Thanks for hopping on here with us. You asked us to keep you posted, and we found something." She held up the photo, not wasting any time. "What do you know about this? It was stashed in her yearbook."

He tried and failed to maintain a neutral expression, like he'd been kicked in the balls and was doing his best to pretend it didn't hurt.

"It's a proof from the yearbook shoot," he said. "I was hanging out in the yearbook room when they were tossing pictures they weren't using, and I grabbed that one and stuck it in her yearbook when I signed it. I don't even know if she saw it. It was funny, you know, how they had us pose like a prom pic. Thought she'd get a laugh out of it."

I flipped it over. "Did you forget you drew a heart on it?"

Kylee snatched it back. "Look at the two of you. It couldn't be more obvious if you had a hard-on showing through your pants." I jabbed her with my elbow and she jabbed me right back. "You said the same thing, Mimi, don't act like you didn't. This doesn't make you look less guilty, Dallas."

Dallas cradled his head in his hands for a long moment, let out a sigh. "Okay, look," he said. "I liked her. She liked me. It wasn't anything serious. We had a lot in common, and we liked hanging out. Flirting, I guess. We both knew it was a temporary thing—we were leaving for different schools in the fall. I understood how it was with her and Levi, and I was never upset with Grace over that. She didn't want to hurt him. There were no jealousies, no strings, nothing like that. It was one of those things where we just . . . clicked. That's it."

"I bet you 'clicked,'" Kylee said.

"Did you love her?" I said.

There were shadows under his eyes that I hadn't noticed before, lines across his brow. He looked tired, almost haggard, as though his perpetual caffeine buzz was wearing off. "Who knows what I felt. We were teenagers. None of it matters now."

I wondered if that was why he was constantly running, constantly working, drinking coffee night and day to keep going. It could have been guilt, trying to escape some unforgivable thing that he'd done. Or it could have been love, the loss of it, the inability to forget what might have been.

"Dallas, last time you said something about Jimmy. That it bothered Grace, him hanging around? Did she say anything specific?"

He rubbed his eyes, and when he opened them again, his focus was back. "Jimmy. Yeah. Her mom pretty much moved him in, there toward the end. She didn't like having him in the house. He made her uncomfortable. She thought . . . a pair of her underwear went missing."

Kylee poked me, her finger gouging into my thigh. She had to be thinking the same thing I was. How Grace's covers were messed up, and Elsie said she didn't go in there anymore. I'd figured Jimmy'd been napping in there. It was much more disturbing to imagine what he was doing in Grace's bed after rifling through her underwear drawer.

"She didn't know for sure it was him," Dallas said. "I mean, maybe they got lost in the laundry. But it made her uneasy, having to wonder. She started to feel like she was the one who didn't belong there, like Elsie had basically traded her in for Jimmy. It just made her all the more eager to get out."

"Okay, how about this," Kylee said, holding up the card I'd found in Grace's desk. "This mean anything to you?"

"No. Where'd you get it?"

"Grace's room. How about the number?"

"I don't recognize it. Did you do a reverse lookup?"

"No," I said.

"Hold on, let me try . . . all right. Looks like it might belong to Bill or William Wheeler? You know the name?"

"Nope."

"There's a ton of Bill Wheelers coming up on Google, but you could probably figure out which one's him."

"Or we could just call him."

"Uh . . . maybe I should do it," Dallas said.

"You think we can't make a phone call, Dallas?" Kylee said.

"No, I just mean you should be careful about cold-calling random strangers if you think they might be involved. You might come across some unsavory character."

Kylee snorted. "*Unsavory character*? Thanks for your concern, but you know we live in Beaumont, right? Where girls go missing and dead bodies get found? We're experts in unsavory characters. You just keep drinking your lattes and working out. We'll handle it."

"Thanks, Dallas," I said. "We really appreciate it. We'll keep you posted." I wasn't sure if he heard the last part before Kylee hung up on him.

"You're a little hard on him, aren't you?" I said. "He's trying to help."

"I don't know when you turned soft, Mimi. You never used to be soft with anybody but me."

"I'm not soft," I said. "I think he really loved her. He's hurting, too."

"So you've crossed him off your list. No way a guy could kill somebody he loved. I know you're not that naïve."

"No, it's not that. I just have a feeling about him. He seems like a decent guy. He puts up with us interrogating him, and he doesn't have to talk to us at all if he doesn't want to."

"Maybe he just enjoys being tortured," she said. She handed me the card. "Let's get this over with."

"Do you think this number's still good after six years?"

"Dial."

"Maybe we should have let Dallas call," I said. "If he wants to help, why not?"

"What if he knows the guy and that's why he offered—what if he's helping to cover something up? We can't trust anyone but ourselves, Mimi."

She tapped in the numbers for me. I was starting to panic about what to say if it went to voicemail, but someone answered right away.

"Is this William?" I asked.

"Who's this?" He had a raspy smoker's voice.

"Um . . . Amelia Crow."

"Crow?" he said. "Where'd you get this number?"

I didn't know what to say except the truth. "From a card we found in my cousin's room. Grace Crow."

"Son of a bitch," he said. "You Shannon's kid?"

I squeezed Kylee's arm. "Yeah. Shannon's my mom ... How do you know that? How did you know Grace?"

"I'm Bill Wheeler," he said. "My niece went missing."

I turned to Kylee. "What?" she mouthed. "What's happening?" I shook my head. "I'm sorry," I said to Bill. "Who's your niece?"

GRACE

TWENTY-TWO

Levi Baylor occupied no space in Grace's thoughts until freshman year, when the English teacher asked for volunteers to read their poems aloud, and Levi was the only one to raise his hand. Regret colored his face almost immediately, but he stood up straight in his flannel shirt and cowboy boots and Wranglers and read a poem he had written about his horse. His voice was hushed, as though he was whispering a story to her, and the cadence of his words built steadily from a canter to a gallop. She was drawn into the rhythm. As she watched him read, his face earnest, the notebook gripped tightly in his hands, she imagined him on his horse, riding through summer fields, the wind rushing over him. When he finished, he looked up and saw her, a moment of shared astonishment, and inside her chest, her heart unfolded itself.

He was her first boyfriend. She had known him all her life, in the way that you can't help but know someone in a small town. They had been in 4-H Club together. His family had horses. His brother, Tyson, had once crashed his dirt bike in front of her house. His grandmother had treated Elsie in the ER when she was stung by a swarm of yellow jackets. She knew Levi, yet there was so much she hadn't known. That he saw poetry in the barnyard. That, up close, he smelled of saddle leather, fresh hay, and sunshine. That his hands were strong, yet gentle. She would watch him brush his horses in the barn, and he would look up at her with the same wonderment as he had that day in English class.

She had never loved a man. She had never even wanted to love one, after seeing how her mother acted when men were around. She didn't know how it was supposed to feel, but she felt warm when she was with him. Safe. The knot in her stomach had loosened, made room for other feelings. The giddy sensation of butterflies.

He took her riding one day after school, and she watched the way his body moved, the way he carried himself. He was a patient teacher, explaining how to work the reins, how to change pace. She fell into the rhythm of hoofbeats. When he helped her down from the horse, the heat of his hands awoke something inside her. She felt fearless. Free. She wanted to kiss him and she did. When they came out of the barn, Tyson was there. He had seen them, and he teased his brother, but it came off sweet. He grinned at Grace, and even as her face burned, she couldn't help laughing.

She no longer woke up worrying about Uncle Norman coming back. She'd stopped counting the days since he left, stopped sniffing the air every morning, stopped creeping down the stairs. He had come through town a few times to ask Elsie for money, to eat the Frito pie she would inevitably make, but he had not spent the night at their house or lingered around. He barely glanced in her direction, turning her invisible again. The belongings he left behind had been packed into boxes and stuffed into the closet in the dying room. The room itself had been taken over by her little cousins, and it smelled of Play-Doh and Hello Kitty nail polish and plastic dolls.

Grace rarely thought of Norman at all, though occasionally certain things would trigger a wave of nausea, a tightness in her chest. Cigarette smoke. Strawberry shampoo. In those moments, she tried to tell herself there was more to her than the things Norman had done to her, the things he made her do. That was only one page of her story, a crumpled piece of paper with scratched-out words. If she tried hard enough, she could let go of the dark weight inside, the anchor that held her down, and find the Beautiful Now. The sun on her shoulders. Owls calling outside her window in the night.

She could witness small wonders, like Mrs. Mummer had taught her. She had figured out by now that it didn't fix anything, that it wasn't a magic cure. The magic lay in finding something to grab on to so she could get through that moment, and the next, and make it to another day. It seemed so simple, even if it wasn't always easy, but that was the secret to living.

TWENTY-THREE

Grace sat in the middle of the Chevy bench seat on the way to the Baylors' river cabin, Tyson driving, a Monster Energy drink between his legs, Levi riding shotgun. The sun blazed through the windshield, and the hills were beginning to green, sprinkled with the ephemeral blossoms of spring beauties, violets, and dogwood trees. They were barely thirty minutes outside of town, yet here in the countryside, it was easy to imagine they were far away from Beaumont.

They turned from one dirt road to another and another, too many for Grace to keep track, the air cooling as they drove deeper into the woods and descended into the river valley. Levi held her hand, his fingers entwined with hers. They hung out at his house most days after school, and went riding on the farm, but this was the first time they'd really gone anywhere together. It felt special somehow, that he'd invited her along to his grandparents' cabin to open it up for the season, something he always did with his brother.

"It's just around the bend," Tyson said. "Hold on!" He sped up and took the curve too fast on purpose, laughing as they slid across the seat, Grace sandwiched between the two of them.

"Every time," Levi sighed, pulling her back.

"Here we are," Tyson said. "What do you think?" He parked the truck near a stand of cottonwoods that must have been a hundred feet tall, and they all got out. The cabin was an actual log cabin with a tin roof and a wide front porch facing the river. It was surrounded by trees, with an over-grown garden bed in a clearing. Wind chimes and bird feeders hung from low branches.

"It's so pretty," Grace said.

"Ain't it, though?" Tyson drained his energy drink and crushed the can. He glanced around at a scattering of fallen branches and dead leaves. "I call dibs on the yard. Y'all can do the housework."

"No way," Levi said. "Grace should get to pick. You're just assuming she's gonna clean house?"

Tyson shook his head, grinning. "No, idiot, I was trying to give you two some privacy, but hey, if Grace wants to help me out in the yard, fine by me. Grace?"

She looked from one to the other, pretending to think it over. "I'd like to see the house," she said, taking Levi's hand.

Tyson got the door open and went inside with them to retrieve a dusty six-pack of Budweiser from the pantry. "I'm gonna set this in the river to cool off for later. I expect you lovebirds to get this place polished up by sup-per." He winked at them on his way out the door.

"He's gonna pick up a few branches and then fish the rest of the day," Levi said.

"Hey, that's okay. We've got the place to ourselves. And it's so homey." The large main room had a high ceiling crossed by wooden beams. There was a stone fireplace at one end with two fat couches and a bookshelf stacked with board games and old copies of *Field and Stream* and *Buck-masters* magazines. A kitchen occupied the other end, with little gingham curtains over the cabinets instead of doors, and cast-iron skillets hanging on hooks, and a long, sturdy farm table that appeared hand hewn. There were deer heads mounted on the walls and a largemouth bass, along with a gun rack and a collection of prize ribbons and medals from 4-H and the youth rodeo. The light fixture hanging in the middle of the room was made of antlers. A film of dust covered everything, but it wouldn't take long to clean.

He showed her the tiny bathroom and his grandparents' bedroom, as well as a guest room with twin beds that he and Tyson shared. The last stop was a small bedroom with a window looking out to the woods. It was less rustic than the others, with a pretty oval mirror on the wall instead of a taxidermy animal head. The old-fashioned iron bed was covered with a patchwork quilt in shades of lavender and yellow and pink.

"Whose room is this?"

"It's all boys in our family," he said. "Granny wanted something girly. Still holding out hope for great-granddaughters, I guess."

Grace smiled. "I could bring my cousins over. They'd love it. We could play in the river." She leaned into him. "It must've been fun for you and Tyson, growing up out here."

"Yeah," he said. "It's been different since my grandpa died. Granny's the only one out here much, anymore. My parents have their own cabin now, farther south on the river. But back when we were little, the whole family used to get together. We'd have a big bonfire, fry up some fish. We were always swimming, hunting, making trails in the woods. I want the same for my kids someday."

"Sounds nice."

Levi squeezed her hand. It was completely quiet in the house. Tyson was outside somewhere, probably getting out the fishing poles like Levi said, cracking a warm beer. She had been alone with Levi before, in the barn, or in his bedroom at home, where his mother would carry a basket of laundry down the hall every ten minutes to make sure the door stayed open, but they had never been alone like this. She glanced at the door, and then reached out and closed it.

Levi drew her close and kissed her, and she grabbed his shirt and pulled him over to the bed. They lay down on the quilt, their bodies pressed together, his hands moving lightly over her clothes. She took his hand and placed it under her sweatshirt and felt him sigh. She loved him—his gentle-ness, his thoughtful nature, the smell of his skin, the way he looked in a cowboy hat. He made her feel safe. She did not disconnect from her body when Levi touched her. She inhabited it fully, in a way she hadn't known was possible, the pleasure of anticipation blotting out anything else.

She slid her fingers down his chest and into his jeans, and he went still for a moment, just long enough for her to feel that she'd made a mistake. Instantly, the knot in her stomach was back. Her memories of Norman had lain dormant for so long, it was almost as though she'd forgotten, and now they all flooded in at once. She pulled away and Levi sat up.

"Are you okay?" he said. "We don't have to . . . do anything, if that's what you think. That's not why I brought you here. I wanted to show you this place."

"No, I know." His sincerity was almost painful. She had never worried that he'd try to push her into anything, and he never had.

"Did I do something wrong?"

"No. It's fine. I'm just . . . We should probably get to work."

"Yeah," he said, watching her carefully. "Okay." He held out his hand to help her up, and she smiled so he wouldn't worry.

They shook out the rugs and swept the plank floors and put fresh linens on the beds. Levi wiped down the windows and she dusted the furniture and swiped spiderwebs from the walls. All the while, she could feel a chasm growing between them, her secret welling up in the dark crevice. They made conversation, but it felt like acting, like she was wearing a mask. She didn't know how to be close to him while keeping a piece of herself hidden.

The sun was setting by the time they finished, an orange glow in the sky as they washed their hands in icy well water at the kitchen sink.

"Tyson's got the fire going," Levi said, nodding out the window. "We brought hot dogs and marshmallows in the cooler."

"Levi," she said.

He turned to her, wiping his hands on his jeans.

"Earlier . . . that wasn't about you—us. I just thought of something that I hadn't thought of in a long time. Something I've never told anyone. And I don't want to keep secrets from you. Even if this changes things."

Those first words were the hardest. After that, the rest spilled out in a rush, relieving some of the pressure that had built up inside her. She couldn't read his face. Anger? Disgust? Pity? Levi wrapped his arms around her and told her how much he loved her, and promised that no one would ever hurt her again, because he would kill anyone who tried. She took his hand and kissed his fingers. She couldn't imagine him hurting anyone, and she liked him that way.

"We can take you home now," he said. "If you want to go."

"I'm fine," she said. "I promise. We can talk more later if you want, but right now I'd rather go outside. Catch the last of the sunset."

Tyson was sitting by the fire, roasting marshmallows on a stick he'd whittled down. "You two want a beer?" he asked.

"I don't know," Levi said, brushing off a log so he and Grace could sit down. "How many have you had? Am I gonna have to drive?"

Tyson chuckled. "He forgets sometimes which one of us is the baby brother. I've had one beer, Levi, and I'm about to have another. Grace, how about you?"

"No thanks, I'm all right."

"Look at you two, cuddled up," Tyson said. "Not even leaving room for Jesus. It's sweet. Gotta admit, I didn't see it playing out this way. Me all alone, Levi with a girlfriend. I wasn't sure it'd ever happen for him. I mean, he's good-looking, obviously—he's my brother. But he's always been kinda shy around the ladies."

"Hang in there," Levi said. "You'll find somebody who can stand you someday."

"Hell," Tyson scoffed. "I just wish I could find a girl who's not batshit crazy. But, you know what they say." He shoved a burnt marshmallow in his mouth. "Wish in one hand, shit in the other. See which one fills up faster. Pardon the language, Grace."

"Shocking the girls aren't lining up for that."

"Hey, nothing wrong with being single," Grace said. "Don't let him bully you, Tyson."

"Ha! I like her, Levi. She's good for you. Don't screw this up."

He skewered fresh marshmallows on the stick and handed it to Grace. The river shushed in the background, and night birds called in the trees. Levi slid his arm around her, held her close. She imagined how it would be, the two of them living out here together in the woods. Building fires in the old stone fireplace, watching the stars from the front porch, wading in the river. Away from town, away from her family, but not so far she couldn't see them whenever she wanted. It wasn't a life she'd pictured until now, but it could be a good one.

"I wish we didn't have to go back tonight," she said.

"Maybe one day," Levi whispered in her ear, "we can stay forever. This'll be home, and you'll never have to leave."

TWENTY-FOUR

There were plenty of annoying songs on the Waffle House jukebox, but some of the worst ones were originals from Waffle Records. Grace imagined a bunch of men in suits sitting around a shiny conference table, trying to come up with dumb ways to spend money while they were only paying their waitresses $2.13 an hour. Probably one of the corporate guys had a son who was into music, so they gave him a record label. Every time a customer dropped a quarter to play "Only at the Waffle House" or "Waffle Do Wop"—which was way more often than she would have thought—she had to remind herself why she was there: her college savings account, which she had recently opened for herself, contained $137. Mrs. Mummer had talked to her about college. She thought Grace had an excellent chance of earning a scholarship, and would definitely qualify for financial aid, but college was expensive, and Elsie hadn't put anything away.

Her coworkers were mostly older, but one of the cooks, Javi, had been in her gym class the year before. They had been partners in the square dance unit, and after two weeks of up-close promenading and do-si-doing, all she knew about him was that his family worked at Savor Meats, same as her mother, and that Javi wore deodorant and washed his gym clothes, unlike most of the other guys in class. She hadn't seen him at school since the previous spring and figured he'd dropped out. He didn't say any more at work than he had at school, though he always nodded hello and goodbye to her, and she knew which jukebox songs he liked because he'd bob his head or wave his spatula in the air when the chorus hit. He had caught her pretending to choke herself when a customer played "Waffle Do Wop" three times in a row, and that was the first time she'd seen him crack a smile. Now they traded sympathetic eye rolls whenever a Waffle House original came on.

Grace checked the clock for the hundredth time. Still half an hour till her shift ended, and the place was dead. She counted the change in her apron. Eighteen dollars in tips. Not a great night, though she'd had worse.

"Hey." Alan emerged from his office and loosened his collar. "It's getting slick out there. I can give you a ride when you get off."

"Oh, thanks, Alan, that's okay. I can walk."

"I know you can walk," her boss teased. "I've seen it with my own eyes." He bugged his eyes for effect. "But wouldn't you rather ride in a warm car?"

She'd heard him bragging about his new car having seat heaters. Bun warmers, he called them. It made her gag. She wondered how much he got paid to sit in his office and play on the computer, which was what he seemed to do when he wasn't nagging the waitresses and saying, "If you got time to lean, you got time to clean!"

"That's all right. It's out of your way. I know you've probably got things to do."

"It's called being nice," Alan said, sidling closer. "You need to learn how to accept goodwill when it's offered to you."

She wanted to shove a handful of sweetener packets down Alan's throat to keep any more words from coming out. "I appreciate it so much," she said. "I really do. But I like to walk. It clears my head, you know?" She smiled at him in a way she hoped would put him at ease, make him see her as a good girl who didn't want to trouble him rather than a woman snubbing his advances. It was the most exhausting part of her job, constantly having to modulate her tone, her expression, to act in exactly the right way to avoid an unwanted reaction from a handsy trucker, a self-important regular, her borderline-inappropriate boss. Camouflaging herself and hiding in plain sight in order to survive and try to break minimum wage.

"Oh, yeah, I get that," Alan said. "Exercise is what keeps me mentally sharp. I'm putting in a home gym, actually."

"That's great," she said.

"It's gonna be lit," Alan said.

"I bet."

"Well, if you don't need a ride, I'm heading out, gonna work on some reports from home."

Grace watched Alan's car leave the parking lot and went back to wiping the counter. Her last two customers lingered in a booth sipping coffee, their bill already paid. She tried to count the change they'd scattered on the table. From a distance, it looked to be at least a dollar's worth.

"You think he really works from home?"

Grace turned around, startled. It was probably the longest sentence she'd ever heard Javi utter at work.

"I doubt it," she said.

"You really like to walk home in the ice?"

"Nope," Grace said.

Javi cracked a smile. "Don't blame you. I wouldn't get in his car either."

The couple from the booth walked out, and Grace went to clear the table, sliding the coins into her palm. "Slow night."

"Overnight shift'll be even slower," Javi said.

"You work a lot of doubles, don't you."

"Yeah."

"So . . . are you not in school anymore?"

"Nah. Don't need to be square dancing all day when I could be working. Gotta take care of my family. Me and my wife got a baby on the way."

"Oh," she said. "Congrats." She hadn't even known he was married.

"What about you?" he said. "Gonna keep working here when you graduate?"

"Well, my mom seems to think I'll get a job at Savor, but I'm actually saving up for college," she said, shaking the change in her apron. "Very, very slowly."

"Yeah," he said. "You gotta do your own thing. My family, they think I'm an idiot, not working at the plant. Pay's better over there. But I'd rather cook. I want to have my own restaurant someday. Work for myself, not somebody like Alan. No boss ever gonna look out for you. They just look out for their own ass. Never gonna get anywhere different when you're cutting meat for somebody else. Figure the more doubles I work, the closer I am to getting outta here."

"Sounds like a good plan," she said.

"Maybe," he said. "Or they're right, and I'm a dumbass. Guess we'll find out."

Grace smiled. "Here's to being short-timers."

One of the night waitresses hurried in, sleet melting on her coat and hair. "Colder'n a witch's tit out there," she said. "Will you clock me in? I gotta hit the toilet."

"Sure thing," Grace said. She took care of the time cards and bundled up in her parka and stocking cap. If Levi hadn't been out of town for a basketball game, she would have called him for a ride, but she didn't regret declining Alan's offer. She'd rather walk through a blizzard than spend ten minutes making awkward conversation in her boss's car.

"Have a good night," she called to Javi.

He waved his spatula. "Careful out there."

She walked along the access road toward home, curtains of sleet billowing in the wind, the icy air burning her throat. A car crept up behind her, and her shadow stretched out like a giant in the headlights. The vehicle turned toward the interstate that led to places she'd never been, roads that would one day carry her away from home.

The glow of the Waffle House faded into darkness as she reached Cutting Road, and she had to watch her steps carefully as she trudged uphill. She hadn't gotten far when the sky lit up above the trees, and then high beams spilled over the hilltop and momentarily blinded her. A truck sped toward her and skidded to a stop in the middle of the empty road. The driver's-side window jerked down with a series of squeaks.

"Hey there, young lady. Need a ride?"

She squinted into the cab, her eyes adjusting. "Tyson?"

"Who else?" he said. "Baby brother was worried about you, so I came to pick you up. Hop on in."

She climbed inside and tugged off her wet hat. Tyson had the heater blasting, all the vents aimed in her direction. He grinned at her. "Good thing I showed up when I did. Looks like you been rode hard and put away wet."

"Wow, thanks," she said, smacking his arm with the hat.

"Sorry!" He laughed. "It's a horse thing."

She hadn't noticed before how his smile looked so much like Levi's.

"Seriously. Thanks, Ty."

"Anything for my brother," he said.

TWENTY-FIVE

G race's lab partner was tearing up again. Sophie cried every time they got their cat out of the black garbage bag it was stored in and claimed she was allergic to formaldehyde. She averted her eyes whenever Grace reached for the scalpel. Grace didn't want to dissect a cat either, but she needed another science class on her transcript. The worst part was that it was taught by Mr. Copeland. She'd had him for health freshman year, and when she got the highest grade on the final, he'd told her she was smart enough to consider becoming a nurse. A nurse, not a doctor. It had grated on her. Not that she thought nurses were inferior, but because he apparently did. Everyone knew that Mr. Copeland's son, Dallas, was going to be Beaumont's next doctor. Dallas had been talking about majoring in pre-med since middle school, before Grace even knew what a major was. She didn't doubt that Dallas would make a good doctor—he was smart and driven and knew what he wanted. If anyone could beat her for valedictorian, it was him. She didn't mind competition either, but now she was stuck competing with her biggest rival in his strongest subject, with his dad keeping score.

Sophie rubbed her eyes. "I'm going to the restroom," she said. "Be right back."

Grace knew by now that was a lie. Sophie would be gone long enough for Grace to do the required cutting by herself. Mr. Copeland was lenient on bathroom breaks for girls, and Grace wasn't sure if he assumed they were all on their periods all the time or simply didn't notice or care when the girls were gone. More than once, he had literally pushed her aside so "the boys" could use the microscope she was using. "The boys" were his son's football teammates.

Grace glanced up at the board where Mr. Copeland kept the top five students' running scores. She'd never had a teacher do that before, and didn't even know if such a thing was allowed, but Mr. Copeland thought it was good for them, that it would inspire them to work harder. She was in second, trailing Dallas by a whole percentage point. She'd briefly been in the lead at the start of the semester, but then Mr. Copeland had decided to add bonus questions to the quizzes. Conveniently, all the bonus questions were about football, and Dallas had pulled ahead. She started checking football scores so she could at least have a chance at guessing the answers, but even with her competitive nature, she knew she'd never beat him that way. She resigned herself to studying as hard as she could, and if she had to dissect the entire cat by herself, she'd get it done. It wasn't the worst thing she'd ever had to do.

Today's lab was starting on the upper digestive system. She consulted the diagram. Mouth, tongue, larynx, pharynx, esophagus. Mr. Copeland was making his way around the room, stopping to explain the difference in tongue papillae between cats and humans and chat with the boys about the upcoming football game. He walked past her table without saying anything. Sophie returned in time to write down the answers and seal the cat back in its bag.

"I've got your tests," Mr. Copeland said as they were cleaning up. "And a new seating chart. Grab them on your way out."

The bell rang and Grace collected her papers. She checked the test first. Mr. Copeland hadn't made any marks or comments on the pages, only the score in crisp red ink at the top: 100 percent. She didn't get any of the bonus credit. She glanced at the seating chart on her way to the lunchroom to meet Levi. According to the diagram, she was no longer seated at the front table with Sophie. She'd been moved to the back of the room, facing the hallway, sharing a table with a notoriously talkative stoner. Dallas remained in the front, facing the board, next to the good microscope. Mr. Copeland hadn't given a reason for the shuffle, though it seemed obvious. She looked at her test again. Maybe she'd overtaken Dallas for head of the class, and his dad was doing everything he could to make it impossible for her to stay there.

Levi waved to her from their table, and she went to set down her things before getting in the lunch line.

"Want to share?" he said. "There's plenty." His mom made his lunch every day, and she packed it like she was still feeding two boys, though Tyson had graduated and was working for Savor at the rendering plant. Grace wouldn't be surprised if Mrs. Baylor still packed his lunch, too.

She sat down next to him, dropping her papers on the table. "What do we have today?"

"Ham sandwiches with pimiento cheese, apple slices, chips, peanut butter crackers, and your favorite, oatmeal cookies with M&M's."

Grace grabbed a sandwich. The ham was stacked on thick slices of homemade bread, cheese oozing at the edges. "You're spoiled," she said.

"You try and tell my mama not to make lunch," he said. "She keeps going on how this is her last year to do it."

"Must be a boy thing," Grace said. "Because my mom is plenty happy for me to wait in the free-lunch line."

Levi pushed the cookies toward her. "How's your day going?"

"Fine, but . . . I think Mr. Copeland is trying to screw up my grade."

Levi nodded at her test, face up on the table, trying not to smile. "I don't think it's working."

"No, I mean, he moved us around, stuck me in the back. I won't even be able to see the board. He's trying to make sure Dallas does better than me."

"That sucks, but, I mean, how much better can he do? Does it matter that much?"

"It does for scholarships. I need a good class rank for my applications."

"I know you're worried about scholarships," he said. "But that's not the only option. It'll be okay no matter what happens. Everything'll work out the way it's supposed to."

"You really believe that, don't you?" she said. "That somehow, you'll get what you need and everything'll be all right in the end." She envied him in that sense. How did a person come to think that way? Maybe it was how your mind worked if nothing terrible had ever happened to you.

"Well, I don't need much," he said. "When I was a kid, I'd get everything on my Christmas list, but I had to narrow it down to the three things I wanted most."

Grace had always had more than three things to unwrap on Christmas morning, though they weren't usually quite what she'd asked for. A box of ugly fake Barbies from the dollar store instead of the one real one she wanted. A frilly dress from the church rummage sale instead of the jeans she'd picked out.

"Three things? That's all it takes to make you happy?"

"I mean, there's things I want. A new truck'd be nice. But if you think on it, what're those few things you really need? Most of it, I already got."

Grace picked up a cookie. "Okay, let's hear it. What's at the top of the list?"

He held up one finger. "A horse."

She laughed. No surprise that was first. She couldn't imagine Levi without his horses.

He extended a second finger. "A place to live." The third finger went up. "Somebody to grow old with."

Her face warmed. She broke the cookie into pieces, crumbs falling on her test.

"How about you?" he said. "What do you want most?"

The din of the cafeteria hummed around her. She wanted to be able to give him a simple list, to tell him that she didn't need much either, but it wasn't true. She wasn't content with what she already had. She wanted to meet people she hadn't known all her life, see places she'd never been. She couldn't tell him what she wanted, because she hadn't saved a place for him in any of it. All of it lay beyond Beaumont.

TWENTY-SIX

Kylee and Amelia fought over Grace's ratty, old dollar-store dolls. Neither wanted to be stuck with the one that had its eyes stamped on wrong, but both of them wanted the silver sparkle dress Grace had put on it. The dolls were the same size as Barbies, but they couldn't wear Barbie shoes or fit into Barbie clothes with sleeves, because their hands and feet weren't shaped right. Grace had made a pattern and sewn a tiny sleeveless dress with material from an old shirt of Shannon's. Now she'd have to hurry up and sew a second one.

"Let's take a break from dolls," she said. "Go on, put them away." Kylee started chucking them toward the bin. The one with the bad eyes hit the wall headfirst and bounced. Amelia picked it up and stuffed it in with the others, its legs overextended in an unsettling version of the splits.

"Okay," Grace said. "What do we want for dinner?"

"Klondike Bar," Amelia said.

"Me, too, but I want a chocolate one," Kylee said.

"That's dessert. You have to eat some real food first." Grace opened the fridge. Elsie had left them meatloaf and a green bean casserole. She made a point to have home-cooked meals for her nieces when they stayed over, because she worried that Shannon only fed them food out of cans, though the girls didn't seem to care one way or the other. They would eat only as much dinner as they had to for Grace to give them ice cream.

"Grace." Amelia tugged on her shirt. "There's something outside."

"Something? Like what? An animal?"

"Somebody's here," Kylee said, pointing out the side window. "Maybe it's Levi."

Shannon and Elsie were both working, and she wasn't expecting Levi, though the girls loved it when he came by. He let them ride around on his back and would play as many hands of old maid or go fish as they wanted. Grace peered through the glass into the darkness but didn't see anyone.

"The door," Amelia said. Grace pulled her back as the kitchen door swung open and Norman strode in. He hadn't changed much in the time he'd been gone, except that his beard had grown long and scraggly, and it was dusted with gray. He locked eyes with Grace and dropped his duffel bag on the floor with a thud.

"Hey, girls."

"Who's that?" Kylee said.

Norman knelt down in front of her. "What? Don't tell me you don't remember me! It's your uncle Norman."

Amelia wrapped her arms around Grace's waist, but Grace barely noticed. She felt as though she was watching a scene in a television show, where a long-lost relative arrives to throw everything off-balance. It felt, for a moment, like she could simply turn it off, choose not to watch.

"I brought you girls something," Norman said, unzipping his bag. He pulled out two packages of sour gummy worms, and Kylee and Amelia rushed forward to grab them.

"Wait!" Grace said. "You haven't had dinner yet."

"It's okay," Norman said. "It's a special occasion."

Kylee ripped open the cellophane package and shoved a bright blue worm into her mouth. Amelia struggled with the wrapper and resorted to using her teeth. Neither girl said thank you, and Grace didn't prompt them. She stared at Norman's duffel bag, considered its heft, the space it was taking up on the floor. His scent was slowly filling the room. Marlboro Reds. Motor oil.

"Where's Elsie at?" he asked.

"Work," Grace said. "I can tell her you came by."

Norman chuckled. "No need. I'm staying awhile."

"There's no bed. The girls have the spare room."

He grinned at her. "Oh, I'm fine on the couch for now. You know me, I can fall asleep anywhere." His attention turned to the girls, playing with their candy worms. Norman untied his boots and kicked them off. They landed in the middle of the floor, where someone was liable to trip on them. "Got any beers around here? What's for supper?"

The refrigerator door still hung open. Grace wasn't about to serve Norman supper, but she had to feed the girls. She got out the meatloaf and green beans, heated up plates for Kylee and Amelia, and left Norman to fix his own. She had no appetite. She leaned against the counter while the kids sat at the table, sneaking looks at their uncle and picking at their food. The smell of ground beef and cigarettes roiled her stomach, but she didn't dare leave the room, leave him alone with her cousins. She slid her phone out of her pocket. *He's back*, she texted to Levi. She couldn't bring herself to type his name, but it didn't matter. Levi would know.

TWENTY-SEVEN

When Norman wasn't ignoring her, he was acting as though everything was completely normal, like he was a doting uncle in town to see his sisters and nieces. He set up in the living room, taking over the couch and coffee table and TV, using empty beer cans as ashtrays and making the house smell like the Elks Lodge on bingo night. Elsie said nothing about the mess. She didn't even seem to notice it. She was too busy making Frito pie and playing cards and drinking Pabst Blue Ribbon with Norman late into the night, their drunken laughter keeping Grace awake.

One week into his stay, Grace came home from work to find the living room tidied up and no sign of Norman's things. Her heart clenched into a fist when she found him sprawled on the girls' pink comforter in the spare room, surrounded by their stuffed animals, his duffel bag disemboweled and the contents strewn on the floor.

It was hard to breathe in the dying room now that he had taken it over. She gathered up some of the dolls and toys while he was out and put them in her room before they could be permeated by Norman's stench. She heard him come into the house one night when she was there alone, and while she wasn't exactly scared of him—it wasn't as if he could coax her into the bathtub now and force her to wash his hair—there was a residual fear in her body that she couldn't tame when he was around. Snakes writhing in her gut, a tightness in her chest. It didn't matter that Norman was no longer her bogeyman. The response was visceral and unaffected by reasoning. She was tense, even with Levi.

"I'll take him down," Levi said. "If he looks at you wrong."

"I know," she said. They sat on the floor of his room, leaning against the bed. Levi's hunting rifle hung on a rack on the wall, freshly cleaned. "I'm not worried about protecting myself. I just don't like him being there. I wish he'd hurry up and leave."

"You could stay over here," Levi said. "With me."

"You think your mom'd go for that?"

"She'd probably rather we were married first," he said. "But if we were married, we could get our own place. You wouldn't have to worry about him at all."

"That shouldn't be a reason to get married."

"It's not the only reason," he said. "You know I want to be with you, Grace. Start a family, grow old together, sit on the porch in rocking chairs, the whole bit."

"You have it all figured out already."

"I do."

"Well, I'm not ready to get married. And I don't know if I'll ever want to have kids."

"You love kids! You've been taking care of your cousins since they were born."

"I love them, yeah, but it's not the same. I don't know if I could be a *mother*. I'd always be worried I wasn't doing it right."

"Well, Shannon's getting by. Because you and Elsie are helping her. You'd have help," he said. "You'd have me. You wouldn't be doing it alone."

"How do you know for sure *you* want kids? We haven't even graduated yet. You might change your mind about what you want."

"My mom and dad got married right out of high school and had Tyson a year later, and that worked out fine. If you wait too long, you won't be around for your grandkids."

"Are you serious? How are you even thinking about grandkids?"

"That's my family. My mom's been talking about grandkids forever. She's always praying for Tyson to meet somebody, settle down. She's worried he's gonna run out of time."

"School's all I can focus on right now."

"When we talk about the future, that's all you talk about. It's always school. Am I in the picture at all?"

"I just don't want to end up like Shannon, or my mom, struggling to take care of kids while I'm working myself to death at some miserable job. I'm trying to plan for something better."

"You'll never be in that kind of situation. I'd take care of you, our kids, our family. If the farm doesn't pan out, I could work at the plant."

"That can't be your dream. You'd hate that. You couldn't stand to be indoors all day."

"Why can't that be the dream? I'm not afraid of hard work. A job's a job. We could have a house out in the country. Maybe a little land. Horses. Family all around. Why does it have to be anything different than that? I want to be with you, make a life here with you. Who cares what I have to do for a paycheck."

She kissed him then, deeply, and drew him close, because she didn't know what else to do. She loved him as much as she ever had, though she wasn't convinced that love was enough. She could go away to school and come back to him, but could she be content to live out her days in Beaumont, where everything had a memory attached, where there was nothing to do but what you'd always done? How hard would it be to do that—to let go of everything else and cling to Levi, to trust him with the rest of her life? It might be impossible. Or it might be easy, in the most ordinary way, like sinking into a warm bath, falling asleep, quietly drowning.

TWENTY-EIGHT

Elsie squirted another greasy glob of Bengay into her palm and rubbed it onto the back of her neck. *Wheel of Fortune* was on, and she and Grace sat in the matching recliners eating what was left of the fried bologna and boiled potatoes Elsie had fixed for supper. Norman had devoured most of it before heading out for the night. The air in the living room was sharp with menthol, and it stung Grace's eyes and throat. She tasted it when she chewed her bologna.

"Buy a vowel already," Elsie said to the big-haired woman on the TV. She squirmed in her seat, unable to find a comfortable position. Her neck and back had been acting up, some problem with her spinal discs that was getting worse. Still, she'd spent her day off at the church, prepping and delivering freezer meals for the sick, the elderly, and families with new babies. Grace knew how hard her mother worked. Elsie was like a machine that never let up, but now various parts of her body were beginning to wear out. A lifetime of tending to others had taken its toll, along with the endless hours on her feet at the meatpacking plant. Her shoulders were hunched, her back bowed, her knees and ankles weak—her whole body reshaped by her labors. So much work, and so little to show for it. It wasn't the sort of life Grace wanted for herself.

"Not *that* vowel," Elsie said. Grace knew the answer to the puzzle, but she didn't say it out loud, because her mother liked to guess.

Wheel of Fortune cut to commercial, and Grace braced herself for what was coming. Her mother had been nagging her at every opportunity all week long. Elsie set her plate down on the coffee table and turned to Grace. "I just don't understand what's wrong with Springfield," she said.

Grace took her time chewing and swallowing a mouthful of potato. On TV, a man in a crown gestured grandly at rolls of carpeting and vinyl while an annoying jingle played in the background. *Carpet King, he's got the cheapest floor covering!* "There's nothing wrong with Springfield, I just don't want to go there."

"And why not?"

"Mama . . ."

"John Goodman went to Missouri State," Elsie said. "You know who that is, don't you? He's a big deal. I think he gave the graduation speech one year."

"That's supposed to convince me to go there?"

Elsie ignored her. "It's a good school, is all I'm saying. So you go to school in Springfield. You won't be so far you couldn't run home for dinner if you wanted. And when you're done with school, you come back. You could find a good job right here in Beaumont. You could be a teacher, like Mrs. Mummer! We need good people here. Look at Dallas Copeland, he's gonna come back home and run the clinic when Dr. Billings retires."

Grace clenched her jaw. She was sick of everyone talking about how Dallas Copeland was going to be a doctor and save the town. Maybe in ten years she'd be the doctor, and Dallas would be teaching high school kids how to dissect cats. "Mama, I'm not coming back here."

"You don't mean that!"

"I'm not saying I won't come visit! You know I'll come see you, but I'm not moving home. You can forget about that. It'll never happen."

"So who's gonna take care of me? When I can't get up and around, can't go to the store, can't get in the shower by myself? Family takes care of family. I'm getting tired, Grace, is all. I'm wore out. I done took care of everybody else and I don't want to be alone when I'm the one who needs help. You're the only child I have. My only daughter. There's no one else left."

"That's not true," Grace said. "Norman's here. What about Shannon? She's not going anywhere. Maybe she should help out for once."

"Shannon does what she can. She's raising two little girls."

"I take care of them more than she does."

A flush of anger crept into Elsie's cheeks. "That's really not fair, Grace. She has to work to support them. That counts as taking care of them, too. You don't know what it's like—how hard it is to be a mother. A *single* mother! The love and care you pour out, emptying yourself bucket by bucket till your well runs dry, and you don't know if it'll ever come back to you, if you'll ever get filled back up again. Used to be, you could count on family. But I don't know anymore."

Elsie rubbed her eyes and immediately cried out.

"Mama?"

Elsie shook her head, blinking back tears. "Got that danged cream in my eyes. Burns like the dickens."

"Want me to get you a wet rag?"

"Don't trouble yourself, Grace," she said, her voice sharp. She pulled her sleeve down and dabbed at her face. "I'll take care of it myself."

There was a shuffling sound at the front door. Not a knock, exactly. Someone lurking on the porch, holding a cardboard box. Grace recognized the slumped shoulders, the stringy orange hair. Jimmy Schultze had graduated a few years before her. She remembered him hanging out with the smokers in the gravel lot outside the art room, his hair already thinning, his jeans sagging, tennis shoes busting open. Jimmy had drifted among the gamers, the burnouts, the art kids, not quite fitting into one particular crowd. She'd sat next to him in geometry, and he'd covered his desk in doodles of marijuana leaves and cartoon characters with bloodshot eyes. A few times, she'd looked up from her work and caught him staring at her.

Elsie pushed herself out of the recliner, and Grace got up, too.

"Why is Jimmy Schultze here?"

Elsie's face was pink from their fight, her eyes still watering. She crossed her arms and uncrossed them, flustered. "He's helping me out with your graduation present," she said finally. "I wanted to get you a computer, but I couldn't get what I wanted brand new. He fixes up old ones, replaces parts. Says it'll be just as fast and good as a new one."

Guilt flooded through Grace. Her mother let Jimmy in and helped him negotiate the box through the doorway. "Hi, Jimmy," Grace said.

"Hey." He stared down at the box he was carrying, shifting from one foot to the other. There was electrical tape on his shoes, holding them together.

"Grace was just going upstairs to do her homework," Elsie said pointedly.

"Yeah," Grace said. "Actually, I'm meeting up with Levi to study. I'll see you later."

She left the paper plate with her half-eaten dinner on the coffee table, grabbed her jacket and backpack, and walked out, Jimmy watching her. She did need to study for her biology test, but she didn't feel like going to Levi's, even though she'd barely seen him all week. He'd probably bring up the future again, and she was tired of talking about it. She kept walking, and when she reached the high school, she crossed the road to Deer Creek Park. The picnic tables in the shelter were chained to the concrete so no one would steal them. All the playground equipment had been destroyed ages ago—swing seats cut in half, teeter-totter cracked—so there were never any little kids hanging around making noise. Perfect for studying.

As she approached the shelter, she discovered someone else had the same idea. Dallas Copeland sat at the best table, the one in the center that never had any bird poop on it, his textbooks, notepads, and folders spread out in front of him. He saw her before she could turn around, and she wasn't going to let him think he'd scared her off.

"Hey, Grace," he said, pushing back his dark floppy hair. He was wearing his blue-and-white Beaumont High letterman jacket, covered with patches and pins from four years of football and clubs and honor rolls. "You here for tutoring?"

"No," she said, bristling. "Shouldn't you be off delivering a baby at the side of the road or something?"

Dallas grinned. "Did that on the way here. It was twins, actually. C-section. Pretty impressive."

She didn't smile back. "I bet."

Dallas looked a little hurt. Probably the first time a girl hadn't laughed at one of his jokes.

"You okay?" he said. "I was joking about the tutoring. I know you don't need my help with anything. But that's my service project. That's why I'm here. Volunteer algebra tutor." He gestured at the empty table. "Nobody showed up, so I'm just doing homework for my dual credit classes."

His unexpected earnestness dulled the edge of her anger. "I knew you were joking," Grace said. "I just . . . I was fighting with my mom a minute ago and your name came up. Wasn't expecting to run into you here."

"Let me guess," he said. "I'm gonna take over the clinic just in time for Dr. Billings to retire, so Beaumont won't have to go without a doctor. Town hero, basically."

"That's it," she said.

"Yeah, that's all my dad. He came up with that. Tells everybody that'll stand still long enough to listen. It's embarrassing as hell."

"Yeah, really embarrassing that everybody thinks you're great. I don't know how you deal with it."

He chuckled. "It's rough." He shoved his books to the side, making room at the table. "Want to sit down?"

"I guess. I was gonna study for bio."

"We could study together," he said. "If you want."

"Sure." She shook off her backpack and sat on the bench across from him.

"Is your boyfriend gonna be mad?" he said.

"Why?"

"You know, you hanging out with another guy."

"He's not like that," she said. "And I doubt he sees you as competition."

Dallas grinned. "All right. If you say so. I know how guys' minds work, is all."

She rolled her eyes. "It's fine. I'm willing to risk being seen with you."

"Me too," he said. "For the record."

He opened his notebook, and she noticed the pages of cramped writing were highlighted in a rainbow of colors, same as hers.

"Hey," Dallas said. "You remember field day in third grade, when we got stuck doing the three-legged race together?"

"Vaguely?"

"You don't remember," he said. "I can tell. That's okay, you can admit it."

"No, I do, I just hadn't thought about it in a long time."

"Well, I remember because it was the only event I was in that day that I didn't win."

"That's pretty sad," she said. "The two most likely to succeed, and we couldn't win a three-legged race?"

"Right? I mean, I was mad about it. Miss B caught me crying. Remember her?"

"World's oldest gym teacher," Grace said. "But she could still knock the wind out of you with a dodgeball."

"Uh-huh. She told me to stop acting like a baby, and then she said you and I were both so competitive, we were competing against each other. Instead of working as a team, like we were supposed to. We were trying to outrun each other with our legs tied together."

"Okay, wait, are you suggesting we team up and agree to be co-valedictorians? Is that where this is going? 'Cause that's not gonna happen."

"No, not at all. I just think . . . we're a lot alike, I guess."

"Except your dad wants you to go be a doctor and my mom wants me to stay home and work at the Kum & Go."

"She does not."

"Well, maybe not Kum & Go, specifically. But she doesn't care what I want to do. She just wants me here, in Beaumont."

"My dad, too. You know, he tells everybody I'm coming back, but I never said I would. He never even asked."

"So that's not your plan?"

"No way," Dallas said. "I want out as bad as you do. But I don't go around telling everybody. See, that's where you went wrong. When you say that, they think *you* think you're too good for this place. There's no point telling people something they don't want to hear. Just pisses them off. When I eventually disappoint everybody, I won't be here to deal with it."

"God, you're as smart as everybody says," she groaned. "So annoying."

"Right? I'm also good-looking and extremely generous."

"I wouldn't go that far."

"Well, what if I told you I know the bonus questions for the test. I saw my dad writing them out. I'll tell you," he said, leaning toward her, "if I can trust you to keep a secret."

"You can trust me," she said.

He held out his hand. "Dad always says a handshake means more than a contract."

Her pulse quickened when their hands met, his fingers squeezing hers, slowly sliding across her palm as he let go. She knew how to keep a secret.

AMELIA

&

KYLEE

TWENTY-NINE

"Why do we have to meet this guy at the stockyards so late at night?" Kylee asked.

"Because I just got off work and that's where he wanted to meet?"

"There is literally a slaughterhouse next door. I could call Tyson. Just in case."

"You said we needed to handle this on our own, Ky. That we couldn't trust anyone else."

"Well, I'd trust Tyson over this Bill guy who we don't even know."

"He sounds like he just wants to help."

"People can sound however they want."

"I know that," I said. I drove to the far end of the gravel lot, where Bill had said to meet, and when my headlights revealed the long lines and sharp edges of a lone vehicle in the darkness, a cold hand reached inside my chest to squeeze my heart. "Do you recognize that car?" I asked Kylee.

She squinted. "Kinda looks like the one that was parked outside our house the other night, super late. Thought Mama had some new broke-ass boyfriend."

"We passed it leaving Elsie's house, too. The night Jimmy had that fit. And it was at the vigil. There was somebody inside smoking, but whoever it was didn't get out. Like they didn't want to be seen."

"Maybe we shouldn't stop," Kylee said. "We don't know if this guy's who he says he is. All we know's his niece went missing. Who knows if that's even true."

"Grace had his card."

"Yeah, and she's missing now, too. I should've called Tyson."

The car's massive driver's-side door swung wide and Kylee grabbed my arm as the man climbed out. I flicked on my brights and he waved. He was bowlegged, an aging cowboy in a snap-front Western shirt with a bolo tie and an oversize rodeo belt buckle holding up his jeans. Long strands of stringy silver hair had been shellacked across his bald spot. He appeared to be carrying a purse, until I saw the tubing and realized it was a portable oxygen tank.

"What do you think, Ky? I feel like we could take him if it comes down to it." She let go of my arm and rolled her eyes.

We got out and introduced ourselves. Cattle lowed in nearby pens, the air thick with the scent of manure. "We've seen your car around," I said. "Were you following us?"

"Not on purpose," he said. "Hope I didn't scare you. I was checking to see if Norman was around. Figured he heard about the bones, too. Thought it might draw him out. That's what brought me back to town."

"You know Norman?"

"Yep. He was engaged to my niece when she was only fourteen years old. They were neighbors since she was about nine or ten." He took out a picture. "That's Annalise."

She looked like a kid in an old Coppertone ad, a wholesome, grinning girl with sun-streaked hair and freckles across her nose and cheeks where the sun would hit.

"There's a word for guys like that, who take up with little girls." He cleared his throat and tucked the picture back in his wallet. "They split up before he could get her to the courthouse, but he wouldn't leave her be, so her and my sister moved to Polk County to get away from him. Half the time Annalise was scared he was coming after her, and the other half she wanted to go back to him. She run off at some point, and she never did come home. Figured maybe she took off with Norman somewheres, but when he finally showed up again, she wasn't with him. I knew he did something to her, felt it down in my gut." He knocked his knuckles against his belt buckle. "Couldn't prove it, of course. But Norman, he was doing concrete work back then, did you know that?"

"I think Elsie's mentioned it before," I said.

"Well, I got it in my head if he did something to her, he probably buried her body in concrete on some job he was doing, so nobody'd find her. That girl they just found, I wouldn't be surprised if it comes out she was buried under concrete, too." Bill turned his head and sprayed tobacco juice, wiped his mouth with the back of his hand. At least he wasn't smoking while attached to his oxygen tank. "I spent some time trying to figure out where all he'd worked from the time Annalise left till Norman came back. There's a parking garage in Joplin. A hospital in Springfield. Some smaller jobs, too, hereabouts. Work he did on the side. Patios. Driveways. I been trying to get somebody to do that ground-penetrating radar, see if there's something underneath. Ain't easy if you don't got the cops on board. Been trying to raise money," he said.

The mention of money made me skeptical. Was he telling the truth or making up a story to fleece us?

Kylee must've been thinking the same thing. "We don't have any money," she blurted.

He tilted his head in the direction of my rusted-out Pontiac. "Didn't figure you did. At this point, I'm about ready to rent a backhoe and start digging shit up myself." He shifted from one foot to the other, his boots scraping the gravel. "Look, I know how it is, the not knowing. Feeling like nobody cares, nobody's doing nothing. My sister overdosed last summer; they found her dead in her car in a Walmart parking lot in the middle of July. That's not something you ever want to see. I'm on my own now, the only one left looking for Annalise. For a while there I wanted to hunt Norman down, put a bullet in his nutsack and another one right through his brain. And I'd do it, still, if I ever came across him. But now I'm just trying to find my niece. Bring her home, lay her to rest. I was thinking you might want to do the same with Grace—see where Norman worked around the time she disappeared. See if you can dig something up."

"I don't think it would help," I said. "Norman left town before Grace went missing."

"Oh, did he now?" Bill chuckled. "You sure about that? That he wasn't hanging around, that he didn't leave and come back? He's a slippery son of a bitch. Always has been. He could be anywhere."

"I get why you think he did something to your niece. Why would he kill Grace, though?" Kylee said.

"It's something I've turned over a lot in my head," he said. "I've got this guilt chewing my gut like an ulcer, because if I never talked to her, maybe she wouldn't be missing, too. I got the feeling she must've said something to him," Bill said. "About Annalise. That she found something out, that she threatened to tell. When I talked to her, I wanted her help. I wanted to know about Norman's movements. Where he'd been. If he'd said anything. Annalise's name was already familiar to her. But when I showed her the picture . . . the way she stared at it. The look on her face. She wanted to help. I could tell that about her."

Kylee squeezed my wrist. That sounded like Grace, all right.

"She wanted to know what happened to my niece," Bill said, "and she was dead set on finding out. So I'm guessing that's what happened. She went after Norman. Folks want to think it's strangers you gotta watch out for, but a place like this, we eat our own."

THIRTY

Mama was draping wet laundry over chairs and hanging underwear from cabinet knobs when I came downstairs the next day.

"Dryer's busted," she said. "Clothes sat in there all night, wet and hot, and now everything smells like a dirty mop."

"Great," I said. I wouldn't have time to wash my uniform before work unless I wanted to wear it wet. I went to open the refrigerator, and she stopped me.

"Don't bother," she said. "Haven't had time to get to the store." I expected her to start screaming about the moldy hot dog like she had the other day, but she didn't even raise her voice. She continued laying out the laundry, humming to herself. She must've taken some gummies to be this mellow.

"Hey, Mama? When's the last time you heard from Uncle Norman?"

"Norman?" She leaned back against the counter, stretched her arms over her head, and yawned. "Jesus, I don't know. Years, I guess. Why?"

"So . . . before or after Grace? I was just wondering."

"Well, he wasn't around when it happened, I know that, so I guess before. But he was always coming and going, and you never know when he'll crop up like head lice you thought you got rid of."

"But he hasn't been back since then? Has he ever been gone that long before?"

"Hard to say," she said. "He's left for years at a time. That's not unlike him. Usually comes back when he's screwed something up or run outta money."

"Where does he go when he's gone? Do you have a way to reach him if you need to?"

"Shit, you want a phone number? Good luck with that. He doesn't keep the same number one day to the next. No point keeping track. He'd probably rather cut off his left nut than talk to one of us on the phone."

"So you haven't even talked to him."

"Nah. Get wind of him every once in a while, that's enough. Friend of his told me he saw Norman at Sturgis a couple years back. Wasn't doing great, apparently—so shit-faced he didn't even recognize his old buddy. Acted like he didn't know his own name when the guy called out to him. Either that or he was just being an asshole. Wouldn't surprise me."

"You miss him at all?"

She snorted. "Norman can choke on a bag of dicks for all I care. Elsie's the only one misses him. She was hurt pretty good when he didn't show up after what happened with Grace, but she still made excuses for him. Maybe he didn't know, she said. My guess, he knew and he didn't care, because he's never given a shit about anybody else, not even with how Elsie caters to him. I guarantee she's got an old bag of Fritos in the cabinet, waiting to make his favorite dinner the minute he darkens her door. She still thinks he didn't get a fair shake."

"Fair shake? What do you mean?"

Mama groaned, swiped wisps of hair off her forehead. "She always felt bad for him because Daddy's family called him a bastard. Mama was already pregnant with him when she married Daddy, and Aunt Iris said he wasn't Daddy's kid. He didn't have green eyes like the rest of us. He's got blue eyes . . . same as Grampa Sellers. Mama's dad." She waited for the words to sink in. "They thought he was inbred, and Norman knew it. Hell, everybody knew it."

"Was he? Green-eyed people can have kids with blue eyes."

Mama flapped her hand at me, unimpressed by basic genetic fact. "I don't know, Amelia, let's dig up your dead granny and ask her the most personal shit you can imagine! Mama never said a word about it, and why would she? If it was true, would you want to tell your kids that? That you were raped? By your own daddy, even? Jesus. Maybe she was just boning some blue-eyed guy right before Daddy came along, and he knocked her up, who knows. That wasn't something she'd bring up at the dinner table either. She didn't treat Norman any different from me and Elsie. If anything, she spoiled him, let him get away with things. It didn't make him any less of an asshole."

"What about him and Grace? Did they get along?"

"They butted heads, same as he did with most everybody else. Norman's not easy to get along with, especially when he's living in your house the way he was there at the end."

"Sure, but was it worse right before he left? Did they have a big fight or anything like that?"

Mama squinted. "Well, I do recall she threw a fit about Norman babysitting you girls. It was kinda ridiculous, but she was real serious about it. She'd been watching you and your sister since you were born, and I guess she didn't want Norman coming in and trying to do it. She thought he was a fuckup, and she was right. He was an unreliable son of a bitch, but hell, you were old enough you didn't need an eye on you every minute. It wasn't like you were babies and he'd forget you in a hot car or something. But Grace didn't have anything to do with him taking off. Didn't bother him one bit if people were pissed at him, if they didn't like him. That kind of thing rolled right off his back." Mama shook out her arms.

"You okay?" I asked.

"Just got a crawly feeling," she said. "Almost like he knows I'm talking about him—like speaking of the devil might summon him right up. Times like this, I wish I was Catholic. I'd be sprinkling holy water around the house right now, waving a rosary around, whatever it is they do to ward off evil shit."

"I've got the children's Bible Elsie gave me around here somewhere," I said.

She rolled her eyes. "Yeah, Amelia, I'm sure a picture Bible works just as good as an exorcist."

I couldn't keep a straight face.

"What?" she said, starting to crack up. "Why do the damn Catholics have all the good stuff? Us Methodists don't get shit. Pray and hope for the best, what the hell kinda plan is that?"

"Throw some salt over your shoulder," I said. "If we have any."

"Think a hot dog'll work?" She was busting up now, slapping the counter, definitely high.

I hadn't seen Mama really laugh in a while. She looked ten years younger when she wasn't scowling.

"Well, I haven't slept yet," she said, once she caught her breath. "I'm going up to bed."

"All right. I'll station a priest outside your door."

"Make it a hot one," she said, heading for the stairs. "The kind that might give in to temptation."

I waited until I heard her door close, and then called Kylee.

"Where are you?" I said.

"With Tyson. At the farm. What's up?"

"Do you remember Uncle Norman babysitting us?"

"Yeah," she said. "Maybe once or twice? Didn't he make us play dress-up or some other dumb thing we didn't want to do?"

"Probably. I remember Grace showing up, putting us to bed. She acted like everything was fine, but there was this feeling . . . like she didn't want him there. She wanted to keep him away from us."

Kylee was quiet for a moment. "Are you thinking, after she found out about Annalise . . ."

"We were around the same age Annalise would've been when she moved in next to Norman. So, when Norman started coming over to baby-sit, Grace wasn't only thinking about what happened to Annalise. She was worried Norman would do something to *us*."

"She was trying to protect us," Kylee said.

"Yeah." I bit down on my lip until I tasted blood. "And maybe that's what got her killed."

THIRTY-ONE

lan was standing at the counter when I walked into work. He wasn't flexing, or doing any of his weird standing pushups. He had his arms crossed rigidly over his chest.

"Hi, Alan," I said. "Busy day?"

"Cutting it kinda close, aren't you?" he asked.

My shift didn't start for another ten minutes, but I figured it wasn't worthwhile to point that out. Most people sprinted in the door with moments to spare, because nobody wanted to be here any longer than they had to. I wasn't late. Something else must have put him in a pissy mood. I did my best to look surprised, apologetic.

"I'm sorry, I must've looked at the clock wrong."

His pinched expression eased slightly. "Timeliness is important for someone who wants to be a manager. I was thinking we should go over the rest of the details for the training program after work tonight."

I vaguely remembered agreeing to meet up again in my rush to get out of his house, though I had no intention of actually going back. Last time, we'd ended up in his bedroom, and I hated to think what he could possibly have in mind after that. A soak in his creepy basement hot tub, surrounded by sharp tools?

"Yeah," I said, smiling warmly. "I guess we'll see how the night plays out."

"Great," he said, his mustache twitching.

I kept smiling, because I didn't know what would happen if I stopped.

He dropped his arms. "You better clock in."

"Right," I said. "On it."

Alan was hovering around the kitchen when I returned, probably looking for things to complain about. Javi focused intently on the grill, far more than was necessary to cook the single order of eggs he was working on. He hadn't waved hello to me.

"Amelia." Alan pointed over my shoulder. "Customers."

I took orders and poured coffee and wiped the counter, glancing back to the grill every chance I got. Javi was definitely ignoring me. He didn't even look up when "Cookin' Down at the Waffle House" played on the jukebox. After an unusual amount of lurking and frowning throughout my shift, Alan had disappeared. His office door was partly open, though I couldn't tell whether he was inside or not. The tables emptied out, along with the parking lot. My stomach hurt, either from nerves or from slamming a large Red Bull on my break without eating anything.

"Javi," I said.

"Yeah." He didn't look up.

"The raccoons are back. They've probably dragged trash all over the parking lot."

"Okay."

"Could you come outside with me for a sec? Please?"

He groaned, set down his spatula, and glanced around before following me out the door.

"Why are you ignoring me?" I said.

He shook his head. "I'm just doing my job, Amelia. There's no raccoons out here. Alan's gonna see I'm not at the grill."

"What's up with him tonight? Something's off."

"Don't know. Figured maybe something happened when you went to his place. Got him worked up. I told you not to mess with him."

"I didn't!"

"Yeah, you did."

"Fine, I did. But I had to. You were right, Javi. He's got something sketchy going on. I don't know what it is, exactly, or if it has anything to do with Grace—"

"Stop. Let it go, Amelia. You're on your way out. Don't mess things up for the rest of us that gotta stay here."

"How can you not even care? It's not about you or me. If he did something to her—"

Javi grabbed my wrist. "Shut. Up," he hissed.

I froze. He'd never touched me before, and now his fingers were digging into my skin. I winced and he let go.

"He's stealing meat from the walk-in. I guess he's selling it or something. Caught him loading up his trunk one night. Not like I was gonna do anything about it anyway, but he threatened all kinds of shit if I didn't keep my mouth shut. He knew I used somebody else's ID to get this job. Threatened to get my whole family deported. Said he'd tell corporate I was the one stealing and they'd believe him. He's done it before."

"I'm sorry, *stealing meat*? That's weird, but . . . is it even that big a deal? Managers probably steal stuff all the time and get away with it."

"That might not be all he's doing—I don't know, and I don't care. But he'll do whatever he's gotta do to keep from getting caught. So drop it. Don't say anything. Don't do anything. Because if you do, it's all gonna come back on me."

"Wait, do you think Grace knew?"

"What does it matter? Do you not hear what I'm saying?"

"Yeah, you said he threatened you, threatened your whole family. What if Grace found out what he was doing and he didn't have anything he could use against her to keep her from talking, like he did with you? How far do you think he'd go to keep her quiet?"

Javi twisted his apron in his hands. The fire had gone out of him. "I don't know. I've gotta get back. But if you think he made Grace disappear, you should think twice about what you're doing."

It was possible that Grace had gotten pulled into Alan's mess, but that didn't explain the way he was acting tonight. The sour mood, the invitation to go back to his house. It was almost as though he was suspicious of Javi and me. Did he think I knew something—that Javi had spilled his secret? Or had Kylee left something out of place in his basement, not put the frozen dinners back just right? I'd been with Alan the entire time I was at his house aside from one drawn-out trip to the bathroom when I was stalling. Maybe he thought I'd snuck down the stairs and gone through his things in those ten minutes, found what he'd been trying to hide? My stomach gurgled uncomfortably, the Red Bull churning in my gut.

I took out my phone to call Kylee. "Alan's acting weird," I said. "I think he might know we were up to something at his house."

"Why do you think that?"

"He's in a bad mood, super tense, and he asked me to come back over tonight."

"That's it? He's probably just frustrated that nothing happened last time and he wants another shot," Kylee said. "Maybe you should go ahead and give him a handy, that might be enough to calm him down. I'd avoid the murder tub, though, if you can."

"Seriously, Ky? You're not funny. Thanks for nothing." I hung up on her, and a sharp cramp twisted my stomach. There was no way I was going to Alan's house, not alone, especially not tonight.

"What are you doing out here? It's not your break time, Amelia." Alan stood between me and the door, a frown ridging his brow. Saliva pooled in my mouth. I turned away, ready to sprint for the weeds at the edge of the parking lot, and he grabbed my elbow and spun me back. I threw up on the walkway, Red Bull and bile splattering Alan's loafers and khaki pants.

THIRTY-TWO

Ketch's army surplus tent was barely visible in the darkness, pitched between two trees. When I called to ask him if I could come over, after explaining what had happened at work, he'd told me he was staying at the campground by the river and not at home.

"How long have you been out here?" I asked, stepping around the firepit. "Why didn't you tell me?"

"Couple weeks," he said. "It's not a big deal."

"Is everything okay?"

"Yeah," he said. "My dad's been hanging around, is all."

Ketch's mom had a restraining order against him, though that didn't stop her from letting him into the house. She didn't want Ketch getting hurt, and she didn't want him trying to protect her either. They got along better, she said, when Ketch wasn't there.

"You could come stay with us," I said. "It's not that much better than here, but we have a real toilet, at least."

"It's okay," he said, holding open the tent flap so I could crawl inside. "I haven't always had indoor plumbing, remember? I don't mind being out here. Weather's pretty good. No mosquitoes yet. I can hear the river."

I stretched out on his sleeping bag, and he lay next to me on a blanket. The ground beneath us was cold and unyielding. Through the open flap, I could see a slice of night sky but no stars.

"You still feel sick?" he asked. "Need some water?"

"No," I said. "I think it was just nerves. The way Alan was acting. When he grabbed my arm, it freaked me out."

"What are you gonna do? Wait and see if his mood passes, if that's all it is? Maybe it's got nothing to do with you."

"I don't know. I told him I was sick, that I wouldn't be in tomorrow. He was too busy cleaning puke off his shoes to argue."

"How about you don't go back at all," Ketch said.

"I need the money. And even if I quit, it's not like Alan wouldn't be able to find me if he wanted to. It's a small town. He knows where I live."

Ketch rolled onto his side, propped himself up on his elbow. "You could leave now instead of later."

"No. Not yet. We're getting closer. I told you about that Wheeler guy, right? I need to ask Aunt Elsie if Norman was doing any concrete work during that time. And I'm thinking we could ask around, see if any of his old friends know how to reach him."

"Maybe he's in the system," Ketch said. "Like, if he's been arrested, gone to jail, had any lawsuits against him. We could try to find him that way."

Nighthawks cried out as they swooped through the trees, and deeper in the woods a whippoorwill sang its repetitive tune over and over and over. Small wonders. I hadn't taken the time to find one in days. Maybe longer.

"Hey, Ketch?"

"Yeah?"

A brisk wind blew off the river and fluttered the tent. The chill made me want to crawl inside the sleeping bag. I was tired, my limbs heavy. "Is it okay if I stay here tonight?" I asked. "I don't think anyone's at home, and I don't want to be alone."

"Of course," he said. "I can stay up if you're worried. Keep watch."

He was a protector, with an inborn desire to keep people safe. He'd protected his mother as much as she'd allow, but no one had been there to protect him. I scooted closer, pulled part of the blanket over us. "I can't believe you'll be gone in a few more weeks," I said.

"Me either."

"As long as I've known you, you've wanted to run off and join the army," I said. "How did you manage to have your life figured out way back then?"

He shrugged. "When I was a kid, I thought soldiers were tough, I guess. They don't get pushed around. They look out for each other. I liked the idea of belonging, having that built-in loyalty . . . kind of like a family, you know?"

"Yeah."

"It's not like I was thinking about careers when I was five years old. It was more of a fantasy. Something better to think about when things weren't great at home. And they never were much good."

I laid my hand on his, remembering how he looked the day we first met on the school bus, in his hand-me-down cowboy shirt and stained jeans, a little boy desperate for something more than a dirt floor, an empty stomach, a closed fist. How I'd known, in that instant, that we'd be friends.

"What'll you miss about Beaumont?" I asked.

He stared out at the darkness and whatever lay beyond. "The woods," he said. "Running the trails." He squeezed my hand. "You."

I curled up next to him, pulled his arm across my body, held on tight. I felt safe with him in this musty tent, on the cold ground, in the dark woods, nothing but a thin veil between us and the night. I hoped he found the same comfort in me—that when we were together, the desperate boy inside him felt safe.

"I'll miss you, too," I said.

THIRTY-THREE

"You didn't come home last night." Kylee's voice was sharp as an ice pick in my ear and I nearly dropped the phone.

"Hold on a sec," I whispered. Ketch was still asleep, so I crept out of the tent, trying not to wake him. It was chilly outside, though not cold enough for frost. Fog hovered over the river. "Why are you calling so early?"

"Some of us have to get to school," she said. "Anyway, I thought about going by Alan's house to see if you shacked up there, or he had you chained to his weight bench, but I'm running late, so I thought I'd just ask."

"I stayed with Ketch," I said. "He's camping."

"Ooh, tell me more."

"Well, I guess it's a good thing I didn't go to Alan's, because he would have chopped me up in the basement before you ever came looking for me."

"You could have told me where you were going."

"You never tell me where you're going."

"True. Because you wouldn't like it. You make that face. But I would really love to hear all about your night in a tent with Ketch."

"Nothing happened."

"Nothing?"

"We kept each other warm," I said. "That's it."

"Clothes on or off? Serious question. You share body heat better if you're naked."

"Kylee."

"I'm just saying, you're more likely to regret things you *don't* do."

"Depends what it is and why you're doing it."

"Look, I'm trying to help you out. Mrs. Mummer told you not to have regrets, right? You're running out of time here."

"Goodbye, Kylee."

Ketch was awake when I crawled back in the tent. "Morning," he said. "You sleep okay?"

I flashed back to some early hour, waking briefly in the dark, his arm still curled around me, his breath warm on my neck. Sometime in the night, our fingers had become intertwined. I'd squeezed his hand, half hoping he'd wake up, too.

"Yeah. I slept great, actually. Better than I usually do in a tent."

"Me too," he said. "I hope you were warm enough. Wish I could make you breakfast or something."

"You going to school today?"

"I could skip," he said. "Why?"

"Nice day for a run. I've got my gear in the car. You up for the High Ridge trail?"

He grinned. "Let's do it."

We were starving by the time we headed back from High Ridge in the afternoon, and I talked Ketch into coming over to eat and take a real shower. We grabbed pizza slices and Gatorades at Kum & Go, because there was still no decent food in the house, and ate on the couch. I was grateful Mama was gone, so I didn't have to worry about her sauntering downstairs with no pants on and making a scene.

"I think I'm starting to feel the effects of sleeping on the ground," I said, rubbing my shoulder. "I don't know how you do that for weeks at a time."

"You get used to it," he said. "Scoot over. Let me help." He pressed his palms to my shoulder blades, his thumbs on either side of my spine.

"Thanks for hanging out today," I said. "I barely even thought about Alan, or anything else."

"Hey, I could do this every day," he said.

"Maybe we should. For the time we've got left." Kylee and her annoying reminders of the ticking clock had gotten into my head.

"Yeah," he said, "why not." His hands worked their way to my neck, sweeping my hair over my shoulder. I closed my eyes as he massaged my stiff muscles and didn't open them until he stopped.

"You can shower first," I said. "I need to throw in some laundry." I followed him upstairs so I could gather my dirty clothes and stripped off my T-shirt to toss in the basket. The water was running in the bathroom when Ketch appeared at the bedroom door, towel around his waist. I'd seen him shirtless plenty of times when we went running, knew every muscle and sinew and scar.

"Uh, I'm sorry," he said, sheepish. "I couldn't figure out how to get the shower part to come on."

"Oh, it's tricky. You have to twist the thing on the faucet. I'll show you."

I followed him into the bathroom and bent down to get the shower going.

"I knew it," Kylee said. She stood at the top of the stairs, ogling us from the hallway. I hadn't realized it was late enough for her to be home from school. I slammed the door in her face, shutting myself in the bathroom with Ketch.

"I'm so sorry," I said. "Just ignore her. She's obsessed with the idea that you and I . . ." My voice trailed off. The water kept running, steaming up the tiny bathroom while we stood face-to-face, me in my sports bra, Ketch half naked in his towel.

"You and I?"

"That we're more than friends."

Ketch didn't flinch. There was no expression of surprise or disbelief. My face tingled, and I knew I was turning red. It was growing warmer in the room, the damp heat slicking my skin. He reached past me to pull back the shower curtain, his arm brushing mine.

"We could really make her wonder," he said.

Neither of us moved. I couldn't tell whether he was serious until he cracked a grin and started laughing. I laughed, too, though part of me wondered what would have happened if I'd done something—anything—instead of nothing. If I'd loosened his towel, let it fall, locked the door. I didn't want to ruin our friendship, but it was hitting me now: in a few weeks, he'd be gone, at the mercy of the army. Who knew where he'd end up? I might never see him again.

Kylee was in the bedroom with the door closed when I came out, and she stayed there most of the afternoon except for a trip to the kitchen, where she complained about the empty refrigerator and carefully surveyed the distance between Ketch and me on the couch as we watched TV. I glared at her as she made obscene gestures that I hoped Ketch didn't see. Later, when I hollered that I was leaving to give Ketch a ride to work, Kylee came bounding down the stairs.

"I'm coming along," she said. "I need you to take me somewhere."

THIRTY-FOUR

"Where are we going, exactly?" It was getting dark, and we'd just passed a mobile home with a Confederate flag duct-taped over the front window and an inflatable Frosty the Snowman in the yard.

"That driveway up there," Kylee said.

I turned in, narrowly avoiding a devil-eyed billy goat with sharp, curved horns. He was chained to a boat anchor, and he took his time getting out of the way, the anchor carving ruts in the dirt. There were high school kids drinking on the porch of a small pale-green house, and a few more messing around on a rusted swing set in the yard.

"Whose place is this, Kylee?"

"I don't know who lives here. I'm meeting Robby."

"Am I dropping you off, or am I waiting for you?"

"Waiting, I think."

"Hurry up," I said. "I'm gonna stay in the car." The goat had followed us and was now staring in through the windshield, chewing, his jaw working back and forth. He had the dull, ornery look all billy goats seemed to have, a look that let you know he didn't give a shit, that he might climb onto the hood and eat the windshield wipers if he felt like it.

"Amelia!" Someone drummed on my window, nearly giving me a stroke. "Hey." Olivia waved, motioned for me to roll the window down. "You want a beer?"

"No thanks," I said. "I'm waiting for my sister."

She bent down to eye level. "I've been watching the news," she said. "They haven't said anything yet about Grace."

"They won't. It's not her."

"Oh. Really? But the hair—"

"You know how you said it looked like a wig? You were right. It was. It's not her."

"Wow. I'm sorry." She set her beer down on the hood. "I just thought . . . I was *sure*, and I thought, if it was me, I'd want to know."

"It's fine. I'm actually glad you said something."

She held on to the car door, clearly tipsy, though nowhere near as drunk as she'd been the last time I'd seen her. "Hey, that guy you were with at the party," she said. "Shaved head? Looked like he was about to ship off to war? Super hot."

"Ketch?"

"Is he your boyfriend?"

"We're just friends," I said.

"You sure? He's totally into you," she said. "It was really obvious." She reached for her beer, but it was no longer sitting on the hood. "Shit," she said. "I think that goat took my beer."

I was about to ask her how she could tell Ketch was into me when Kylee returned, dragging Robby with her.

"Mimi!" she said. "Come here a minute." She scooted Olivia out of the way and I got out of the car. Olivia stood there as though she was part of the conversation until Kylee glared and pushed her farther back. "Go on, Robby, tell her."

"Okay," he said. "So, my cousin plays video games with Jimmy sometimes. He said they got high one night, and they were talking about Grace. Jimmy was saying some weird shit. He was talking about some pictures he had of her, back at the house."

"What kind of pictures?" I asked.

"Fuck if I know. He was kinda talking around it, and it came off real weird, like he wanted to say, but he didn't."

Dallas had told us how Jimmy made Grace uncomfortable. How she thought he'd stolen her underwear. Had he been taking pictures of her, too?

"Let's go," Kylee said, getting in the car.

"You owe me twenty bucks," Robby said.

"Mimi?"

I groaned and dug the last of my cash out of my pocket. My phone pinged. Olivia had added me on Snapchat. I maneuvered around the goat and got back on the road into town.

"Now we know what he's hiding in his office," Kylee said. "We're going over there right now."

"What if they're home?"

"I don't care. We'll figure it out. We need to see those pictures."

Elsie's car wasn't there when we arrived, so she was probably at work, but the red truck she'd bought Jimmy was parked out back. Kylee got out and started for the front door.

"He's home," I said.

"We'll tell him we're stopping by to get Elsie's pudding recipe or something," she said. "I don't know. Dipshit's probably napping or playing video games, he'll barely notice we're there."

"He'll notice if we get anywhere near his office. He couldn't get us outta there fast enough last time."

There were no lights on in the living room. We peered in the front window to make sure and didn't see anyone. Kylee opened the door and we crept in and made our way to the hall. The house was quiet. The bathroom door was open, but the doors to the bedroom and office were closed. I pressed my ear to the bedroom door and heard the whoosh of the fan. Kylee listened at the office door and then got down on the floor to see if there was any light coming from underneath.

"I think he's asleep," I whispered.

Kylee twisted the knob, pausing as it squeaked, and then eased the door open. We hurried inside and closed it behind us, switching on the desk lamp for light. Kylee plopped down in Jimmy's gaming chair and started pulling out drawers.

"What if they're on his computer?" I said. "Who prints out pictures anymore?"

"If they were on his computer, he wouldn't be worried. No way he'd have a password we could guess. I think they're in his desk because he was freaking out every time I came close to touching a drawer handle. Here, help me."

I dug into one of the drawers. "Junk mail. Used Kleenexes." Kylee made a gagging sound. "This one's just a bunch of trash."

"Top one's locked," Kylee said.

"He's gotta have a paperclip around here." I rifled through the trays and mugs on top of the desk until I found one. Kylee unbent it and twisted it around in the lock until it popped open. We both started pulling things out. I opened a folder full of Pokémon cards. Kylee grabbed the manila envelope beneath it.

"Amelia." Kylee's eyes bugged wide. "Jesus ever-loving Christ." She stared at a photo in her hand. "I thought maybe he sneaked pics of Grace changing clothes or something creepy like that. But this . . . What is this?" She held it out to me and I took it from her. There was a little girl sitting naked on a bed, her knees pulled up to her chest, arms wrapped around her legs. Her bare skin was pale, overexposed by the flash. Her head dipped down, dark hair falling over her face.

"That's Grace," I said.

"No, it's not."

"Look." I pointed to the edge of the photo. "On the nightstand." It was Great-Aunt Iris's crocheted tissue box cover. "It's this room. Before it was ours, before Elsie changed out the bedding and made everything pink and purple for us. That's Grace."

There was another picture beneath the first one, showing part of her face. And another. Half a dozen or more, progressively worse, more disturbing. Kylee shuffled through them. Then she was out of the chair, across the hall, pounding on the bedroom door. I went after her, moving slowly, like I was half frozen, my body turning to ice.

"Get out here, motherfucker!" She kept hammering the door until Jimmy opened it in a panic, his hair sticking out every which way, eyes wide with alarm.

"You sick fuck," she growled, slapping the pictures against his chest.

"Oh, God," he said, when he saw what she had. "It's not what you think! It's not what you think!"

"What is it then, Jimmy! Why don't you tell us!"

"Listen!" he bellowed. "Listen, and I'll tell you!"

I put my hand on Kylee's shoulder. Her whole body shook. "Go ahead," I said. "Explain it."

"They're not mine," Jimmy said.

"Then why did we find them locked in a drawer in your desk?"

"They were in my desk, but they're not mine. I found them in a box of Norman's things," he said. "I was clearing out the closet to make room for some of my collectibles. Elsie didn't want me to throw out any of his stuff, but it looked like junk and I didn't figure he'd miss it. I was emptying a box into the garbage and these fell out."

Norman. It was him. Uncle Norman had taken these pictures of Grace.

"And you thought you'd just hold on to them," Kylee said.

"I wasn't keeping them to look at. I was keeping them for evidence."

"If they're evidence, why didn't you turn them in to the police?"

"Because of Elsie," he said, twisting his hands. "It'd kill her. She'd never believe Norman did something like that. She'd rather go to her grave not knowing than to think it was him that hurt Grace."

"So you were just gonna sit on those pictures till Elsie dies."

"I don't know what I was gonna do! I just knew I couldn't throw them out. I liked Grace. I don't know if she liked me much, but she was nicer to me than most people."

"Kylee," I said. "Remember when I talked to Mrs. Mummer? She said Grace was having some kind of trouble at home, back when she was in her class. She didn't know what was wrong, exactly, but Grace was really upset."

"That had to have been around when these were taken," Kylee said.

"She was jumpy," Jimmy said. "Before she disappeared. I thought maybe it was because of me—she wasn't used to me being in the house. Elsie had me come over one night, and she was late getting off work, and Grace didn't know I was here. We ran into each other in the kitchen, and I scared her. I didn't mean to. She scared me, too. The way she was looking at me. I thought she knew what I'd done."

"What did you do, Jimmy?"

"I . . . I took a pair of her underwear. But it was an accident."

"An *accident*? Is anything your fault? What the *fuck*, Jimmy," Kylee hissed.

"I got them out of the laundry! I thought they were Elsie's, and I . . ." His face was redder than I'd ever seen it.

"You what? Jerked off with them? Put them on?"

"You can skip that part," I said. "What happened, Jimmy?"

Jimmy clapped his hands over his face and talked through them. "When I figured out they weren't Elsie's, I couldn't put them back. I burned them out in the burn barrel. It wasn't long after that, she was gone. It wasn't till I found the pictures I thought maybe it wasn't me she was scared of."

It was hard to picture Grace afraid. I imagined her, before she disappeared, bravely searching for Annalise, fighting to keep me and Kylee safe. But she must have feared for herself. She knew what Norman was capable of, the terrible things he could do to little girls. What would he do to her when she was no longer powerless, when she was strong enough to push back, to pose a threat?

"So where is he now?" Kylee said. "Where. The fuck. Is Norman."

THIRTY-FIVE

I picked Ketch up from work in the morning, and we stopped at Kum & Go for Red Bulls and day-old doughnuts and a jug of milk. Kylee was up waiting for us when we returned.

"Gimme," she said, grabbing the sack of pastries and rifling through it.

"They're all the same," I said. "And they're all stale."

"I don't care," she said. "I'm starving." She crammed a doughnut in her mouth and bit it nearly in half, groaning with pleasure. Dried glaze flaked off on her lips. "All right," she said, talking with her mouth full. "What did you find out?"

Ketch sipped his Red Bull. "Next to nothing," he said. "Norman hasn't been arrested, ticketed, sued . . . nothing in the system since Grace disappeared. But—there was nothing on him for years before that either, so it doesn't mean he's not out there."

"Didn't Mama say he's paranoid, likes to stay under the radar? He doesn't use credit cards, smartphones, anything where he could be tracked."

"Then how are we supposed to find him?" Kylee said.

"Well, I talked to one of the guys at the station. He and Norman were old friends from school. Said he had sort of a circuit he made when he was on the road. He'd head west through Kansas and Colorado in the spring, north to the Dakotas to hit Sturgis in the summer, then shoot down to Texas in the fall and stay for the winter if he found enough work."

"Mama said one of his buddies saw him at Sturgis a few years back," I said.

"So what, we go to a biker rally and hunt him down?"

"Maybe," I said.

"Shut up down there!" Mama hollered. "I'm trying to sleep."

"We're not even being loud!" Kylee screamed back.

"Ketch is here," I said. "We brought breakfast."

Mama's feet hit the floor and moments later she came barreling down the stairs, hell-bent for leather. She appeared thinner than usual, almost gaunt. I hoped she had underwear on beneath her Milwaukee's Best shirt, for all our sakes. "Oh, hallelujah." She raised her hands in praise. "Somebody finally got milk." She took a mug out of the sink and filled it up, grabbed herself a doughnut.

"Mama," I said. "You told me somebody saw Norman at Sturgis, right? Do you remember what year it was?"

She frowned. "Why are we talking about Norman again?"

"Somebody was looking for him to do a concrete job, I think," Kylee said. "They remembered he did some other work around here, would've been quite a few years ago."

"Who was it?"

"Bill something," I said.

"Well, Norman did a lot of that work back in the day. Elsie got him some jobs when he needed it. He poured the driveway at her church. Hell, he even did that back patio when Elsie put the pool in. Pretty sure he skimmed supplies from some other job to do it."

Kylee jabbed a finger into my ribs.

"He did the patio?" I said. "When was that?"

Mama licked her fingers. "Hell, I don't know—before you were born."

"That long ago?"

"Yeah. You ever remember the pool not being there? You don't. It's been that long. You'd have to ask Elsie what year."

If it was poured before we were born, it was too long ago for Grace to be buried under the patio. But, depending on the year, it could have been Annalise.

THIRTY-SIX

"I don't know," Jimmy said. "I don't know, I don't know." He paced back and forth on the patio, putting his hands on his hips and then on top of his head and then back on his hips. Huge sweat rings had formed on his Thor shirt at the neck and armpits. His face was turning the color of raw hamburger.

"Come on, Jimmy," I said. "Get out of the way. We have to do this."

He stopped pacing and tugged his shirt down over his belly. "What am I supposed to tell Elsie?"

"That her beloved brother, Norman, is a murderous pedo who buried his girlfriend in her backyard," Kylee said, leaning on the sledgehammer we'd borrowed from Olivia. Olivia had been happy to loan us the necessary tools from their construction site, as long as we promised to return them before her dad found out. Construction was on hold anyway, the yellow caution tape still up around Brielle's grave.

"Elsie's been wanting to get this pool outta here for years," I said. "You can tell her it's an early birthday surprise."

"The pool!" Jimmy said. "Not the patio. What do I tell her when she gets home from work and sees the whole thing's wrecked?"

"I know," said Ketch. "Tell her when we moved the pool, the concrete was all cracked underneath, and we had to tear it out. It'd be a big mess otherwise."

"It's still gonna be a big mess," Kylee said. I pinched her arm.

"You can tell her," Jimmy said. "I'm not telling her."

"Fine," I said. Jimmy turned to go in the house and I grabbed his sleeve. "It'll go faster if you help."

The four of us got to work taking the pool frame apart, which was more difficult than we had anticipated, and finally we gave up on doing a tidy job and used the sledgehammer to smash the pieces that wouldn't come loose. It was getting dark when we finally managed to drag what was left of the pool off the concrete pad and into the yard.

"Ketch," I said. "You were right. There's big cracks."

"Should make it easier to break," he said. He started up the jackhammer and it nearly rattled his skeleton out of his skin. It took him a few tries to begin to get the hang of it. As he broke the concrete into manageable pieces, Kylee and I used pry bars to push them up from the ground, and Jimmy helped move them out of the way. The slab was only a few inches thick, but it was still a lot of work. We were all sweating, the first mosquitoes of the season humming in our ears. Finally, we were able to clear most of the area where the pool had been.

"All right," I said. "Shovel time."

"I need a break," Jimmy huffed. "I think I pulled something." He doubled over and his jeans sagged down in the back, his underwear showing.

"Wait," Kylee said. She turned on her phone light and handed it to me, then got down on her knees, picking at a disturbed patch of dirt with her bare hands. I aimed the light where she was digging, and she gently tugged something out of the ground. A decaying strip of canvas fabric. She gave it to Ketch.

"Part of a tarp?" he said. Jimmy hobbled off to fetch a lantern, and Ketch and I dropped down to help Kylee carefully chip away the packed earth with the pry bars. It was nearly as hard to break up as the concrete.

We found the edge of the tarp and dug down no more than a foot in that spot before we reached whatever was wrapped in it.

"Lazy son of a bitch," Kylee said. "Guess we got lucky."

"Jimmy," I said. "Get the shovel. We'll have to be careful."

Jimmy didn't move. "Oh, God."

"We should leave it how it is," Ketch said. "Shouldn't we? So we don't destroy any evidence?"

"I don't know. Maybe we should call the police. Can you call David?"

Kylee wiped her hands on her shirt. "Do we really want the cops here?"

"We need to clean up this mess," Jimmy rasped, his chest heaving like he was about to hyperventilate. "Before Elsie gets back."

"That's not gonna happen," I said. "We have to be sure."

I knelt next to the hole we had made and pressed my palm against the dirt-crusted canvas, telling myself it could be anything, though only one thing made sense: that it was Annalise, that Norman had killed her and buried her in his sister's backyard years ago, that he had hidden her where he thought she'd never be found. I tore at the layers of disintegrating fabric, stripped them away in ribbons, my fingers burrowing in like spiders to crawl over the bones that lay beneath.

"We have to call Bill," I said, staggering to my feet.

Ketch steadied me, his arm around my waist, and aimed the light down into the hole. I didn't need to look. I didn't want to see.

"Mimi." Kylee grabbed my elbow, her dirt-crusted nails digging in. "Grace always hated this pool."

It was true. She swam in the river, but never the pool in her own backyard. She told us it wasn't safe, the bottom too slick, the water too cold because it never escaped the shade. She'd braved it to save me from drowning, and that was the only time I had ever seen her get in. Maybe somehow she had sensed it, that Annalise lay below, buried in the dark, beneath the earth, beneath the concrete, beneath the thousands of gallons of water. From this impossible depth, Annalise had reached out, made herself known, tried to send a warning.

THIRTY-SEVEN

"Where's your sister?" Mama said when I walked in. At this late hour, she'd usually be at work or asleep. I couldn't remember ever coming home to find her like this, on the couch waiting up for us. I'd hastily scrubbed my face and arms at the spigot in Elsie's backyard, but I hadn't been able to brush all the dirt and concrete dust off my clothes. Maybe she wouldn't notice in the lamplight.

"Kylee's with a friend," I said. I'd tried to get her to come home with me, but she had gone to see Tyson instead. I'd warned her not to say anything to him. I didn't want Levi finding out until we knew if Annalise had any connection to Grace, if Norman had killed them both.

"Your boss came to the house tonight," Mama said. "Mr. Mustache."

"Alan was here?"

"Yeah, he was lurking around outside. Felt like I was getting a migraine, so I had all the lights off. He probably thought nobody was home. Came right up to the door and had his hand on the knob. Shocked the shit out of him when I yanked it open."

"What was he doing?"

"Seemed to me he was about to come in the house without being invited. I asked him what the hell he was up to, sneaking around in the dark, and he said he came to check on you. That you were sick. Hadn't been to work. Something seemed off, though." She gave me a pointed look. "You and him got something going on?"

"What? No! God, Mama. You didn't tell him I was out, did you?"

"You think I'd rat you out to your boss?"

"What did you tell him?"

"Same thing I used to tell the school when you were faking sick." She smirked. "That you had real bad diarrhea. Then I stayed up and kept watch to make sure he wouldn't come sneaking in anyway."

"Do you think he bought it?"

"Hell if I know." She glanced at my dirt-streaked jeans. I tucked my shaking hands under my armpits, but she'd already taken notice. "You want to tell me what's going on?"

Where would I even start? There was no easy way to tell her we'd dug up Annalise's remains under Elsie's pool, that Norman was the only one who could have put them there.

"Mama," I said. "You never seemed like you cared much for Norman. Not the way Elsie does, at least."

She scoffed. "Understatement. What's he got to do with this?"

"Did he do something in particular to get on your bad side?"

"He was an asshole from day one," she said.

"Would you . . . believe he did something awful?"

"Like what?" she said. "Stop playing around and spit it out."

"Okay," I said. I sat down on the couch, folded my hands on my lap. "We think Norman killed Annalise. And Brielle, too. Maybe Grace. We can't rule out Alan for her and Brielle, but Annalise . . . we're sure it was Norman."

Mama didn't blink. Her jaw tightened, twitched. "What makes you so sure?"

"There's someone buried under Elsie's pool. We dug up bones tonight. You said Norman poured the concrete."

She was quiet, her eyes glimmering in the lamplight. "You say anything to Elsie about that?"

"No," I said. "Jimmy knows. He hasn't told her yet." She didn't ask whether we'd called the cops. We'd taken a vote and decided to wait until we could talk to Bill Wheeler and Jimmy could get Elsie out of town for a couple of days, so she wouldn't be there when the police came. She'd find out soon enough, but we all thought it was best if she didn't know until the body was gone.

Mama rose from the couch as though possessed, her body moving unnaturally, mechanically, her gaze locked straight ahead. She ascended the stairs, her footfalls barely making a sound.

I texted Kylee to ask her to call me. I wanted to tell her about Mama, and about Alan coming to the house. I figured she was busy with Tyson, but her reply came immediately.

Levi's freaking out.

That could only mean one thing. *You told him??*

No. He was here.

You told Tyson.

Just get here, Mimi. Ty's trying to calm him down. I need a ride home.

The three of them were out in the dirt road when I got there, Kylee standing in the ditch, Tyson with his arms stretched wide, trying to herd Levi back to the house. Kylee turned toward me, and Levi broke past Tyson and sprinted to the car.

"Amelia!" he hollered. His lip was bleeding, swollen, the collar of his T-shirt ripped.

"Are you all right?"

"He's drunk," Kylee said, getting in the passenger side. "Starting fights. He punched Tyson in the face, twice."

That was hard to believe. I couldn't imagine him hitting anyone, doing anything remotely violent. Levi leaned in my open window, breathing hard. Sweat slicked his face. "I don't know about that other girl. But Norman didn't kill Grace. It wasn't him. Norman was already dead."

Kylee shook her head.

"What are you talking about, Levi?" I said. He'd been drunk at the river, but I'd never seen him like this. His breath could peel paint. He was deep in the bait shop whiskey. "Norman's not dead. Or he wasn't back then, anyway. People have seen him around."

"No," he said. "They haven't."

"One of his old buddies just saw him at Sturgis a couple years back."

"Really?" Levi said. "Some old drunk thinks he saw another old drunk in a crowd? How many guys were out there in greasy bandanas, sunglasses, bushy beards? Could've been anybody. Could've been a thousand other guys. I'm telling you, it wasn't Norman."

"How would you know, Levi?" Kylee said, a sharp edge in her voice. "How would you know he was dead?"

Levi leaned over me, his eyes dark, his body tensed to the point of vibrating. "Why don't you ask my brother," he muttered. "Ask him what happened."

Tyson grabbed him from behind, yanked him back, spun him around.

"They should know!" Levi yelled.

Tyson shoved him toward the house, then shoved him again, until Levi shuffled backward and fell in the dirt, throwing punches on the way down.

GRACE

THIRTY-EIGHT

Grace slid plates of pecan waffles and buttered grits onto the counter, checked the clock, and slipped into the restroom to use her phone. They were slammed, and her replacement was running late, so she couldn't leave. She was supposed to be at Shannon's to watch the girls, but no one was answering the phone at the house. She tried Shannon's cell and finally got her to pick up.

"Hey," Grace said. "Can you tell the girls I'll be there as soon as I can?"

"Didn't you get my message?" Shannon asked.

"No. We've been busy, I just snuck out to make a call."

"Well, don't worry about it, Norman's watching the kids tonight."

"What? Norman?" A cold stab of fear in the center of her chest. "Why is Norman watching them?"

"I dunno. You been busy. He offered to help out. Trying to make himself useful for once."

"I said I'd do it. I can leave in a few minutes."

"No need," Shannon said. "He's already there."

Grace stuck her phone back in her apron and hurried out to see if the waitress had shown up yet. "Javi," she asked, "did Faith say when she'd get here?"

"She was waiting on a ride," he said. "That's the last I heard."

"Shit. I should've known."

"Something wrong?"

"I need to go," she said.

"We could call somebody else in?"

"Probably wouldn't be any quicker." She grabbed the coffeepot and went to top off cups near the front window so she could see into the parking lot. "I think that's her," she said, squinting. It was possible that Faith was in the van that had just pulled up, though she really couldn't tell, and didn't care. She slammed the coffeepot back in the machine. "Gotta run."

When Grace burst into Shannon's house, water was filling the tub upstairs, and her insides twisted at the memory of the first bath, Norman shedding his clothes and climbing in with her, his hands at her waist as she washed his hair. She sprinted up the stairs, calling to the girls, her voice loud and bright. "Kylee! Amelia! I'm here!"

The bathroom door at the top of the stairs was closed, and she couldn't hear anything but water gushing. She tried the knob and it wouldn't turn, so she pounded on the door with both fists. It was flimsy, hollow, and she knew she could break through it if she had to.

"Girls! It's Grace, open up!"

The door creaked open and Kylee peered out through the crack. She was wearing one of Shannon's old T-shirts, the lettering peeling off. Grace couldn't see the whole thing, but she knew what it said: "Tequila: It might not be the answer, but it's worth a shot."

"Grace?"

"Hey! What's up?" She pushed her way in. Norman was sitting at the edge of the tub, fully clothed, looking bemused.

"We didn't think you were coming," Amelia said.

"What? I'm here. Of course I'm here." She hugged both of them to her. "You had a bath last night, you don't need one tonight."

"I told him I didn't want a bath," Kylee said.

Amelia sighed. "You never want a bath."

"Okay, you girls go on and get in bed, and I'll be right there to read to you," Grace said.

She closed the door behind them, shutting herself in the bathroom with Norman. The walls felt too close, and she had to clench her hands into fists to keep them from shaking.

"What are you doing?" she said.

Norman twisted the knobs to shut off the water. "What do you mean, Gracie?"

"You know what I mean. What do you think you're doing with them?"

He rolled up his sleeve and reached down below the surface to pull the plug. The water made slurping sounds as it swirled down the drain. "What's wrong?" Norman said. "Are you jealous?"

There was a burning sensation in her belly, working its way up her throat. She'd been stupid to ignore him, to assume he wouldn't hurt her because she was old enough now to protect herself. Shannon had compared Norman to a cicada, going underground for years at a time. Like a cicada, he'd been waiting for the right time to return. It was no coincidence that he'd surfaced before the girls were too grown-up.

"I'll turn you in," she snarled. "You'll get sent away and you won't be able to touch them."

"Yeah?" he said. "Turn me in for what?"

"What you did to me."

"I took care of you," he said. "Now I'm taking care of them. I've never laid an unkind hand on those girls. I'm helping out their mama. My sister. It's the right thing to do. And I hear you'll be gone soon, Grace—who do you think's gonna watch 'em then?"

She lunged at him, her body moving before she even realized she was going to do it, but Norman was ready. He grabbed her arms and held tight, a smirk on his face. Grace wrenched herself away from him. "You need to leave," she said.

"Tell the girls good night for me. I'll see 'em soon."

Grace leaned against the girls' bedroom door and watched him descend the stairs, then waited for the sound of his truck pulling away. When she was sure he was gone, she climbed into bed between Kylee and Amelia and read to them from *Anne of Green Gables*.

She managed to read the words, but her mind drifted elsewhere. She'd often fantasized about what she'd do if Norman tried to hurt her again. She'd get a rifle, shoot him in the balls. It was easy to think those things, not as easy to follow through. Whatever she did would have consequences. If she shot Norman, she'd go to prison instead of college. And she was so close to getting away, she didn't want to do anything to ruin it. She couldn't be with her cousins every minute even when they were in the same town. She had to make sure that Norman would stay away from them. How could she do that if she wasn't around?

She thought of Norman's truck on that bitter day, years ago. Her foot on the gas, her hand on the gearshift. She hadn't been brave enough to do it. She'd failed herself. But she'd been so young, then, and scared. A bit younger than her cousins were now. How brave were they, how strong? She couldn't leave them to those terrible decisions, a chance moment where they might be able to do something she could not. She couldn't fail them, though in a way, she already had. Maybe if she'd said something back then, he wouldn't be here now.

Grace put the book down and tucked the girls into bed. She would figure it out.

"You didn't fluff the quilt right," Kylee said.

"Oh, sorry. I'll redo it." She shook out the covers, let them drift down over the girls' small bodies.

"Don't forget to tickle my back," Amelia said.

"I would never."

Grace sat at the edge of the bed and ran her fingernails over Amelia's shoulder blades and down her spine, across and down and back. She'd miss her cousins terribly when she left, though part of her—a small, yet urgent part—longed to leave everything behind, to live her life with no attachments, no one depending on her to feed them dinner or keep them safe or make sure they had brushed their teeth. The admission came with a veneer of guilt, but she couldn't deny that it would be a relief. Or, it would have been, if not for Norman.

THIRTY-NINE

Grace's head throbbed from lack of sleep, and she wished she could shut off the alarm and go back to bed, but there was too much to do, so she got up and dressed for school. She hadn't been home much over the past week, and when she was, she stayed in her room, trying to avoid running into her uncle. She'd been working extra hours on the nights she wasn't watching Kylee and Amelia, and all her spare time was spent studying and trying to figure out what to do about Norman.

The smell of fried sausage greeted her as she headed downstairs. Maybe her mother had finally forgiven her and decided to make a nice breakfast as a peace offering. She'd barely seen Elsie since their argument. When she walked into the kitchen, though, it wasn't her mother who was seated at the head of the table, in the good chair with the padded seat, demolishing a plate of biscuits and gravy. It wasn't Norman, either. It was Jimmy, wearing a Batman shirt and the same saggy jeans he'd had on the last time she'd seen him.

While she hadn't expected to see Jimmy first thing in the morning, she wasn't surprised that Elsie was feeding him, because Elsie tried to feed anyone who came within five feet of the house, whether it was a neighbor or a random Jehovah's Witness going door to door. What was more surprising was that Jimmy had started his own computer business and was apparently taking it seriously. In the time since he'd graduated, Grace had seen him hanging out on his bike in the school parking lot, buying scratcher tickets at Kum & Go, and playing games on his phone at the laundromat. She'd never seen him working anywhere and doubted he'd ever held a job before.

"Good morning," Grace said.

"Hey," Jimmy replied, his mouth full.

She couldn't tell whether he was embarrassed, because his face was always red, his cheeks splotched with acne and rosacea. He shifted in his seat, and that was when she noticed that he was barefoot. Jimmy's feet were blindingly white, and they were planted awkwardly on the linoleum, glowing like albino cave creatures that had never seen the sun.

"Are you . . ." She wasn't sure how to formulate the question. She didn't want to make any assumptions. "Are you here to work on the computer?"

"Um?" He fidgeted with his fork, scraping it back and forth across the plate. "Uh. No?"

Grace stared at him, waiting for him to elaborate so she wouldn't have to ask.

"We're, um, hanging out?"

"We?"

"Elsie? And me?" Every sentence sounded like a question he was scared to ask.

"You're hanging out. With my mom."

"Yeah?"

His face grew redder. Or maybe not. *Hanging out.* Jimmy and her mother were hanging out. At seven in the morning. Barefoot. The tips of Grace's ears burned.

"Where is she?"

"Getting dressed?" Jimmy said.

Sweet Lord. What was her mother thinking? She didn't want to assume the worst, but whatever had happened, there was no reason for Jimmy to still be in her kitchen. He needed to find his crusty old shoes and get out.

"Right," she said. "Well, we've all gotta get going." She grabbed his plate and dumped what was left in a plastic baggie. "Here. Could you . . . wait outside for Elsie? Or . . . did you ride your bike here? You could go."

"Uh?"

"Thanks, Jimmy. I'll tell her you said goodbye."

Grace headed down the hall to her mother's room. Jimmy's chair scraped against the linoleum. Hopefully he was on his way out.

"Mama," she said, shoving the door open. "Why was Jimmy Schultze in our kitchen just now?"

Elsie blushed furiously and Grace knew the answer.

"I told you before," Elsie began. "He's helping me—"

"Nope. He said he wasn't."

Elsie sighed and dug through her sock drawer. "Grace . . . he's sweet. And he's smart—he knows everything about computers. He's an artist, too. Look."

She plucked a piece of notebook paper from the top of the dresser and handed it to Grace. It was a cartoonish sketch of Elsie that made her look half her age, flowers in her hair, shy smile on her face. Was that truly how he saw her, or was he only trying to flatter her? It had probably been a long time since a man had made Elsie feel the way Jimmy's drawing apparently did. Was Jimmy smart enough to know that, to play her? Maybe he saw her as an easy mark—a nurturing, hardworking woman who'd support him and take care of him, so he'd never have to get a job. It was hard to picture Jimmy making a move on her mother, though, unless Elsie had made a move first.

Grace handed back the drawing. "He's barely older than me."

"Oh, don't give me that. He's an adult! He's a *man*, Grace. It's nice to have a man around sometimes."

"You've got Norman living here."

Elsie frowned. "You know what I mean. And Norman'll be gone soon. What do you care, anyhow? You'll be gone, too."

"I don't get it—are you trying to punish me for leaving?"

"Grow up, Grace. Everything's not about you."

"What is this about, then? Are you telling me you have some kind of feelings for Jimmy? He came over to fix a computer and you threw yourself at him?"

"I don't want to be alone!" Elsie bellowed.

"You don't want to be alone? That's why you're doing this?"

Elsie sat on the edge of the bed to put on her socks. "I don't expect you to understand, but I can't come home to an empty house every day for the rest of my life and know that it'll always be empty. I don't think I can stand it. I always wanted to be surrounded by family, a houseful of kids, grand-kids. You know how important family is to me. You don't want to be here, Grace. As much as it kills me, you've made it clear. Fine. But I'm not gonna sit here in an empty house and die alone."

"Die alone? That's kind of a stretch, isn't it? I'm still here! Your nieces are over here all the time. I come home and Shannon's digging through the refrigerator. You've never spent a day alone in your life."

"And I don't want to," Elsie said. She yanked her shoes on and walked out.

Grace waited until she heard the door slam and her mother's car start before leaving the room. It was hard to believe that her mother was replac-ing her before she had even graduated. Not with a cat or a new hobby, the way a normal empty nester might, but with a boyfriend who was barely old enough to buy beer. Someone to warm her bed and take up space at the kitchen table and let her guess the *Wheel of Fortune* puzzles. Someone for her to take care of until the time came that she needed him to take care of her. Jimmy was probably the last person Grace would count on for that. She didn't trust him to stick around when their positions were reversed, unless he had a long game in mind—maybe he was planning to marry Elsie and wait for her to die so he could get her house and sit around for the rest of his life playing video games.

Grace's phone vibrated in her pocket. It was Dallas, asking if she wanted to meet up to do homework later. She said *Maybe*, and he wrote back *You owe me*, followed by a winky face. She'd edged him out by half a point on the bio test, which wouldn't have happened if he hadn't shared the bonus questions.

She typed *What do I owe you, exactly?* but hesitated before sending. They'd already racked up a long string of texts, and they'd fallen into a playful back-and-forth of sarcasm, taunts, and mildly inappropriate humor. It was just the way they talked to each other. She didn't see anything wrong with it. It was lighthearted and meaningless, a welcome distraction from everything else going on in her life. She clicked Send and then deleted the message thread. She wasn't doing anything wrong, but someone might read something into it that wasn't there. It could be misinterpreted. She knew if Levi saw it, he wouldn't understand.

FORTY

Tyson had his standard can of Monster Energy between his legs and a second in the cup holder. "Got you a drink," he said, handing her a sweating can of Monster Ultra Violet. "Figured you needed it with all you got going on. I never tried that flavor before, but I know you like purple."

"Aw, thanks, Ty. And thanks for giving me a ride."

"Hey, anytime. It's an honor to chauffer Miss Most Likely to Succeed around town. I feel like I should put streamers on the truck or something. Make sure everybody knows who I got in here."

"Please don't. It doesn't mean anything to anybody."

"It does to us," he said. "We're proud of you. You're making us look good."

"Right."

"Gotta ask, though, why are they taking these pictures out in the woods?"

"Just cause it looks pretty, I think? It was the yearbook people's idea. They always try to do something different for the senior personalities."

He glanced over at her, his gaze flitting down to her form-fitting dress, her bare legs. He cleared his throat. "Well, you look pretty already," he said. "Don't need a buncha trees behind you to make you look good."

"You're awful sweet today, Ty," she said.

"I got my moments."

Grace cracked open the energy drink and took a sip. It tasted like fake sugar. She didn't know how he drank so many of them.

"Everything going all right with you and Levi?" he asked.

"Yeah, I think so. Why?"

"I dunno, he's been kinda moody lately. Thought maybe you two'd had a fight."

"We're not fighting," she said. "Just talking about the future. Trying to figure things out."

"Okay. Well, I know how I hope it turns out. There's anything I can do to help, you tell me," he said. "I mean that."

"I know you do, Tyson."

He parked in the gravel lot at the trailhead.

"Sure you don't need a ride home? I could swing back by when you're done, pick you up. Or I could wait."

"That's okay. I don't have any idea when we'll finish up. I'll catch a ride."

"With Mr. Most Likely?"

"Maybe."

"Do I need to get out and intimidate him a bit? I don't mind." Tyson flexed his arms and she laughed.

"I appreciate the offer," she said. "But definitely not."

After he left, she realized she'd forgotten to take the drink he'd given her and hoped it wouldn't hurt his feelings when he noticed it was still full. He was more sensitive than Levi gave him credit for. Dallas pulled up then and waved to her. He was wearing a navy suit with a pink-and-blue striped tie, his hair combed back, and any thought of Tyson or Levi slipped from her mind.

"Dang," he said, walking up to her. "I feel like I should've gotten you a corsage or something."

"Well, now I'm disappointed."

"Hey, everybody." The yearbook photographer clapped his hands. "We're gonna be in this clearing right over here. You can check the clipboard to see what order you're in. We're starting with Class Clowns."

Grace pushed her way to the front to get a look at the list and then reported back. "We're up next," she said. "I wonder what kind of weird props they've got for us. Looks like they have actual clown wigs for the clowns."

Dallas was scrolling on his phone and didn't look up. "Do you have service out here? I'm waiting for a message from Missouri State and I've only got one bar."

"No," Grace said. "Sorry. Can you hold on to my phone for me? I don't have any pockets."

"Sure. So, have you decided where you're going yet?"

"No. Somewhere out of state, if I get enough aid. If not, I'll be down in Springfield, I guess. Maybe Mizzou. Just waiting to see what's doable."

"Why'd you wrinkle up your nose when you said Mizzou? It's in my top three. Maybe we'll end up at the same place."

"Not if I can help it."

"Really. You know what I think?"

"What?"

Dallas adjusted his tie. "I think you'll miss me."

"Lord," Grace said.

Dallas grinned. "It's almost our turn. Let's show these clowns how it's done."

The photographer pointed out the spot where he wanted them to stand. "How about . . . go back to back with your arms crossed. Do kind of a serious expression. More like you're pissed off. Good. Got it. Okay, now do one of those poses like at prom, maybe. Dallas, you get behind her and, you know, put your hands . . . yeah, like that. Move in closer."

Dallas was at her back, his body solid as a wall, his hands at her waist. Grace could feel him breathing. She tried not to move, not to think about the way he pressed against her, nothing between them but a thin layer of fabric.

"You two make a cute couple!" the photographer said. He snapped several shots, turned the camera to the side, took some more. "All right, I think we got enough. Thanks, guys. Stick around, we're doing the whole group at the end."

They walked back toward the parking lot, away from the crowd. "Do we really have to stay?" he said as they passed his truck. "Do we care that much about the group picture? I'm kinda bitter I didn't get Most Athletic."

"Doesn't matter to me," she said. "I'm ready to get out of this dress anytime now."

"I'm not even gonna make a joke," Dallas said, digging her phone out of his pocket and handing it back to her. "You make it too easy."

Grace smacked his arm. "Hey, I've got service," she said. "Barely. Maybe if we go up the hill a bit." They continued along the trail until they got a stronger signal.

"Well, that was pointless," Dallas said. "No new messages."

"Wait, I got something," Grace said.

"What?"

"Iowa."

"And?"

"Hold on."

"What'd they offer? How much?"

"They came through. Everything I needed."

"Are you serious?"

"Yeah." She was half in shock, her limbs tingling. "It's happening. I'm really getting out of here."

"Hell yeah, you are. We gotta celebrate. Come on, get excited!" He shook her by the shoulders. "Grace, you did it!"

She squealed and threw her arms around his neck, and he spun her around, and when they stopped spinning, he kissed her. Grace was dizzy from the spinning or the kiss or the good news. Maybe all of it. They stared at each other, breathless, stunned.

They would have missed the group picture by now. Everyone else would be leaving. They might notice Dallas's truck in the parking lot and wonder where the two of them had disappeared to. Had anyone seen them walk off together? Could someone have spied them up here from the parking lot? They would have seen that she hadn't fought Dallas off, hadn't put up any resistance at all. That she'd clung to him, kissed him back with an unknown hunger. What would happen if Levi found out? Her heart clenched tight as a fist and a familiar fear pumped through her: that her most shameful secrets would be revealed, that people would know just by looking, a neon light illuminating everything she wanted to keep hidden.

FORTY-ONE

Dallas turned around and caught her eye from his seat at the front of the class. He smiled and her face warmed. She dropped her gaze to her notebook, highlighted some things that didn't need highlighting.

Guilt gnawed at her every day, an insistent creature with sharp teeth, though it hadn't stopped her from studying with Dallas. They had briefly discussed the kiss and agreed they'd gotten caught up in the moment—that it wasn't worth hurting Levi over because it wouldn't happen again. It took some effort to ignore what was simmering between them. Grace was hyperaware of every interaction. Any physical contact took on new weight, whether she smacked his arm over a sarcastic comment or he leaned against her shoulder to check her notes. She overanalyzed her texts, resisted responding with a heart when Dallas said that if they partnered in a three-legged race now, no one could beat them. She sent a smiley face instead, then wondered if she should have gone with a generic thumbs-up.

It wasn't fair to Levi, and she knew she needed to be honest with him. He was her first love and her best friend, and she didn't want to hurt him, but there was no way to reconcile the life she wanted with the one he had in mind. That had nothing to do with Dallas—it wouldn't have worked out with her and Levi, regardless. The situation with Dallas was something else altogether. He understood her in a way Levi never could. They were alike, they wanted the same things. In the fall, they'd be leaving, starting fresh, and if they wanted to stay in touch, see what might happen, the possibility was there. Part of the excitement lay in the unknown, having choices, a chance to plot her own life.

The bell rang, and as she gathered her things to leave, Mr. Copeland approached the table and blocked her way. "Grace, stay after a minute."

Sophie, her old lab partner, avoided eye contact as she moved past with the stream of students exiting the room, as though she wanted to avoid trouble by association. Dallas was the last to leave, lingering until his dad waved him out, clearly as clueless as she was. Grace wrapped her arms around her notebook and Mr. Copeland shut the door.

"I graded the exams," he said, "and I noticed that your seatmate, Jed, had several of the same answers as you. Correct answers. Which is not normally the case."

"Oh," she said. "I helped him with the study guide. We worked on it together in class. And I taught him some of the mnemonic devices I use. He must have been paying attention."

"That's not what I think happened," Mr. Copeland intoned gravely, his jaw twitching. "I think what has happened here is that you let him copy off your test. I think, Grace, that you helped him cheat."

Heat blazed up her neck to her ears. "Why would I do that?"

"You two seem to get along well back here."

"You put me here. I didn't choose to sit by him, and I didn't let him cheat off me."

"How could he have cheated off your paper without you letting him?"

"What makes you so sure he cheated?"

He laid the tests down side by side. "Explain why his answers are the same."

"I told you, I helped him study."

He shook his head. "I'm sorry, Grace. This isn't something I can over-look. There may be disciplinary action."

The only thing keeping her rage in check was disbelief. Grace had never gotten in trouble at school, not once, and now she was being accused of something she hadn't done but couldn't disprove. "You think he looked at my test, and I'm the one in trouble? Did you even ask him if he did it, or if I let him?"

"Jed's already failing," Mr. Copeland said. "He's got nothing to lose."

She wondered what he meant exactly by disciplinary action. A failing grade for the semester that would ruin her GPA? Or something worse?

"You could drop the class," he said. "You don't need it to graduate."

Suddenly, it all made sense. He knew she hadn't cheated. He'd been looking for a way to knock her down, and he'd finally found it. Copeland wanted his son to have the highest grade, to be class valedictorian, to win the Bender Scholarship. He hadn't been able to make that happen by giving Dallas an advantage on the exams, or by moving Grace to the back of the room and saddling her with Jed, so now he was trying to force her to quit. He probably thought he was justified, because Grace didn't even need this class—she wasn't the one who wanted to be a doctor, the one who would stay and take care of the town.

Grace clenched her jaw, her teeth grinding together. Every time she felt like she was in control of her own life, someone reminded her of her place.

FORTY-TWO

Grace couldn't stop fuming about Mr. Copeland all through her shift. She slammed a coffee mug down on the counter, and Javi shot her a look of concern. If Mr. Copeland wanted to threaten her, she would threaten him right back. It was a blatant conflict of interest, and completely unethical, him favoring his own son, putting his thumb on the scale. It wouldn't look good for him if she took it up with the principal, the superintendent. He could make up lies about her, but he had no proof that she'd cheated, that she'd done anything wrong. She wanted to talk to Dallas. Not that he could help her—what his father did wasn't his fault.

The guy sitting at the counter flagged Grace down yet again. He wore an outdated suit and large wire-rimmed glasses, and his cowboy boots and watch looked so flashy they had to be knockoffs. She'd lost track of how many times she'd refilled his coffee cup. He would drink just enough that she would have to top it off, and then he'd start in on some story she wasn't in the mood to listen to.

"Hey," he said. "Want to see a picture of my pride and joy?"

Grace hesitated, because it could go either way. Would it be a photo of grandkids, or a dick pic? She didn't want to know.

"Actually—" she said.

He pulled a card out of his wallet and thrust it in her face. It wasn't grandkids or genitals or even a dog or a sports car. It was a picture of Pride furniture wax and Joy dish soap. He chortled, obviously proud of the stale joke he'd probably told every woman who'd had the misfortune of serving him food over the past thirty years.

"I don't got any kids or grandkids," he said. "I thought I'd get married, but it wasn't in the cards for me. Got too much baggage weighing me down. Missed my chance. Look, before I got into sales, I was a shy little pecker-wood. I never woulda talked to a pretty young thing like you. Used to be, I wouldn't say shit if I had a mouthful. Can you believe that?"

"No," she said. "I really can't." He'd been telling her pointless, self-aggrandizing stories for the past hour and a half and it was becoming increasingly difficult not to let her murderous thoughts show on her face. It was part of the job, listening to men talk. Some were lonely and craved conversation, but most of them didn't actually want you to say anything in return. They wanted your attention, your kind smiles and nods and laughs, a captive audience to feign interest, concern, delight. They clung to that power until the check came, and waitresses had little choice but to play along, hoping that their patient suffering would be rewarded with a decent tip.

Grace didn't expect that Mr. Pride and Joy was a good tipper, only because the odds were against it. Few good tippers patronized the Beaumont Waffle House, and you couldn't predict who they were by the clothes they wore or how much money they appeared to have. At this point, she didn't care if the guy pulled a hundred-dollar bill out of his boot, she was done smiling and nodding and refilling his coffee a tablespoon at a time. She dropped his check on the counter without stopping. "Oh, hey," he said. "I was thinking you looked kinda familiar." He kept talking as she walked away, his voice growing louder, more plaintive when she didn't turn back.

He lingered at his seat for several more minutes, swirling his coffee cup, and when Grace returned from a bathroom break she found five pennies laid out on the counter like a smiley face, two for the eyes, three for the mouth. She swept them off the table into her palm, sticky with syrup, imagining herself rushing out to the parking lot, hurling them at his car as he sped away. *You forgot your fucking pennies!* She swatted the nearly full coffee mug and it spun off the counter and crashed to the floor. Javi looked up from the grill.

Grace clutched the coins in her fist. "Be right back," she said.

The man leaned against the trunk of an old Lincoln Continental at the far end of the parking lot, smoking a cigarette, and Grace wondered if he'd been waiting for her, if he'd made a bet with himself about whether or not she'd follow him outside. She couldn't tell from his expression if he was surprised to see her.

She nearly lost her nerve and went back in, but she was still angry, and her anger was bigger than any fear, an iceberg of devastating mass lurking beneath the surface, its cold weight a lifetime of compressed rage.

She got close enough to breathe in his cigarette smoke. The smell wakened the restless snakes in her belly. "You forgot your change," she said, holding it out to him.

The man curled his fingers around her hand. His skin felt like sandpaper.

"You keep it," he said, smoke leaking from his mouth. His eyes gleamed in the darkness. "You earned that, Grace."

Grace yanked her hand away, the pennies falling to the pavement. She forced herself to walk away from him slowly, as though she wasn't afraid, but she felt him watching her the entire time, her skin prickling, adrenaline urging her to run.

Javi was sweeping up the broken mug when she came back in. "Everything okay?" he said.

"Yeah."

"You look funny."

"What? I'm fine."

"You know that guy?"

"No," she said, grabbing a rag to wipe up splattered coffee. "Just an annoying customer. He forgot something."

"Forgot to tip?" Javi said.

"I was in a bad mood, he just set me off. Please don't tell on me."

Javi made a zipper motion across his mouth. "Whatever you did," he said, "I bet he deserved it."

"Thanks, Javi."

"Hello, hello!" Alan's twangy voice rang out from the direction of his office.

Javi immediately went stone-faced. He took the broom and dustpan and slid past Alan to disappear into the back. Alan sidled up to the counter, staring after Javi before turning his attention to Grace.

"Good to see you cleaning, Grace, I love that initiative. I think you missed a spot down there." Grace didn't move. "Right . . . down . . . there." Alan pointed. If he was waiting for her to bend over in front of him, he'd be waiting until they both turned to stone. His grin faded and he leaned closer. He was always leaning closer, into her personal space. "Your review's coming up, Grace," he said. "We'll have to talk about your future here."

She bared her teeth in the best approximation of a smile she could muster in the moment. "Sure, Alan."

He whispered conspiratorially, "And keep an eye on him for me."

"What?"

He jerked his head in the direction of the kitchen, where Javi was back on the grill. "Some things have gone missing. I've got my suspicions."

She waited for Alan to retreat to his office, like a snail oozing back into its shell, and then went to wash her hands. The heart Amelia had drawn on the inside of her wrist the day before had nearly washed away. The girls had asked Grace if she could come over again tonight, even though Shannon was off work. She figured they probably hadn't gone to bed yet, because Shannon didn't enforce bedtime unless the girls were bothering her, so she got out her phone to call and tell them good night. Before she could dial, she saw there were two missed calls from Shannon's house. No messages. She called back and no one answered, so she tried again. Each time it went to voicemail, an anonymous robotic voice telling her no one was available to take her call, because Shannon had never bothered to set it up.

FORTY-THREE

"Thanks for the ride, Tyson." He'd arrived to pick her up within a couple of minutes of her call, after she hadn't been able to reach Levi, who'd gone fishing at the river cabin. Either Tyson had been nearby, or he'd sped the entire way.

"Always happy to help out," he said. "Levi ought to be back in the morning."

Grace was relieved to see Shannon's car in the driveway when they pulled up.

"You okay? Want me to come in with you?"

"You don't have to, Tyson."

He got out anyway, and they walked in the front door together. The TV was on, but no one was watching it.

"Hello!" Grace called. "Shannon! Girls?"

She jogged up the stairs to their room, where a bin of old Halloween costumes lay tipped over on the floor, and there was Norman, sitting on Kylee's bed, a plastic tiara on his head. Kylee wore a cowgirl outfit with a tulle princess skirt over the top. Amelia was in her underwear and one of Shannon's old Budweiser tees, her hair wet.

"Everything okay? Where's your mom?"

"Yeah," Norman said, adjusting the tiara. "We're good. Shannon took off for a bit. We're just hanging out."

"Great. You can go now. I'm sure you've got other things to do."

"Nah, I told Shannon I'd stay till she got back. Might be late."

"That's okay," Grace said. "I can stay."

Tyson stepped forward, towering over everyone. "We got it from here, man."

Norman smirked, looking from Tyson to Grace and back. "All righty, then. If you insist." As he walked past Grace to the stairs, he muttered to her: "Clock's ticking. We'll sure miss you when you're gone."

Tyson followed him down to see that he left, and Grace stayed upstairs with the girls to put them to bed.

"How was your night?" she asked, picking up the discarded costumes.

"Boring," Kylee said.

"Amelia, your hair's wet. Did you take a bath?"

"I washed my hair. Kylee got paint in it."

"So . . . which one of you called me?"

"Mama did," Amelia said. "You didn't answer."

"I was at work. Was everything okay with Norman?"

"Mostly we watched TV."

"And we did a photo shoot," Kylee said.

"What do you mean, a photo shoot?"

"With the costumes."

"I didn't do it," Amelia said. "Dress-up's for babies. He said next time we could do different kinds of pictures, something more grown-up."

"No," Grace said. She hadn't meant to say it aloud. She teetered between the urgent need to warn them and her desire to keep them from having to know such things for as long as possible. It was a dangerous fantasy, she decided, the idea that she could protect them and still keep them in the dark. "If Uncle Norman ever tries to touch you, or help with your bath, or get you to take off your clothes for any reason . . . that's inappropriate. You know that, yeah? It's not okay. If he ever makes you uncomfort-

able in any way, you get away from him. You tell me immediately. You tell
your mother. You tell anybody who'll listen."

The girls stared at her.

"Do you get what I'm saying?"

They nodded, though she wasn't sure they really understood.

After she tucked them in, she went down to wait for Shannon. Tyson
was sitting on the couch, taking up most of it, arms spread across the back,
knees out.

"Oh, hey," she said. "You didn't have to wait."

"Not a problem. You want to tell me what's going on?" He made room
for her and patted the seat beside him. She reluctantly sat down.

"He's . . . not a good person," she said, hoping to keep things as vague
and simple as possible. "I don't like having him around, and I really don't
trust him with the girls. He's in my house now. I can't get away from him."

Tyson squinted at her, and she wondered what he knew, what he could
guess from reading her face. "He one of the reasons you want to leave
town?"

She shrugged. "I keep hoping he'll disappear again, take off like he usually does."

"Have you talked to Levi about it?"

"There's nothing he can do."

"You know I work in rendering?" Tyson said with a wry smile. "In case
you ever need to get rid of a body. Just saying."

She laughed faintly, and Tyson rested his hand on her knee.

"I'm here for you," he said. "Me and Levi, we both are. Things'll work
out, Grace, one way or another."

They sat there together, watching TV, until they began to nod off.
Grace woke with a start, her head on Tyson's shoulder, his arm wrapped
protectively around her. Headlights illuminated the living room and she
peeked outside to see Shannon fall out of a car. It was well past closing
time. Grace shook Tyson awake and convinced him that he could go
home, that she'd be okay now.

Tyson slipped out and Shannon stumbled in, dropping her purse on the floor and then tripping over it and spewing a string of garbled curse words.

"Hey," Grace said.

Shannon pulled herself upright. "Grace?"

"I need to talk to you."

"I'm kinda tired," she said, leaning against the arm of the couch.

"It's important. Here, you can sit down."

Shannon groaned and flopped over next to her, knocking a pillow onto the floor. She smelled like an ashtray.

"Why was Norman watching the girls?"

"Okay, look," Shannon slurred. "I didn't invite him. He came over here and started eating my food, I guess because Elsie's ginger boyfriend was over at your place. Friend of mine wanted to go out for a drink, and I called you like you said, figured you were working, and Norman was already here and said he'd stay."

"Shannon. They're not safe with him. You can't leave him alone with them."

"Jesus, can I not have one drink, one night out? I never get a break."

"It's not that. I'll watch them whenever you want. This is about Norman."

"Yeah, he's an asshole. We all know it. Doesn't mean he can't make himself useful once in a while."

"He told me that he used to give you baths when you were little. Do you remember that? Said he played games with you in the bathtub."

"What?" she sputtered. "I don't know what you're talking about."

"Do you really want him giving baths to your kids?"

Shannon's face reddened. "What are you saying? You think I'm a bad mother?"

"No—this isn't about you! I just need you to listen to me."

"You're not their mom," Shannon snapped. "I take good care of my kids." She got up and wobbled to the stairs, dragging her purse behind her, loose change spilling out onto the floor.

"Aunt Shannon—"

"Get out!" she yelled, pounding her fist against the wall.

Grace walked out into the darkness. Talking to Shannon hadn't helped, but she could try again when her aunt was sober and maybe she wouldn't get so defensive. If she couldn't trust Shannon to keep the girls safe, she'd have to figure out a way to get Norman to leave. He hadn't flinched at her threats to report him for what he'd done to her—it had been too long, she had no evidence, he'd been friends with the sheriff since grade school. If she could find the pictures he'd taken of her, though, maybe that would be enough. Or she could secretly record him, try to get him to admit what he'd done, to confess. It might not be that hard. He was probably proud of himself, what he'd gotten away with.

She was so focused on Norman on the walk home that she didn't notice the silhouette among the cedar trees until it was almost too late.

FORTY-FOUR

She thought at first that he'd followed her from work to Shannon's and then home, but that wasn't right. He'd gotten here first. He knew where she lived.

"Hello, Grace," the man from Waffle House said, emerging from the shadows.

A prickling sensation rushed from head to toe, as though someone had dumped ice water on her. She pivoted toward the house. She was close enough, she could probably make it.

"Don't run," he said, crossing into her path. "I just want to talk."

She eased backward. She could bolt into the darkness. He couldn't outrun her in cowboy boots, could he? "How do you know my name?"

"I'm not here to hurt you," he said, dropping a cigarette and crushing it under his heel. "I heard Norman's back in town."

Norman. Of course. "If he owes you money, that's between you and him. All I've got's a pocket of change." She glared at him. "The tips are shit."

"It's not money he owes me," the man said.

Grace glanced at the house. All the lights were off.

"He here?" the man asked. "Haven't seen his truck."

"It's in the shop," she said. He'd already asked Elsie to pay for the repairs, and Grace knew she would. "I don't know where he is now." She was tempted to lead him to Norman's bedroom window, let the man do what he would, though she didn't know what else he might do if he got in the house. Mama was in there, too, asleep.

"Where's he been, all this time he's been gone?"

"I can't help you," she said. "He doesn't tell me anything. I don't care if you wait here and see if he shows up. Just leave me out of it." The trees swayed in the wind, branches creaking. The house stayed dark, quiet.

"I'm looking for a girl," he said. "Maybe you've seen her."

She shook her head. "He showed up alone. I haven't seen anyone."

The man reached in his pocket and Grace flinched, scooted back on her heels.

"Wait," he said. "Just tell me if you recognize her. If she looks familiar. She'd be older now." He held out a photo and came close enough for Grace to grab it.

She tilted it to catch the moonlight and nearly dropped it, like a lit match that burned her hand. She recognized the girl in the picture. She was older than she had been the last time Grace had seen her, her expression different, a bright smile, but her eyes were the same. Unreadable, as they had been in the other photograph, the one Norman had shown her.

"Who is this?"

"My niece. Her name's Annalise."

A phantom ache spread through her, the reopening of a familiar wound.

"She's missing," he said. "I think he done something to her. She went off after him and never come back."

She thought of the little girl clutching a white ferret to her naked chest. She thought of the name tattooed low on Norman's belly, grown over with matted hair. She thought of the things Norman had done to her in the dying room while she imagined her own death. How close had she come?

The man gave her the card he'd shown her earlier at the restaurant, his Pride and Joy, phone number scrawled on the back, and she fumbled it, her fingers numb. It couldn't go on like this.

FORTY-FIVE

L evi knew something was wrong. He had apologized for not being there when she needed him, when he had missed her call, but she brushed it off. She had already forgotten about that, and she hadn't been upset in the first place. Her moodiness had nothing to do with him. She couldn't sleep knowing Norman was in the spare room downstairs, and whenever he left the house, she worried that he would go to Shannon's, that he would do something to her cousins. Every time she opened her desk drawer, there was the card from Annalise's uncle, until finally she stuffed it into a stack of other cards so she wouldn't have to see it. She'd been ignoring Dallas's texts, no matter how badly she wanted to talk to him, and they were a constant reminder that she needed to finally end things with Levi. She dreaded it, but it was becoming unavoidable. Every time they spoke, it inevitably led to the same old argument, the same back-and-forth about him wanting her to stay, his refusal to understand why she couldn't.

It seemed impossible that with everything going on, she still needed to study for finals. She stared at her notes, unable to focus. Her stomach was growling, and she realized she hadn't eaten all day. She'd barely left her room in an effort to avoid running into Norman. She listened at her door, heard someone moving through the house. Elsie was working late, probably to make extra money so she could pay for the new transmission in Norman's truck. She was running out of time and she knew it. Something had to be done, before it was too late. She couldn't hide in her room, hoping he would go away. She set her phone to record, stuffed it in the pocket of her sweatshirt, and headed downstairs before she could change her mind.

Norman stood in the hall, gnawing on a fried chicken leg.

"You need to stop," she said. "Kylee and Amelia. I know what you're doing, and you're gonna stop."

Norman smirked, his lips gleaming with grease. "What the hell are you talking about?"

"You know what I'm talking about. The things you did to me. The baths, the pictures. Everything else. And now you're trying to do the same to them. You started with the bath. I walked in on you trying to put them in the tub."

"That's hogwash. I was just helping my sister out. Babysitting. I didn't do nothing wrong."

"Maybe not yet. But you want to. What about me, Norman? What you did to me when I was younger than them? I don't expect an apology. I know better than that. People get sent to prison for what you did. You're a pedophile. A child molester. You could at least own up to it. Have the balls to do that much."

Norman sucked his teeth, his eyes narrowing. He stepped closer. "What are you doing, girl?"

"The pictures," she said. "That's child pornography. They could put you away."

"Prove it," he said. "Show me what you got." He waited, smug. He knew she had nothing.

"I know about Annalise," she said finally, the name spilling out into the room. "I know what you did. I know everything. Her uncle knows, too, and he's coming after you."

Norman's head cocked to the side. Angry red splotches mottled his face. Grace's legs wobbled, went weak. It was like a veil had been removed and something she had vaguely known all along was revealed with startling clarity. Annalise's uncle was right. His niece was dead. Norman had killed her.

Norman lunged at her then, and she stumbled up the stairs to her room. He pushed his way in before she could shut the door, his hands clawing at her pockets, and he snatched her phone as she tried to slap him away. He swiped at the screen and then slammed the phone against her dresser.

"Did you think you were gonna tell the cops?" he said. "You think my buddies in the sheriff's office'd cuff me and take me in? You've got no idea the shit I've got on them. You've got nothing."

He grabbed her wrists and twisted, pushing her backward. She screamed, though she knew no one was home, no one would hear her.

"You've got no proof," he growled, shoving her onto the bed. "Nobody'd believe you."

He was on her before she could move. She thrashed, kicking her legs, but she could not escape the weight of his body, the smell of him. It roused old fears, ones she had foolishly packed away. She had never been safe. He would always find new ways to hurt her. She should not have doubted that. There was a fleeting thought, that if he raped her now, she would have evidence. She could go to the police, get him taken away. If she survived. If he let her live. He wasn't that stupid.

As she continued to struggle, his forearm across her throat, she could feel herself detaching, the way she had done as a child, floating away from what was happening. She saw light dancing on the wall in a pretty pattern, a reflection of the sinking sun, and she thought of Mrs. Mummer. *Look! Let the universe speak to us! See the Beautiful Now!* Mrs. Mummer had taught her to look for tiny miracles, hidden beauties, especially in times of darkness. Her body grew numb, and Grace focused on the light, blocking out everything else, quieting her mind so she could see. As she watched the shifting patterns, it made her think of the objects reflecting the sun. Her trophies lined the shelf on top of her headboard. The math contest, the science fair, all the spelling bees she had won.

With her remaining strength, she twisted her body and wrenched her arm free. In one fluid movement, she grabbed a trophy and smashed it into the side of Norman's skull. His body went slack, slumping half on top of her and half on the bed. She shoved him off and he rolled awkwardly to the floor, headfirst, his skull clunking on the hardwood. The sound made her stomach lurch. She peeked over the edge of the bed. He appeared to be out, for now.

She sat there clutching the trophy for a moment, half dazed, and then spied her phone on the floor across the room. She stepped over Norman and hurried to retrieve it. It was still functional, despite a spiderweb crack in the screen, but Norman had trashed the recording. Not that it mattered. He hadn't admitted anything. Not only had she gotten no evidence, she had made things so much worse. Norman would be furious when he came to, which might be any moment now, and she couldn't escape him by leaving. If she left, there would be no one to protect Kylee and Amelia.

She turned to look at him. He had landed oddly, his neck at an angle, his eyes slightly open. She waited for him to blink, for his limbs to move. As she watched for signs that he was waking up, she realized that his chest didn't appear to be rising and falling. She had thought that it was, before, but now she wasn't sure. Grace got down on her knees to feel for his pulse and couldn't find it. He wasn't breathing. She shook him, attempted a few chest compressions, but couldn't bring herself to place her mouth on his to give him air. There was no blood that she could see, though maybe he'd bled inside his skull. Or maybe his neck had broken when he fell, and nothing she did would help. He was dead, and she had killed him.

There was a low hum building in her ears, something far away and growing closer. A swarm of locusts. A revving engine. Her fingers were cold, tingling, like when she'd sat in the cab of Norman's pickup as a little girl, her hand on the gearshift, and he told her to punch the gas. All those years ago, she couldn't slip the truck into drive, couldn't protect herself. She thought she'd finally found a way to keep her cousins safe and make Norman pay, but she'd only wanted to get evidence from him, not kill him.

This was different from the truck—it was self-defense—though intentions might not matter. They wouldn't simply take her at her word. There would be an investigation into his death. She would have to tell her side of the story, all the ways that Norman had abused her, none of which she could prove, and then everyone in Beaumont would know her worst humiliations, her darkest shames. They would ask why she didn't report the abuse until after she had bludgeoned him to death with a spelling bee trophy, why she'd remained silent until he conveniently couldn't defend himself. Her mother wouldn't believe her beloved brother would do such a thing. If Norman was telling the truth about his friend in the sheriff's office, the cops wouldn't listen to her either. There could be a trial. Instead of going to college, she might be fighting to stay out of prison. Norman would keep haunting her even after he was dead, ruining everything she had worked for.

Or. It wasn't unusual for him to disappear for years at a time, going underground like the cicadas, not contacting anyone. He changed phone numbers the way most people changed underwear. No one would think anything of it if he left town without warning, if they couldn't get ahold of him. He was already dead, and she couldn't undo it. Norman had caused her enough suffering to last a lifetime. Whatever punishment she deserved for his death, she had already paid the price.

The trophy lay on the bed where she'd left it. There was no blood, but she wiped it down anyway, in case any trace of Uncle Norman remained, and placed it back on the shelf. Then she wiped the dust from the rest of the trophies so they all looked the same.

She opened the contacts on her phone, her fingertip hovering, scrolling, hovering again. She dropped it on her pillow and sank down next to it. One of Norman's legs was still propped against the bed, his boot caught in the blanket. Looking down, she noticed that his pants were unzipped. He must have done it after he threw her on the bed, just before she hit him. It was probably the reason she'd been able to get her hand free, because he reached down to undo his zipper. Any trace of uncertainty dissolved. She shoved Norman's leg and the boot thudded on the floor. Then she picked up the phone and tapped the shattered screen to make the call before she could change her mind.

FORTY-SIX

Tyson stood on the doorstep in the gathering dusk with an armload of contractors' garbage bags, the big, heavy-duty kind, his cheeks ruddy from the wind.

"I parked out back," he said.

She ushered him upstairs, where Norman still lay on the floor by her bed. Though she knew it was impossible, part of her had expected him to be gone, like a villain in a horror film. It wouldn't be unlike Norman to disappear and leave her with the fear that he might come back at any time, that she'd hear cicadas keening some spring night and find him at her door.

Tyson knelt beside the body, staring. "Damn," he said. "You must've got him just right."

"I didn't mean—"

"He deserved it," Tyson said, tucking his hair behind his ears and donning work gloves. "You did what you had to do." He straightened Norman's legs and shook out a trash bag to open it up. "If I'd been here, I would've done it for you."

"Thank you," she said. "For helping me, Ty. I didn't know what else to do."

He nodded. "Of course."

"You're sure...you're sure they won't find him? And you won't get caught? I don't want you to get in any trouble because of me. I could still call the police. Maybe I should." Tyson started to pull off Norman's boots. Tremors worked their way through her. What was she doing? She grabbed his shoulder. "You should go. I shouldn't have asked you to do this. It's my mess, not yours."

"Hey," Tyson said softly. He took her hand and stood up to look her in the eye. "You're practically family, Grace. You were looking out for your family, and I'm looking out for mine. He'll go right in with the rest of the scraps. They'll never find him, because there won't be anything left to find."

"Levi...," she said.

"He doesn't need to know."

Grace crumpled, the enormity of what she'd done finally hitting her. Tyson held her to his chest. "All we're doing is making things right," he murmured. "Everything'll be okay now. It'll all be fine. Everything'll turn out how it's supposed to."

"What if someone sees you?"

"Roadkill. Found a dead deer on the way to work. Happens all the time." His voice was steady. He wasn't shaken at all.

She knew it was wrong to get Tyson involved, to burden him with what she'd done, but she also knew he could handle it. He wouldn't be haunted by it. It was different with Levi. He would never look at her the same if he knew. Levi couldn't dump a body into a rendering pit, watch it disappear. It would ruin him, and she didn't want him ruined.

Tyson finished stripping Norman and fit the bottom half of his naked body into one bag and covered the top with another. She was glad when she could no longer see his face, though the tattoo was still partly visible, the top half of "Annalise." When Tyson hoisted him up, her stomach lurched, and she held her arms tight around her middle as if that might keep her from puking. She wasn't sorry for what she'd done—it was an accident, and he'd given her no choice. Still, it didn't feel good to have killed someone, even someone whose death she'd wished for since she was a child. The only good thing was that he was no longer a threat to anyone. Kylee and Amelia were safe, as safe as she could make them before leaving town. They would have a chance to be little girls awhile longer. That was the best gift she could give them. For their sake, she could carry this secret. It would settle atop the others, layers of grit and sediment that formed a hidden landscape inside her.

After Tyson drove away, she put Norman's clothes in the hamper in his room and took his flip phone and his wallet and duffel bag out to the burn barrel with the kitchen trash. There was no need to worry about his truck, since it was still in the shop. She opened the wallet in the light of the fire. There were no credit cards, no ATM cards. Norman didn't like to be tracked if he could help it. His driver's license was expired, and he had thirty-seven dollars in cash. In a separate flap behind the bills, she found a small photograph—a school picture, the edges cut unevenly with safety scissors. It was stuck to the side, long forgotten, and she had to pry it out. The little girl was missing her front teeth, her hair pulled tight into two neat braids. Grace had printed her name on the back years before, her pencil carving deep grooves so the letters were still readable even though most of the lead had worn away. She let the picture slip through her fingers into the flaming barrel, then threw his belongings in the fire and watched them burn.

Heading back to the house, she tried to think of loose ends. It couldn't be that easy to get away with something, even if Norman had been getting away with things for years. It was dark in the kitchen when she stepped inside, and as she went to wash her hands, she let out a little scream. Jimmy stood by the refrigerator, watching her, a half-eaten drumstick dangling from his hand. Was it the one Norman had dropped when he came after her? She'd forgotten about it, forgotten to find it and throw it out. How long had Jimmy been there? What had he seen?

AMELIA
&
KYLEE

FORTY-SEVEN

I t took two days after digging up Aunt Elsie's patio to get our plan in place. We promised her we would rent a dumpster and clean up her yard, and Jimmy convinced her that he had planned a surprise early birthday trip to Branson for her all along. Because Elsie had been dying to go, he got tickets to Dolly Parton's Stampede, where you eat dinner with your bare hands, and booked a night in a roadside motel. Jimmy didn't have any money of his own, so he lied and told Elsie he'd been doing some freelance work to pay for the trip, and Ketch and Kylee and I had to pitch in to cover it. Once they left for Branson, we'd call Bill and tell him what we'd found, and leave it up to him to decide what he wanted to do. In those two days, while we made our plans, I didn't see Mama once. She wasn't around.

I had just gotten off the phone with Jimmy, confirming what time he and Elsie would be leaving the next day, when Ketch stopped by on his way home from work with Kum & Go breakfast pizza and a carton of orange juice.

"Thought you all might be hungry," he said.

"How'd you know?" Kylee swooped in to grab the first slice. "For future reference, I prefer SunnyD. We're not used to real juice around here. But A for effort."

"Thanks, Ketch," I said.

Kylee made a kissy face behind his back.

"My pleasure," he said. "I'll do better next time."

I got up to fetch glasses, and my phone rang, another call from Alan. He'd been leaving stern voicemails saying he needed to speak to me, and I kept avoiding them. I'd tried getting ahold of Javi, but he wouldn't text me back. I knew he didn't want to get involved, didn't want to get in trouble, but he was the only person who might be able to tell me what was going on with Alan. If he was just pissed about me missing work for a few days, he could fire me. It had to be something else.

"Hey," Kylee said. "Did you tell Ketch about what happened with Levi the other night after we left Elsie's?"

"You mean how you told Tyson about what we dug up, even though we promised not to talk about it, and then Levi freaked out and said Norman was dead and I had to come pick you up?"

"Yeah," Kylee said. "That. What do you think, Ketch?"

"I don't know. What if Levi found out about those pictures? About what Norman did to Grace? Maybe he lost it, like how they say people snap? Maybe he snapped and killed him."

I poured juice for me and Ketch, and Kylee snatched mine to take a drink. "If it's true, though, and Norman was already dead when Grace went missing, where does that leave us? Who's left that would've wanted to hurt her?"

"Alan," Kylee said. "Javi. Mr. Copeland. Dallas. *Levi.*"

"When you asked how he knew Norman was dead, he said to ask Tyson about it."

"Yeah. Ty said Levi's delusional. Drinking way too much. The whole thing with Grace really wrecked him. He's never been able to move on. Guess that's why we never see him out unless he's with Tyson. Ty's taking him out to their granny's river cabin, trying to calm him down, dry him out. Levi's lucky to have his brother looking after him." She helped herself to two more slices of pizza. "Now, I hate to leave you two unsupervised, but I'm off to the stables," she said. "Thanks again, Ketch."

"You didn't thank him a first time."

I checked my messages and saw that Alan had left a new voicemail. He didn't mention anything about me being sick, missing work. He insisted on seeing me in person. It was urgent. He wanted to talk.

"What's wrong?" Ketch said, studying my face.

"Nothing. Just Alan again."

"He's still calling?"

"Yeah. He wants to talk to me, but he won't say what it's about."

"I wouldn't talk to Alan until we're sure he didn't have anything to do with what happened to Brielle or Grace."

"I don't know how long I can avoid him. Now he's saying he wants to meet and talk in person."

"How about I meet up with him instead," Ketch said, "and convince him to leave you alone."

I thought of the pistol he carried, the trouble he could get into if he went after Alan with a gun. He was so close to getting out of this place and living the life he had dreamed of. I couldn't let anything ruin that. I couldn't be the reason he got stuck here and couldn't go.

"I'm serious, Amelia," he said.

I knew that he was, that he'd do anything to protect me, without hesitation. That he'd bring me food if I was hungry. That he'd shelter me, keep me warm in a freezing tent, stay up all night so I'd feel safe, and expect nothing in return. Maybe Kylee had been right about Ketch, as she often was about men and the things they wanted: there was something more between us than friendship. It hit me that all those years when I'd had a girlish crush on Levi, it wasn't Levi I'd wanted, but someone who'd love me the way he loved Grace. Someone who'd look at me the way he looked at her—the way Ketch was looking at me now.

I grabbed him by the shirt and kissed him, hard. "I know you're leaving," I said when I pulled away. "But I hope it's not too late."

He stared at me for the briefest moment before his mouth was on mine, his hands in my hair, my fingers frantically unbuttoning his work shirt.

FORTY-EIGHT

Later that night, after Ketch had gone back to the campground, I heard someone scrabbling around downstairs. I knew the door was locked because I'd locked it myself, and Kylee had gone out after work. Fear tingled in my chest. What if Alan had come back, broken into the house? I grabbed my phone and Kylee's deer-skinning knife and crept partway down the stairs, weak with relief when I saw it was only Mama. I hadn't seen her since I told her about Norman, about what we'd found under Elsie's pool. I set the knife down on the table with a loud click and said hello, but she ignored me, digging through the drawers of the old desk in the living room, upending the couch cushions and sticking her hands down into the crumb-filled crevices.

"What are you doing?"

"Nothing."

"Haven't seen you in a while. Did I . . . upset you, with what I said the other day?"

"Nope. Been busy," she said.

"I forged your name on the history test Kylee failed. She left it out for you to sign. Guess you didn't see it."

"I can't even think about shit like that right now, Amelia."

"What, got a new boyfriend taking up all your time?"

"Really? That's what you think? I'm out pissing around? You want to know what's going on? I been busting my ass all over hell's half acre trying to find extra work. Rent went up and we're behind. We'll get kicked out of here and I don't know where we'll go. Fucking trailer park rent's outrageous."

"Are you serious? We've been here forever. Can't you work something out with Phil?"

"Tried. Turns out he doesn't want to screw me."

"Mama."

"What else am I supposed to work out? I'm doing everything I can."

"How far behind are we?"

"Really fucking far."

"Maybe we could stay with Aunt Elsie. Me and Ky'll be out of here soon. You won't need this whole house, anyway."

"We're not staying with Elsie."

"What, you'd rather live in a car? We've got to go somewhere. It'd just be temporary, until you get caught up."

She covered her mouth with her hands and crumpled into a chair, bawling. It was only the second time in my life that I'd seen her break down and cry like that. "I was so close," she wailed. "I almost did it. Nobody thought I could. Not Elsie. Not anybody. I raised two kids on my own. Kept you in school. You're not pregnant. You're not in jail. You're not riding a pole like me. I was feeling pretty damn good about that. All ready to rub it in people's faces. And now . . ."

"So . . . you raised us out of spite?"

I was hoping to get a laugh, but she only cried harder.

"Mama. Mama, hey." I leaned down, wrapped my arms around her shoulders. "It'll be okay."

"I won't go to Elsie's. I won't. We're not doing that. She's been judging me my whole life."

"We'll figure something out." I let go of her to grab a napkin to wipe her face. She absently traced the tattoo on her forearm, sniffling.

"It's not just the rent," she mumbled. "Had to get that crown on my back tooth, root canal. Transmission went out on the car. I'm an old stripper and I'm only getting older. Even if we find a place to stay, where'm I gonna go from here?"

All the anger had drained out of her, leaving nothing but defeat. She huddled in the chair, tears dripping down, not bothering to wipe them away. I knew she'd tried. That it hadn't been easy. She hadn't always been the sort of mother I would have chosen, but she'd done what she could to take care of us.

"I was thinking about what you said. About Norman, the other day." She balled her hands into fists, pressed them to her eye sockets. "I never told this to anybody. I kinda pushed it back in my head. When I was little, we had one of those plastic kiddie pools in the front yard under the persimmon tree. Norman'd get in there and splash me, kick all the water out, take my toys, whatever he could do to piss me off. Ripped the tail off the plastic mermaid I got for my birthday. One day, Daddy came out with Popsicles for us, and he saw Norman doing something to me and he dropped those Popsicles in the dirt and bent Norman's finger back and broke it. He threatened worse if he ever touched me like that again, and he didn't. Guess I figured that cured him. Didn't think of it much after that."

She unclenched her fists, wiped her nose. "I was so fucking stupid, Amelia. Had him over here, with you and your sister, alone in the house. Grace tried to tell me. I remember now, when she was little, she was asking me, once, about Annalise. I thought she must've heard the name from Elsie, but . . . Norman had her name tattooed on his privates. I didn't even think about it, that she might have seen it. How did it never cross my goddamn mind?"

There'd been men in the house sometimes when we were little, men Mama brought back from Sweet Jane's, though we didn't know it at the time. We'd hear them in the bedroom, the springs straining, headboard smacking the wall, but we never saw them. Mama told us they were ghosts, moaning and rattling chains like on *Scooby-Doo*, and we believed it for probably too long. There were footsteps on the stairs, doors eased shut in the early hours. One time on the bus, I was telling Ketch that our mother's room was haunted, and an older kid sitting behind us smirked and said Mama was screwing customers in there.

Later on, she was less careful, or the men were, and we'd catch them in the act of fleeing. They'd avoid looking directly at us. Occasionally there would be a man in the kitchen wiping his face on the dishtowel, scrubbing at an unknown stain on the front of his shirt or the crotch of his pants. Some wore wedding rings they hadn't bothered to twist off. We sometimes saw faces we recognized, and the more nervous among them might offer a reason why they were there as they hurried out the door. They were inspecting the house, or spraying for termites, or helping our mother unclog a sink.

As Grace would say about snakes, they were more scared of us than we were of them. Most of them did not want to be alone with two little girls dressed only in beer T-shirts and cartoon underwear. They did not want us looking at them and seeing a new daddy. Kylee and I delighted in our power to terrify them, watching them stumble over a pile of stuffed animals as they ran for the door. Not all snakes are scared, though, and not all the men were afraid. There was one who had come into our bedroom in the thin light of dawn and stood at the foot of our bed. Kylee had screamed and screamed, and her piercing shriek was what finally drove him away, though it did not summon our mother to help. We found her passed out in a nest of twisted sheets, the musky animal scent of sex pervading her room. She woke later with a terrible headache and didn't remember the night before, and that was the first time I had ever seen her break down crying, the only time I had seen her look scared. Seeing her that way almost felt worse than having the man in our room.

"Norman," I said. "He never touched us."

Mama grabbed me, clamped her scrawny arms around my neck, and didn't let go.

"I've got that money I've been saving up," I said, my cheek pressed to hers so tight it hurt. "You can have it, as much as you need."

Mama started sobbing again, and I felt like I'd been caught up in a whirlpool, swirling toward the drain. I'd finally convinced Kylee to leave, and now, without that money, we couldn't go anywhere. We couldn't even afford to move out of this house. I had nothing left to offer her, and Tyson would be waiting to swoop in.

It wasn't as if I had a choice. Despite everything our mother had done or failed to do, she had never abandoned us, and I couldn't leave her to the wolves now. Even if that meant losing our only way out.

FORTY-NINE

I woke up thinking of Ketch, what had happened the day before. How right it had felt to lie close to him, to feel his hands on my bare skin, his lips on mine. Before he left, he had asked me again to come with him, to meet him wherever he ended up after boot camp, but I couldn't say yes. I'd wasted so much time, waited too long, and now I couldn't promise him anything, because I'd already promised my sister. We'd made our plan. We'd stick together.

"Ketch didn't bring us breakfast today?" Kylee said. "Disappointing. He was really starting to grow on me." She set her backpack on the table. She was already showered and dressed and had fixed her hair. It was nearly noon, but early for her to be up and around on a Saturday.

"No breakfast. But there's some orange juice, still, if you want it."

"Nah. You can have it. You got anything going on today?"

"Well, Jimmy and Elsie are on their way to Branson, so I called Bill and told him what we found. Told him he can do whatever he wants—call the cops, finish digging the hole himself. But I don't want to be around for any of that, so I'll probably call Ketch, see if he wants to go for a run if the weather holds. And I might stay out at the campground with him tonight.

Alan's still trying to track me down, and I'd rather not be home if he comes looking. What are you up to?"

"I do have something planned, actually." Her cheeks pinked a little, and she chewed her lip. "Tyson and I are taking a little trip. All that talk about Branson, planning Elsie's getaway, we thought it'd be fun to get out of town. Maybe go to Silver Dollar City."

"Oh. Sounds great."

"Yeah. I was gonna see if you could give me a ride. He's supposed to pick me up, and I thought he'd be here by now, but I can't get ahold of him. I don't think he gets good service out at the cabin."

"Isn't he out there with Levi?"

"Yeah."

"Maybe something's going on with him and that's why Tyson's not answering. Might not be the best idea to just show up out there."

"I'm pretty sure Levi was going hunting today. It'll be fine. He's probably just running behind."

"All right. If you're that antsy to get outta here, I guess I can give you a ride. I need to shower first, though, pack a bag for tonight."

"Thanks, Mimi." She squeezed my arm. "I'm gonna take care of something real quick while you do that. Be right back."

It was early afternoon when we started out. I drove and Kylee navigated. The fields and hills outside of town were finally fully green. True spring was here, which meant the short, tender season was already ticking down, soon to be suffocated by sweltering heat. My stomach felt off, which could have been caused by any number of things given the circumstances, but in the quiet of the drive, the reason suddenly surfaced. I hadn't told Kylee about the money. I felt sick inside, the secret a toxin my body was desperate to purge.

"I've gotta tell you something," I said. "Mama's behind on rent. We were close to getting kicked out, nowhere to go. That's why she hasn't been around much. She was trying to find extra work, figure something out."

"Fuck," Kylee said. "Why didn't she say anything?"

"I know," I said. "And I'm so sorry, Ky. I know we were planning to leave, but . . . I couldn't take off and leave Mama with nothing, nowhere to go. So I gave her the money. Everything I've been saving for us." I braced myself for her anger, her disbelief that I could blow up our plans after I'd finally convinced her to leave. "I promise I'll fix this," I said. "I'll work twice as hard. I'll get a job at the plant. It'll just take a little time."

"It's fine," she said, disturbingly calm. "We don't need the money."

"Yes, we do. Did you hear what I said? It's all gone, and we can't get out of here without it. What you have isn't anywhere near enough. We're not gonna make it out, Kylee. We're stuck here with Alan and Mama and everything else. We have to start all over again."

"Mimi, listen." She reached out and squeezed my knee. "We don't need to worry about money. We've got plenty of cash. We just need to hurry up and get out of town before Alan figures it out. I hope you packed your toothbrush, because we can't go back."

"Wait, *Alan?* What are you talking about? What did you do?"

"You gotta make hay while the sun shines," she said, flicking her hair back. "And it hardly ever shines on us."

"Tell me *right now.*"

Kylee draped her arm out the window, let her hand ride the wind. "Remember all that money I found in his freezer? I took it. Some of it. A lot. As much as I could fit in my backpack, however much that is."

"What? Kylee! That's why he's after me! He's been calling me nonstop, trying to sneak into our house. I thought he was gonna kill me! Maybe he is. And all this time you knew why. Why didn't you say something?"

"I was going to, later," she said. "I figured it'd be easier that way—if you didn't know, you wouldn't have anything to hide. You wouldn't act suspicious around him."

"We can't keep that money."

"I *knew* you'd say that."

"He's not gonna let it go!"

"What's he gonna do?" Kylee said. "He stole it in the first place! It's not even his. And he can't come after us if he doesn't know where we are. That shouldn't be a problem, because even we don't know where we're going."

"I can't believe you didn't tell me. That you'd keep a secret that big from me."

"You didn't say anything to me before you gave all our cash to Mama."

"That's completely different! And what about Grace? We were gonna do everything we could before we left. We're not done yet."

"What else is there for us to do? Ketch can tell David everything we know. They can hunt Norman down, see if he's dead or alive. Now that we know he killed Annalise, maybe they can figure out if he killed Brielle and Grace, or buried girls in other states on his cross-country trips pouring concrete. He can try to get them to look at Alan, too, see if he's up to something worse than stealing T-bone steaks and harassing waitresses. We're not the law. We can dig stuff up, make some noise, but we can't do much about it. Somebody else has to take it from here."

She was right; maybe we'd done all we could. Still, it wasn't enough. Two girls had been found, but Grace was still missing.

"Ky."

"Yeah?"

"If we're leaving town right now, why're we going to Tyson's? To say goodbye?"

"That's the other thing," she said, angling toward me.

I didn't want to hear whatever she was about to say. My stomach twisted. "Don't," I said.

"Mimi . . . we're leaving, just like we always talked about. But not together. I'm going with Tyson."

Her words cut into me, sharp as her deer-skinning blade. My sister, ever since we were little, always wanting the same thing, but different.

"Say something."

"What do you want me to say, Kylee?"

"Come on, Mimi, you're the soft one. You, of all people, can't get mad at me for falling in love."

"You think you're in *love* with Tyson? So you're running off with him? How well do you even know him?"

Her look was almost pitying. "Sometimes you know things without having to think them through," she said. "Haven't you ever felt that? Love's a *feeling*, Mimi, it's not a checklist or a résumé or a quiz with right and wrong answers. I love him. I feel it. I know it. I don't want to hurt you, but I hope you can understand."

It hurt that she didn't think I knew what love was, how it felt. Maybe I'd never experienced the improbable, impulsive love she had with Tyson, but I knew love born of instinct, love that went unquestioned, that pumped through my heart like blood. I had loved my sister every minute of her life. It hurt that she wanted to leave without me, though I understood, despite it all.

She'd always been my other half, the two of us taking care of each other, especially after Grace was gone. I hadn't bothered to consider my life without her, to think about what I would want, what I would do, if she wasn't there. Would I have made different promises to Ketch, if not for the plans I'd made with Kylee? Would I have gone away to school if I hadn't worried about leaving her behind? Now it was as though she had walked through a hidden door and left it open. I could walk through it, too, and emerge wherever I wanted. Had that been possible all along? We had been taught that life was hard, knew it for a fact. It felt foolish—sinful, even—to think otherwise. Maybe, though, sometimes, even people like us got lucky. Sometimes, your back aching from work, the smell of manure in the air, you scraped the silver coating off a scratcher with your thumbnail and won a free ticket, a chance for a do-over. Maybe that wasn't too much to hope for.

FIFTY

"Are you sure the map's right?" I said, breaking the silence. "This is barely a road. It doesn't look like there's anything out here."

"Map froze after that last turn," Kylee said.

"Well, did he give you any kind of directions, or just the address?"

"He didn't actually give me the address," Kylee hedged. "I found it by tracking his phone."

"Kylee! Are you serious?"

"It's fine," she said. "I think this is it. The river's gotta be up there through the trees."

"I hope so. I don't want to get lost out here." The sky had gone overcast, the clouds gray and rippled like ocean waves. Not that I'd ever seen the ocean.

"Are you mad at me?" Kylee asked.

"Yeah," I said. "A little. I'll get over it."

"What do you think's happening at Elsie's?" she said.

"I think Bill's over there with his oxygen tank and a garden spade." He'd made a promise to his sister that he'd find Annalise, and he insisted he be the one to dig her up, not the police. He said he'd call them after, though there wasn't much they could do beyond confirm what we already knew. If Norman was truly dead, it was too late for any justice aside from laying her to rest in a proper grave. "Maybe we should send Ketch over to see if he needs help. I hate the thought of him doing that all on his own."

"Oh! That reminds me." Kylee put her phone down, giving up on navigation. "Ketch gave me something to give to you. Don't let me forget. It's in my purse."

"When did you see Ketch?"

"While you were in the shower. And he said not to worry about Alan, he was gonna take care of it."

"*Take care of it?* What does that mean? I told him to stay out of it. If he shows up with his pistol and threatens Alan—"

"He won't," Kylee said. We rounded a sharp curve, and as the road straightened out, a cabin came into view. "Tyson's here," she said, craning her neck. "There's his truck."

"Levi's, too."

By the time I got the car parked, Tyson had come out to greet us. Kylee stood on her tiptoes to throw her arms around his neck. "Are you surprised?" she said.

"Uh, yeah," he said. "I thought I was gonna pick you up."

"Well, I got tired of waiting, and you talked about bringing me out here someday, meeting Granny Velda, and since we might not have a chance again, I figured why not."

"It's not a good time for that," Tyson said. "That's why I was running late. She's not feeling very well today."

Kylee's smile faded. "We're still going, though, right?"

"Yeah," he said. "I just need to check on her. See if she needs anything."

"Hey, there she is," Kylee said, leaning around Tyson to wave.

His granny saw us and backtracked toward the cabin door, but Kylee was already bounding across the yard, introducing herself. Realizing she couldn't sneak back inside, Velda came off the porch and into the yard to greet her. Tyson turned to join them, and I grabbed his sleeve.

"So, where're you taking my sister? What're you gonna do? Got any sort of plan?"

He glanced over at Kylee and his granny, who were talking under the cottonwood trees. The two of them began walking slowly toward the river, away from the cabin.

"Do you love her?" I said.

Tyson kept her in his sight. Kylee was gesturing to his granny, talking with her hands, a habit she'd picked up from Tyson.

"You know," he said, "she tries to come across all venom and barbed wire, almost like she wants to scare people off. But I don't scare easy. Lucky for me, neither does she."

I let go of his sleeve.

Kylee and Velda finished their conversation and headed their separate ways, Velda returning to the cabin. When Kylee reached us, she tucked her hand in the crook of Tyson's arm.

"She just wanted some fresh air. She's going back in to lie down," she said.

"Is Levi around?" I said.

"Yeah. He's been out hunting all morning. Not sure when he's coming back." Tyson put his arm around Kylee. "We'll probably be gone by then."

A breeze shuddered the cottonwoods, bringing the scent of rain from the hills. I thought of Levi alone in the woods, invisible to his prey, watching the storm approach.

"Is he doing better?"

"Better? I don't know. He's calmed down, I guess."

"That night, when he was out in the road, saying Norman was dead . . . he told me to ask you about it."

Tyson groaned, rubbed his neck. "He was all worked up. He gets that way sometimes."

"I told you that, Mimi," Kylee said, leaning into Tyson's chest.

She had, but it still didn't sit right with me. There had been a raw, aching intensity radiating from Levi that night, an unmistakable urgency in his voice. I didn't buy Tyson's claim that it meant nothing.

"Please, Tyson," I said. "If you know something, we deserve to know. That's what Levi said. I can wait and ask him when he gets back. But he told me to ask you. Why is that? Is there any point in us looking for Norman? Is he really dead?" I paused. "Did Levi kill him? Did you help him? I don't care if Norman's dead. I just want to know whether or not he killed Grace."

"Amelia." Kylee frowned at me.

It stunned me for a moment, how easily she'd switched to his side. I hadn't expected that, even if I should have seen it coming. "Don't give me that look," I said. "Don't you want to know?"

"If Tyson knew something," she said coldly, "he'd tell us."

"Well?" I turned to Tyson. "You have anything to say? Guess I'll just hang out here with your granny, wait for Levi." I started toward the cabin, and Tyson grabbed my shoulder, spun me back.

"Wait," he said, his hands out. "Look, I made a promise, too. To Grace. She never wanted you to know, not any of it. But . . . Levi's right."

"Ty?" Kylee's hair tangled in the shifting breeze, lashing her face, dark strands catching her open mouth.

"You can stop looking for Norman," Tyson said. "You won't find him."

"You mean . . . ?"

"He's dead. It's true. But it wasn't Levi. It was Grace that killed him."

A few raindrops fell, cold, sporadic, given weight by the wind.

"No," I said. "Grace would never."

"She was protecting you. You and Kylee."

It was hard to breathe. My lungs filled with lead, my chest refusing to expand. Grace had kept us safe time and again. As much as I hated to think it had come to that, it wasn't so hard to believe that she would kill someone to save us.

"She killed him," he said. "And I know because I helped with the body. Took him to rendering, turned him into fertilizer. I'm the one she called, the one she trusted. But afterward, she was scared Jimmy knew. He'd been there that night, she didn't know what he'd seen. She was afraid he'd turn her in, so she made up her mind to leave. She . . . wanted to make it look like she couldn't have survived. So she could just go missing. She thought that'd be better, if nobody expected to find her alive. So people wouldn't be so keen to go looking."

It took a minute for his words to sink in. Kylee chewed her lip, and I wondered if she was thinking the same thing. There had been so much blood in the kitchen, more than enough to make it look like a crime scene. If she truly set out to fake her death, maybe she'd gone too far trying to make it convincing. What if she accidentally cut too deep and couldn't control the bleeding?

"Do you know where she went?" I said. "If she was bleeding that much, maybe she lost consciousness and bled out somewhere." I imagined the life draining from her body in the river, or the woods beyond the field, her bones waiting all these years to be uncovered by hunters.

He shook his head. "She didn't tell me where she was going. All I know is, the last I saw Grace, she was still alive."

No one said anything for a long, empty minute. Kylee had gone mute. "Does Levi know all of that?" I asked.

"Yeah," he said. "You can ask him. We can go out in the woods and find him if you want."

"No," Kylee said, shaking her head. "Where would she go? Why would she stay gone so long if nobody ever reported Norman missing?"

"She told us not to look back," I said. "Not for anything. Not for any-one."

"Not even for us?"

I didn't want to believe she would have left us like that, never letting us know she was alive, though until recently, I wouldn't have believed she'd loved anyone but Levi, or that she could kill someone. We didn't know who she was to other people, only who she was to us. None of us were saints. She wasn't so different from Kylee and me—a girl with her share of secrets, trying to make her way out of a den of snakes, not knowing which one was about to strike.

"Why was Levi acting so crazy about it?" Kylee said.

"Just flares up sometimes," Tyson said. "He's still mad. Hurt. Because it was me she came to for help, not him." He stroked Kylee's arm. "I'm gonna check on Granny before we go, make sure she'll be all right. Wait here."

Kylee crossed and uncrossed her arms. She watched Tyson until the door of the cabin closed behind him. "Do you buy that?"

"I don't know," I said. "It's a lot."

"If Grace was alive, she would have found a way to let us know by now."

"Maybe."

"What if Tyson's covering for Levi? He's always helping him out, watching over him. And Levi clearly has issues—you should have seen him going after Tyson that night, when he was punching him. He was in a full-out rage. He's capable of hurting somebody, Amelia. He could've found out about Grace and Dallas, or just been mad that she was leaving him. Tyson wouldn't have wanted to turn him in. He'd do anything to protect his little brother. I know you get it, right? You're my big sister. You'd do the same for me."

"I'll wait for Levi," I said. "I want to talk to him myself."

"I bet he's not out hunting," Kylee said. "You notice neither of them wants us near the cabin? I bet he's hiding in there—that they're keeping him hidden. I'm gonna ask to use the bathroom."

"You think it's a good idea to go in a remote cabin with a possible killer and two people hell-bent on keeping a secret?"

"I don't need to get inside. I just need to see if they'll *let* me in. If not, we know something's up. We'll know Tyson's lying, that he's protecting Levi."

Kylee approached the cabin and stepped onto the porch, knocked. She pressed her ear to the door, listening. No one opened it. She crept around the far side of the building, into the woods and out of sight. I was about to call out for her when she screamed my name. I sprinted for the trees, toward the sound of her voice.

FIFTY-ONE

Tyson hauled us into the cabin, dragging me and Kylee by our wrists. I hadn't seen anything. Kylee had climbed a tree to peer in the top of a boarded-up window and claimed she had seen someone in bed, in a flowered nightgown, before Tyson clamped his big hands on our shoulders and pulled us away.

"Is that *Grace*? What did you do to her? Why is she here? What the fuck is going on?" Kylee kept up her steady barrage of questions as she squirmed to break free.

Tyson's voice boomed in the vaulted space, repeating the same thing over and over again. "It was an accident! It was an accident!"

"You tell us what happened right now, Tyson," Kylee hollered, finally ripping out of his grasp. "Right the fuck now."

Tyson let go of my wrist and waved his arms, shushing us. "Stop screaming," he said. "Calm down. Listen. Listen."

Kylee shut her mouth, waited, red-faced, her hair wild. I looked around for Tyson's granny, wondered where she'd disappeared to, if she'd shut herself in the room with Grace.

"Okay," Tyson said, pushing his hair back. "I didn't want to tell you this, but you deserve to know. You do. It was Levi," he said. "He didn't mean to. He'd been drinking, and he was upset, and it was all an accident. I swear to you."

He went on to explain what had happened the night Grace disappeared, filling in details, but one thing stuck in my mind: Levi. I had never believed he could hurt her, though I'd been wrong about many things. It made sense, in a way. His anger, his guilt, his pain. How he said he was trapped here, that he could never leave.

"As soon as it happened," Tyson continued, "he took her to get help. He brought her here, and Granny saved her life."

"Saved her life?" I said. "Boarding her up in a room—what kind of life is that?"

"Why didn't he take her to a *hospital?*" Kylee shrieked.

"Nearest hospital's in the next county. You know that. Beaumont General had closed down. Roads were flooding. There wasn't time. She was bleeding out."

"What's wrong with her?" Kylee said. "What's she doing in that bed? Can she walk? Can she talk? Let us see her."

"She lost so much blood . . . Granny didn't think she'd make it. It was a miracle she survived the night. But when it looked like she wouldn't get better . . . this just seemed to be the best thing. Granny was a nurse for years. She took care of our grandpa out here. She knows what she's doing. We take good care of her. Better than what she'd get in some nursing home."

"Are you serious?" I said. "Don't act like you did it for Grace. You did it to protect your brother. You should have told us. You should have told her *family*. Grace would never want this—she wouldn't want to be rotting away in this place."

"Is this any better than being dead?" Kylee said. "If there's nothing left of her, that's not living. What's the point? She'd want us to help her. To set her free."

"We just found her alive, and you want to *kill* her?"

"No, not kill. I'm saying, if Grace isn't Grace anymore, her life's already over. We're not any better than them if we keep her alive for us. Velda's gotta have something that'd do it. Painkillers? Sedatives? But not here." Kylee grabbed my arm. "We have to take her with us, get her out. We can't let her die here. We've gotta get her out of Beaumont."

"We don't even know what's wrong with her," I said. "If there's some kind of treatment, if she can get better. Maybe they're giving her something that's keeping her like this and she'll be fine if we get her away from here. Maybe she's in a coma and could still wake up. We need to get her to a hospital."

"There's no point!" Tyson slammed his fist into a wooden beam. "There's nothing they can do."

"How do you know that!" Kylee screamed. "You're not a fucking brain doctor!"

"We've got to get her out of here," I said. "Now."

"If we take her to a hospital and there's nothing they can do, we won't be able to help her die. She'll be stuck there, same as she's stuck here. Elsie'd never let her go."

"Stop talking about her dying!" I said. "She's alive, and Elsie's her mother, it's not up to us. We'll call Dallas."

"He's not a doctor!"

"He works at a hospital, and you know it's a good one or he wouldn't be there. He said something about neurology. He can go with us." I had no doubt he'd help us, that he'd do anything to help Grace.

"Tyson," Velda said, appearing in the hall. "They can't leave here. You can't let them go."

GRACE

FIFTY-TWO

Shannon was working the closing shift at Sweet Jane's. It was cold outside, too cold for spring, rain pelting the house. Grace fed the woodstove and it was putting out a fierce heat, but you had to be close to feel it. The chill seeped in through the thin walls of the farmhouse on all sides and wind whistled through unseen cracks. Kylee and Amelia dragged a kitchen chair as close as they dared and sat together, holding their hands and feet out to the stove's black belly until the heat made their skin tight and itchy.

Grace was frazzled, though she was careful not to let it show. At home, Elsie had grown increasingly moody and argumentative about her leaving, and Jimmy had taken to hanging around the house even when Elsie was at work. He jangled her nerves every time he appeared, pink-faced and mute, staring at her in that creepy way of his. Once she saw him in the backyard, poking around the burn barrel. She wanted to confront him, ask him what he knew, but if he hadn't actually seen anything the night Norman died, that would only make things worse. At the very least, he'd likely spied her by the fire from the kitchen window, but she kept hoping he wasn't quick-witted enough to connect that with Norman's absence and point a finger at her.

The other thing was Levi. She'd finally told him that it would really be over between them when she left, that she loved him, but she wouldn't be coming back. The look on his face had bruised her heart—the hurt, the disappointment, the bitterness that followed. He'd immediately closed himself off to her, which should have made things easier, but didn't. Dallas was the only person she could confide in now, and he was busy studying.

She poked through Shannon's cabinets, examining the meager options among the cans and boxes, trying to find something to feed the girls for supper.

"Do you want SpaghettiOs or mac and cheese?" she said. They didn't actually have SpaghettiOs, but it sounded better than Best Value Pasta Circles.

"Orange circles or orange elbows," Amelia said.

"Orange circles!" Kylee yelled.

"SpaghettiOs it is."

"I'll make the toast," Amelia said. She fed slices of white bread into the toaster while Grace microwaved the fake SpaghettiOs. Kylee helped smear butter on the toast and cut each piece into four triangles.

The three of them sat around the woodstove eating their dinner off plastic plates and drinking grape Flavor Aid out of the last clean glass while the wind rattled the windows.

"It sounds like a tornado," Kylee said, her lips purple from the drink. "Like it's gonna pop the roof off and suck us out."

"No," Amelia said. "If it's really a tornado, it'll sound like a freight train. That's when you get in the tub. I'll lay on top of you so you don't blow away."

Grace stifled a laugh. The girls were practically the same size and together might weigh less than she did. If a tornado hit, the rickety farmhouse would explode into confetti and everything in it would be swept away. "I'd lie on top of both of you," she said. "It's too cold for tornadoes, anyway."

"Spring's a frigid bitch," Kylee said. "That's what Uncle Norman says."

Grace smirked. She'd never have to hear him say it again. "I'm gonna miss you girls so much when I leave."

"But you'll come see us," Amelia said.

"Of course! I mean, I don't have a car. So I can't come back all the time. Christmas, though, for sure. I can catch a ride."

"Christmas? That's forever! You're gonna forget all about us."

"I'll write you letters!" Grace said. "And you can write back."

Kylee frowned. There was orange sauce at the corners of her mouth. "There's nothing to write about here."

"Sure there is. You can send me your small wonders. Look for one every day and write it down."

Kylee swung her feet, hammering her heels against the chair legs. "No," she grumbled.

Amelia glared at her sister.

"Hey, who wants their hair braided?" Grace said.

Both girls' hands shot up.

"Okay, why don't we go get your pajamas on, and you can do your reading while I braid."

Grace followed them up to their room and sat on the bed while she waited for them to change into their pajamas. Tonight, Kylee won the battle for the Hamm's beer shirt with the cute cartoon bear, and Amelia was stuck with "Old Milwaukee: It doesn't get any better than this!"

"Regular or French braids?" Grace asked.

Kylee bounded onto the bed first. "French!" she said.

"I wanted French," Amelia said. .

"You can both have French."

"I changed my mind," Kylee said, glowering at her sister. "I want *Dutch*."

"No problem," Grace said. "I can do both."

"And make 'em real tight so our hair's all crimpy when we undo it."

"Yeah," Kylee added.

"You got it."

When the reading and braiding were finished, Grace fluffed the quilts and sat at the foot of the bed. "Are you warm enough?"

The girls nodded, though their noses were pink with cold. Rain slashed at the window.

"Okay," she said. "What were your Beautiful Nows today? Mine was the smell of rain. It smells fresh and new, like the beginning of something."

Amelia raised her hand. "When I got up this morning, the sky was lavender, and the moon was still all big and bright like it was nighttime."

"Oh, that's a good one. Ky, how about you?"

Kylee picked at the quilt ties. "I don't have one."

Grace wiggled Kylee's foot through the covers. "Come on, are you sure?"

"I don't. You said sometimes we can't see it. You said that yourself."

"You're right," she said. "But you have to keep looking. I bet you'll have one tomorrow."

"I don't want you to go."

"Well, I'm not leaving *now*. There's still lots of time for us to hang out."

"Why do you have to leave at all?"

"You know why. We've talked about it. There are things I want to do that I can't do here. And it'll be the same for you. You can't stay here forever—there's nothing here for girls like us. When it's your turn, you'll leave and you won't look back."

"Take us with you," Amelia said.

"I wish I could. But you'll be okay. Just stick together. You have each other." Grace hugged each of the girls, and they turned on their sides so she could scratch their backs, tracing hearts and wings across their nightshirts with her fingernails. She looked at them one last time before she switched off the light. Amelia had her arm around Kylee, the two of them facing the window, the rain thundering down outside. She could not promise that they were safe, but they were safe from the monster she knew, as safe as she could make them in the days to come, when she wouldn't be here to protect them.

Back downstairs, she cleaned up the dishes and tidied the kitchen for

Shannon and then got out her biology notes, though she wasn't sure she could focus. She thought about calling Dallas, asking if he wanted to come over so they could study together. She went to listen at the foot of the stairs to see if the girls had fallen asleep, but if they were still up and making noise, the rain and wind were too loud for her to hear it.

Headlights traced across the wall, someone pulling into the gravel drive. It was way too early to be Shannon. She imagined Bill Wheeler at the door, looking for Norman. What would she tell him? Or maybe it was Levi, wanting to talk again.

When she answered the knock, it was Tyson who stood in the doorway, thoroughly drenched. "Hey," he said.

"Hey. Come on in, you're soaking." A puddle grew around his feet when he stepped inside. "Is everything all right?"

He looked a bit stunned, his eyes wide. He wiped off his face with his palms. "I was talking to Levi. He's pretty upset."

"Oh . . . yeah, I thought maybe you were him. Coming over to talk."

He sighed heavily, and she caught the liquor on his breath.

"Grace—I did what I did because I thought it meant you'd stay. I did it for my brother. You made me think Norman was the reason you couldn't be here, and now Norman's gone and you're still planning on leaving." His voice rose at the word "leaving," his arms flying up, water droplets flicking her face.

She held out her hand and shushed him. "Please. The girls are sleeping. I didn't mean to mislead you. I needed to keep him away from Kylee and Amelia."

Tyson rubbed the back of his neck, staggered a little. She couldn't tell if his eyes were bleary from drinking or if he was tearing up. "I dumped a body for you."

"I know, and I'm so sorry I ever got you involved. I shouldn't have, and I regret it more than you know. But it was never only about Norman. That was part of it. This whole town . . . I can't separate it from what happened to me here. That hasn't changed. And I finally have the chance to go away to school, like I always wanted. I can't turn it down."

"What about Levi?" he growled. "You're all he ever wanted. Why doesn't he get to be happy? Why can't he get what he wants?"

"I can't make somebody else happy, Tyson. It doesn't work that way. I can't stay here for Levi. I won't."

"Then what about me." He stepped closer.

"What about you, Tyson?"

"You think he's the only one who loves you?"

He whispered the words, but Grace heard them through the gusting wind, the clattering rain. For a moment, she was frozen in place, unable to blink, unable to breathe.

"You don't love me," she said. "You're just drunk."

He shook his head, reaching out to her. "The whole time you've been with Levi, I wished I could find a girl like you. I tried, I did. I finally figured out why it never worked. Nobody else measures up, Grace. I love my brother, but I couldn't help wanting you."

"Tyson, I appreciate everything you've done for me. I've always cared about you, you know that."

"I could deal with it," he said. "Because you were both so happy. You were gonna be part of the family. But you ruined it."

"I don't know what you want from me, Ty."

"If you leave," he said, "I'll tell them you killed Norman."

"Why would you do that?"

"It's the truth, isn't it?"

The words stung. He knew what had happened, what Norman had done, why he was dead. Tyson thought he loved her, but this wasn't love. He had an idea of what she should be, how she could fill a certain need, and that was the only version of Grace he wanted. A fantasy.

"You're not thinking this through," she said. "If you're gonna say I killed him, you're the one who got rid of the body. You're an accessory to murder."

He slid his hunting knife out and flipped open the blade, nearly dropping it in the process. "I'll go cut Levi's heart out right now, because that's what you're doing to him."

"Put it down," she said. "Come on. You've had too much to drink. You're gonna hurt yourself."

Tyson held the blade up to his throat. "Hurt myself? You're killing me, Grace. Maybe I should finish the job. Get it over with quicker."

"Stop," she said, holding out her hands, inching closer. "Don't do this, Tyson. The girls are upstairs. Everything'll be okay. Come sit down."

He bit his lip, pressed the sharp point of the knife to his jugular.

"Give me the knife, *now*."

She reached for it, and he slapped her away, too strong, too drunk to realize what he was doing. His hand came down with the knife still in it, and the blade drew a line down the soft flesh inside her forearm.

Grace watched, stunned, as blood seeped from the wound and kept coming, too much, too fast.

"Oh, God," Tyson said. "No, no, no, no, no." He whirled around, grabbed the kitchen towel off the handle of the stove, wrapped her arm with it. Then he scooped her up and carried her out, Grace fighting him, clinging to the doorframe until she had to let loose.

FIFTY-THREE

The low-water bridge was completely covered by the rising creek when Tyson crossed it, the truck struggling but staying its course. He headed west, the windshield wipers shrieking against the onslaught. The clumsy tourniquet he'd made with his belt hadn't been tight enough, and the kitchen towel he'd pressed against Grace's cut had gone dark and dripping. Her fighting him hadn't helped. She'd stopped struggling now, but she wasn't keeping enough pressure on the wound.

"Ty," she mumbled. "Lemme out."

"I told you, we're gonna get help. Just hold on. We'll be there soon." They passed the shuttered hospital at the edge of town and jounced over a series of potholes where the edge of the blacktop had crumbled away. There were no other cars on the road.

Grace rested her head against the fogged-up window, her eyes closed. "Don't let me die."

"I won't. You won't. I promise. Here, put your hand here. Hold tight."

He turned on one dirt road after another, relying on habit more than anything else to find his way, because it was nearly impossible to see where he was going. He knew they were almost there when he hit the last turn, and he took it too fast, as always, in a rush to get to his grandmother's cabin, where lights gleamed through the rain.

Tyson pulled close to the porch, hauled Grace out of the truck, and carried her inside, hollering for help. Velda sprang up from her chair at the sight of them, both soaking wet, Grace slumped in Tyson's arms, her clothes stained with blood.

"There was an accident," he said. "She's still bleeding."

"Lay her on the table," Velda said. "Hurry now." She removed the kitchen towel and grabbed the edge of the tablecloth to stanch the blood. "Hold it tight. I'll get my things."

Tyson clamped his hands around Grace's arm and she winced but didn't open her eyes. He couldn't tell whether she was conscious or not. "We made it," he said. "It'll be okay."

Grace didn't respond.

Velda returned with her medical kit and hurried to start an IV in Grace's good arm, then came around the table to take over from Tyson. "Let go now," she said. "I'll do my best."

"What do I do?" he said.

"Pray," she said, not looking at him. "And fetch the lanterns, case the power goes out. It's already flickering."

When Velda had done what she could, Grace lay motionless on the kitchen table, her skin pale in the lantern light.

"Is she . . . ?"

"Lost a pulse at one point. Heart's still beating, for now," Velda said. "I'll keep a close eye on her. Come daylight, we'll see where we're at, what we can do. I expect the road'll be flooded tonight if it isn't already. Nobody's getting anywhere." She carefully began to remove Grace's bloody shirt, but stopped when she saw Tyson staring.

"We need to talk," she said. "About what happened. What kind of accident this was. Meantime, clean yourself up . . . and clean out the truck."

"Yes, ma'am," he said.

Velda sighed. "There's bleach and rags in the cupboard."

By the time Tyson finished with the truck, he was soaked to the bone and shivering. Before going inside, he sloshed through the dark to the edge of the swollen river and hurled the knife into the foaming current. Velda sent him to shower and set out some of his grandfather's hunting clothes for him to change into. Afterward, he helped her move Grace into the back bedroom, the one with the pink-and-yellow-and-lavender quilt. Velda had dressed her in one of her own housecoats, the kind that snaps up the front. They laid her down on the bed and Velda tucked a heavy afghan around her to keep her warm.

"Sit with her a minute," Velda said. "I've got to get the blood up off the kitchen floor."

She left the door open when she stepped out. Tyson stood at the edge of the bed, studying Grace in the lantern light. Velda had cleaned her up. Her arm was bandaged, her eyes still closed. He wondered if his grandmother had given Grace something to keep her asleep, or if she might wake up at any moment. She'd be angry with him. She'd want to get out of here. Or maybe she wouldn't remember what had happened. She would only know he'd brought her here, saved her life. She'd be grateful. He touched her face, his palm against her cheek. Her skin felt clammy, cool.

"Grace," he said.

There was no response. He slapped her face lightly. Her chest rose and fell. He resisted the urge to slap her harder. Tyson checked his phone for the first time in hours and was glad to discover it was dead, so he wouldn't have to see any messages from Levi.

FIFTY-FOUR

Velda set out a fresh bouquet of tickseed and spiderwort, the first of the spring flowers, on the nightstand. She did her best to make the room nice for Grace, even if she couldn't let in fresh air, or much natural light. A sheet of plywood covered the bottom three-quarters of the window, a pretty curtain over that. She straightened the quilt, wiped flyspecks from the oval mirror, and settled into the wingback chair to read aloud from the Bible, but her hands were too shaky and she had to put it down. Grace lay flat in the bed, a sheepskin throw beneath her feet to keep her from getting bedsores on her heels. Velda said a prayer that the end was close, because she'd nearly reached the end of what she could bear.

She hadn't expected Grace to survive that first night, when the road was out and they couldn't get anywhere. She thought she'd be driving her body to the closest hospital as soon as the water went down. It had simply been a terrible accident, and her grandson had taken her to the one place he knew she could get help. Velda was a highly qualified nurse, after all. She'd been an EMT and worked in the hospital emergency room before moving on to long-term and nursing home care. She'd nursed her husband through the final year of his illness in this very cabin and had a stockpile of medical supplies on hand. She'd saved Grace's life. The girl would've died if Tyson had tried to drive her to the nearest hospital in the next county on the flooded roads.

The next morning, Grace seemed to be fading, and Velda doubted she had much time. The water began to recede as word spread of the bloody scene at Shannon Crow's house and the news that Grace was missing. The reports were unsettling. They didn't seem to match her grandson's account. He'd used the word "accident." He'd said nothing about a struggle.

This would have been the time to bring the girl forward, but instead of driving to the hospital, Velda called her favorite police officer, who had grown up playing baseball with her son and riding horses on the Baylors' farm. She volunteered to clean Shannon's house so she and her girls wouldn't have to come home to such horror. She asked a few careful questions in regard to the cleanup—Was there blood on multiple surfaces? Was it confined to one room?—in an attempt to determine just how big a mess Tyson was in. The officer said he would pass her offer on to the family once they had finished processing the scene and collecting evidence.

As the days went on and Grace clung to life, it became harder to figure out what to do. She was alive, though still not conscious. Velda didn't know the extent of the damage from blood loss or lack of oxygen to the brain, but she feared Grace had suffered a stroke. Was her mind still working? Did she understand what was happening? If Grace regained consciousness—if she remembered what happened, if she could talk—that would be a problem. Velda didn't think it was likely.

If she continued on as she was, she wouldn't last long. There was only so much Velda could do. She could run a feeding tube if necessary, but she didn't have access to a ventilator. When Grace stopped breathing, it would be God's will. Velda was certain that Grace's mother wouldn't want to see her like this. Elsie had taken up with a boy her own daughter's age and wouldn't have the time or the wherewithal to care properly for an invalid. Grace would likely spend what little time she had left in a nursing home.

Velda knew the kinds of things that happened to pretty young girls in those places when they were incapacitated. She'd heard stories, seen it in the news. There'd been a shameful incident, in fact, with an elderly woman in a facility where she had worked. Velda had the skill, and access to medical supplies. Grace would be comfortable here as she prepared to go home to Jesus.

In those early days, it had made sense. There was Tyson's future to think about. Even if it had been an accident, some might not see it that way. It wouldn't fix anything to ruin his life over a mistake. And Velda had been nursing patients her whole adult life. She'd been lonely and restless after her husband's death, after a year spent at his bedside. Having Grace there almost felt routine after a while. No one came out to the cabin anymore, except, occasionally, the boys.

The hardest part was explaining it to Levi. The accident, the aftermath. They kept it from him as long as they could, longer than she'd thought possible, but in the end, Tyson was the one to tell him. Velda had to explain that there was no chance of her getting better. Too much time had passed to return the girl now, and it would do no good anyhow. They'd go to prison, her and Tyson both. No one had wanted this to happen. It was a tragedy all around. It had broken something inside her younger grandson. She prayed it wasn't irreparable, that Levi could eventually heal.

As time wore on, it grew more difficult to reconcile what she had done. She had acted on instinct, at first, to protect her grandson. Once she realized she was wrong about Grace's prognosis, she had kept her there to protect herself. The girl might've had a chance to recover if she'd gotten her help, and now it was far too late. She prayed every day for forgiveness, for mercy. When her knees wore out, she prayed for God to take one of them—Grace, or herself. She wanted it all to be over. She needed it to end. It might have been her imagination, but eventually it seemed that Grace had begun to wither, her body losing its will. Velda dared to believe that Grace was finally preparing to die. Instead, she opened her eyes.

It was a fluke, and then it wasn't. The girl would have moments of dazed semi-consciousness. She would try to make sounds. Velda had sedatives to give her when the boys were around, but that wouldn't last. What would happen if Grace continued to improve, if she could no longer keep her confined to the bed, if Levi found out? The answers were bad and worse. There were no good ones. God was punishing her. This was the bitter fruit she was left to harvest.

AMELIA

&

KYLEE

FIFTY-FIVE

"She's right," Tyson said, agitated. He paced back and forth in front of the door. "You can't leave. You know that." Tyson nodded to Velda. "I'll handle it," he said. "You stay with Grace." Then he turned to us. "Come on. Outside."

"Tyson!" Kylee said. "No! What are you doing?"

"Outside," he growled. "Now."

He let go of my wrist when we got out the door, and the moment I felt the pressure release, I grabbed Kylee's hand to make a run for the car. Tyson locked his arms around her and wouldn't let go. Kylee twisted and kicked, struggling to break free.

"You can go, Amelia," he said. "Go on. I won't stop you."

"Let her go," I said.

"Ky." He held her chin so she had to look at him. "We can get out of here now," he said. "You and me. Like we planned. Get as far away from here as we can. We'll leave. Not look back."

Kylee smacked his chest and jerked away, and he loosened his grip. "You scared the shit out of me! I can't go with you now. Amelia and I have to take Grace. Help us get her out of there, or get out of the way and we'll do it ourselves."

Tyson frowned, his eyes going dark. "You promised. You promised me. We promised each other."

She shook her head. "Everything's changed, don't you get it? You of all people should understand about family. You've been protecting yours all this time. I can't leave her behind. Mimi, come on, let's get Grace."

"I can't let you take her," he said, pushing her back a step.

She shoved him back. "What are you gonna do to stop me?"

"You crazy bitch." He grabbed her by the throat, and then they were on the ground, Tyson rolling on top of her and pinning her down.

"Mimi!" she gasped. "My purse! Go!"

I had no idea what she had in her bag—mace? her deer knife?—but I ran for the car and snatched it off the floorboard. It was heavier than I'd expected, and when I fumbled it open, I saw why. Ketch's pistol was tucked inside, beneath an envelope with my name on it. I grabbed the gun and took off running.

"Amelia."

His voice stopped me. I turned to see Levi at the edge of the clearing, emerging from the woods. He was dressed in camouflage, a crossbow in his hands. Fear flooded through me, weakening my limbs, but I had to keep going. I ran for Kylee, the gun heavy in my hand. Ketch had taught me how to shoot using beer bottles and tin cans as targets. He had told me never to aim at a living thing unless I was willing to kill it. I just wanted Tyson to let my sister go.

"Stop!"

I whirled around. Levi held his bow at the ready, arrow in place, staring me down. I leveled the gun at him and he shook his head. Somewhere, in the hidden chambers of my heart, I had always known it wasn't him, that he could never hurt Grace. I didn't know whether or not he would hurt me, but I couldn't do it. I couldn't shoot him.

I turned back to Kylee, Tyson's meaty hands on her throat. She was pinned to the ground, but she clawed up dead leaves, tried to stuff them in his mouth, while he screamed at her to stop, *just stop*. I took aim, tried to steady my hands, and then Tyson went mute, toppling to the side, his legs still draped over Kylee, an arrow through his eye.

Levi sprinted toward us. "Wait here," he called to me. "I'll bring her out."

I pulled Kylee to her feet, gasping, wiped specks of blood from her face. Levi emerged from the cabin moments later with Grace in his arms, head lolling, limbs dangling, Velda close behind. She was caterwauling and pummeling him, trying to drag him back inside, and then she saw Tyson's body on the ground, the arrow sticking straight up. She ran to him, sobbing, feeling for a pulse, searching for breath, crying out to Jesus for help.

We met Levi halfway. He cradled Grace to his chest. "I didn't know," he said. "For the longest time, I didn't know. And then . . ." He shook his head. "I'm sorry. Go." He laid her gently in our arms, and together, Kylee and I rushed her to the car. She was almost weightless, skin and bone, shadow and air, but she was warm, breathing. Alive.

Levi stood in the yard, watching us carry her away, though he wasn't looking at us, he was looking at Grace. I thought of the day at the farm when we were still little girls, when he had led us on the horses and couldn't look away from her, the sun on his face, flushed with love.

FIFTY-SIX

t a fork in the road, while Kylee refreshed the map, I unfolded the
message that Ketch had sent for me along with the pistol. He'd
written my name in fancy cursive at the top. *Amelia—First, don't
worry about Alan. I told David to go scare the shit out of him. Intimidation's
his favorite part of the job, so I'm sure he'll have fun with it. Kylee told me
you're leaving. I won't say goodbye, because we'll see each other before long.
We'll be living in color, like Dorothy in Oz, just like we said. You can write to
me at boot camp. I'll call when they let me. I don't know where I'll end up after
training, but as soon as I can live off base, I'll have a place for you to stay. If you
want. I hope you will. Because I'm yours. I always have been. It's never too late.*

"Go left," Kylee said from the back seat, Grace's head resting in her
lap. "And then one more left to the main road. Elsie's not answering—she's
probably deep-throating a turkey leg at the Stampede and can't hear the
phone. I'm calling Dallas. Let's hope Mr. Most Likely to Succeed is as
smart as he thinks he is."

"Call Mrs. Mummer next," I said. "Tell her Grace is alive, and that's all
we know." She could have one last Beautiful Now, and maybe she would
pass peacefully before any ugly details came out.

The tires spit gravel as I hit the gas, putting distance between us and the cabin. I couldn't stop thinking of Levi, the look on his face as we left, the part of me that wanted to take him with us, that worried about leaving him behind. I didn't know what would happen to him now, whether he could survive it. It would be all over the news, the whole story would come out. Everyone would know about Velda. About Tyson. And Levi, too. I would make sure they knew, in the end, that he helped us—that he helped Grace.

"Dallas," Kylee said. "My sister trusts you, so I'm gonna have to trust you, too. It's your time to shine. We need your help."

We had to go back through town to hit the highway, and we drove down Cutting Road, passing all the landmarks. The abandoned hospital where we had been born. Savor Meats, where Aunt Elsie carved up carcasses while her body broke down part by part. At the Waffle House, Alan would be standing too close to a waitress, Javi at the grill, dreaming of being anywhere else. The flashing sign at Sweet Jane's made me think of Mama, the hard lines of her face, which still softened when she laughed. I looked in the direction of Elsie's house, where Annalise was finally being set free, and slowed down to the speed limit as we passed the police station, which was quiet and calm, though probably not for long. Last was Beaumont Memorial Cemetery, the final resting place for most of my family—all but Norman, who'd ended up right where he belonged. The whole path from birth to death, trod into deep ruts by generations of Crows, a short distance but a lifelong journey to the only place they knew to go.

I glanced at Kylee in the rearview mirror. She stared straight ahead, her face stoic but streaked with tears, her hair swirling in the breeze from the open windows. Dots of blood formed constellations on her shirt. The smell of the stockyards and the meatpacking plant, the familiar odor of manure and blood and dirt, began to fade, little by little, as we closed in on the county line.

"This is it," I said. "Say goodbye to Beaumont." It would always be the place I came from, but it would never be my home again.

"Don't let the door hit ya where the Good Lord split ya," Kylee said.

A butterfly swooped toward the windshield and disappeared, and I didn't look back to see if it had survived, if it kept going. It was here and gone, its presence necessarily fleeting, same as our own. It was a wonder to witness its flight, a miracle that it existed at all. I had learned that from Grace. She had been with me, her voice in my heart, all the time she'd been missing.

The road ahead held unknown horror and hope, endless twists to navigate. Now that we had the freedom to turn the wheel, I didn't know what the next bend would bring. There would be beauty and bitterness and all things in between, and we would do our best to feel every bit of it. We would curse it and embrace it and wake up again the next morning, if we were lucky, to do it again. That was life, like Mrs. Mummer had said. That's how you knew you were living.

ACKNOWLEDGMENTS

Writing might feel like solitary work, but I'm never alone. I'm so grateful to my family; my friends; my writing besties; my daughters, Harper and Piper; my readers; and my sweet dog for bringing so much light to my life. I'm amazed every day by your kindness and generosity and unwavering support. I love you all.

I never forget how lucky I am that I get to do this. Everyone at Random House is an absolute joy to work with. Huge thanks to all who helped bring this book into the world, especially my wonderful editor, Andrea Walker, Noa Shapiro, Robert Siek, Amy Ryan, Meghan O'Leary, Jo Anne Metsch, Ella Laytham, and my agent, Sally Wofford-Girand.

As always, my deepest gratitude to the librarians, booksellers, reviewers, and readers who spread the word about the books they love. You make all of this possible. Thank you for everything you do to support books and authors.

ABOUT THE AUTHOR

Laura McHugh is the internationally bestselling author of *The Weight of Blood,* winner of the International Thriller Writers Award and Silver Falchion Award for best first novel; *Arrowood,* an International Thriller Writers Award finalist for best novel; *The Wolf Wants In;* and *What's Done in Darkness.* McHugh lives in Missouri with her daughters.

Facebook.com/lauramchughauthor
Twitter: @LauraSMcHugh
Instagram: @lauramchughauthor
TikTok: @lauramchughauthor